THE GINGERBREAD MAN

Richard Powell

This is a work of fiction. All the characters here are a product of the authors imagination alone. Any resemblance to real people is a pure accident. There is no such place as Jergen County, but Memphis and Tunica are real and are great places to live and work.

ISBN: 1549822292
ISBN-13: 978-1549822292

ALSO BY RICHARD POWELLL

THE JERGEN COUNTY SERIES:
Murder Club

THE BRIDGE CLUB SERIES
Old Age and Treachery
Harvesting the Angels
Little Lucifer

This book is dedicated to my Mother Marie Powell and my Aunt Irene Zickle. As a child they let me play with a typewriter and if I wrote something made it a big deal. If this book fails to please don't blame them. They did their best. It was me that let them down.

*****

ACKNOWLEDGMENTS

First, I want to thank my Beta Reader Cammie Adams for her excellent feedback she gave me on this project. The fact that it is the second book in a series was her suggestion. Again, thank you for all your work and the kind way you redirect my missteps and hopefully someday I will see the dog with at least one eye open.

Also my thanks to Lynn Maples, Larry Hoy, and Jackie Flaum for their critiques. You have all offered excellent suggestions and if this product has fault it is mine, because God knows you tried.

CHAPTER ONE

"Sorry, guys, I was on my way home when I got the call. Looks like all the troops are here already. Whattaya got?" Jordan asked as he strode to the open motel room door. The uniformed officer standing in the doorway grimaced then shook his head.

"Body. Baby Pro we've seen workin' the streets around here a few times. It's bad, Bob. Paramedics and Crime Scene are in there now. Not much room." The officer turned to the open door.

"Hey, guys, can some of you clear out? Homicide's here!"

Glancing over his shoulder, a paramedic tapped the other next to him on the shoulder. When the other turned around, he pointed with his thumb over his shoulder then stepped away from the bed.

"Nothin' we can do. Coroner'll be here to pick up the body." The paramedic took his bag and strode to the door, trailed by his partner.

As Jordan turned, his jaw dropped. His knees weakened. The naked girl on the bed turned her head to him. Blood trailed down her chin. She smiled. "Hi, Daddy. Can you take me home?"

Jordan awoke, trembling. Covered in sweat. Confused, he studied his surroundings. Charmain, sleeping next to him, stirred but stayed asleep. Not wanting to disturb her, he slipped from the bed. Grabbed his slacks from the pile in the corner then left the room. As he turned the trousers right side out, he found his mouth dry, and his hands still trembled from the nightmare. He'd just slip them on then find his cigarettes. Step out on the balcony. Smoke while he waited for the images to fade.

A pack lay on the coffee table next to his badge and gun. He tossed them there earlier as they wrestled with their clothes in a passionate dash for the bedroom. Before he closed the bedroom door, he studied her face in the moonlight. She looked at peace. Undisturbed by the nightmare that had entered the bedroom and shattered his sleep. Sheets and blankets piled at the bed's foot, where they'd kicked them during their passionate romp. Her brown skin contrasting with the white covering sheet. The thought of its velvety texture stirring his arousal. But then guilt quenched it, as he recalled the dream. He gathered a blanket from the pile and spread it over her. She stirred but did not wake. On tip-toe, he gathered his remaining clothes. Smoking on the balcony, even this late, required clothes.

He pulled the door shut, hoping the sound would not disturb her. Why invite someone else into his private hell?

After slipping on his clothes, he stepped to the railing, closing the apartment door behind him. He lit up and let the first drag sink deep into his lungs. Almost six months sober, he wondered if maybe he should think about giving up this habit as well.

"We'll see," he said to himself. "Too much of a good thing might be bad for me as well."

Finishing the smoke, he flipped the butt over the railing. His stomach rumbled, reminding him that in their haste, they had not eaten anything. Returning to the apartment, he searched the kitchen. Something he could nibble on. Opening and closing cupboard doors, he hoped she maybe had crackers, peanut butter. Anything.

One cupboard contained two file folders. A photograph clipped to one caught his attention. After pulling it closer, his jaw dropped. He groaned. A tear came to his eye. His daughter's last school picture. She stared back at him. The smile that never failed to melt his heart. The sparkle of life and hope in her eyes.

Pulling the folder out, Jordan flipped it open. The contents spilled on the floor. As he gathered them up, he examined each sheet. Copies. Police reports of her death and the investigation. The coroner's report. News clippings describing the crime. A note from a publisher. They accepted Charmain's book proposal. Looked forward to seeing the manuscript detailing this true crime story.

Reading the note, his hand trembled. "Why was Charmain doing this? Could she be just like her mentor?" Not interested in him? Only wanting a first-row seat on some story that would catapult her to fame?" He chided himself. The second file's contents chronicled his downfall from Memphis Homicide. As he read, despair, anger, sorrow coursed through his body. Feeling foolish and betrayed, he set the folders on the kitchen table. Gathered up the rest of his belongings, then strode out the door, slamming it behind him.

*****

The slamming door jolted Charmain awake.

"Bob? Bob?" she called in the dark.

No answer, she slipped out of bed. She smiled, realizing that he had covered her with a blanket. After seeing him viscously attack in her defense, his tenderness always amazed her. In the moonlight, she spotted her robe mixed with the sheets still lying on the floor. The sight reminded her of the rush of passion when he arrived. The hungry lovemaking, driving both to exhaustion.

She first met Jordan as he investigated the murder of a prominent author. A television reporter, Charmain, worked the media covering the case. During this adventure, Jordan and Charmain fell in love.

They talked about moving in together. He lived in Davis City, an hour away, so they often went several days without seeing each other. He did not seem to mind the separations, but she yearned to be with him more. Greet him when he got off duty. Maybe even cook him a meal—TV dinners. Maybe heat up a can of soup. Hopeless in the kitchen, she could manage without starting a major fire. Nothing bound her to Memphis. She only needed to be here once a week for her radio show on Saturday evenings. The rest of the time, she could be with him in Davis City.

She also hoped that being close to him, she could support him in battling his personal demons. On his own, he appeared to be on his way to sobriety. Now she wanted to help him come to peace with his daughter's death.

Murdered several years ago, the police failed to bring her killer to justice. Charmain believed finding the killer might bring him peace. With this in mind, she decided to keep the story alive. Use her position as a journalist to put pressure on the police.

Tonight, their lust had been more potent than usual. Working overtime, investigating farm equipment thefts, they had not been together in two weeks. They planned on going out for dinner then return for an evening of romance. Their plans swiftly changed.

Thrilled by the news that a publisher wanted to see her book's manuscript, she ambushed him at the door. She planned to first tell him about the book and then ravage his body. But the second part came first. Both had drifted off to sleep before she could share the news.

Slipping into the robe, she thought, at this point, she might be able to hold his attention. At least discuss the book. Confess about nagging Archer to work the case. The book would give her added leverage. But now he needed to know.

She hoped he would be pleased. She wished she had told him about it earlier. But the time had never been right. But it must do it now. Forget putting it off.

Leaving the bedroom, she searched for him. She paused before entering the living room, wondering if maybe she should just coax him back to bed at this point. Talk about the book tomorrow.

Inside the living room, she found his gun and his badge gone. Maybe he had gotten called into work. Typical for detectives. He claimed the Chicken rustlers never slept. So, the forces of Truth and

Goodness must always be on their toes, he'd say. But she had not heard his phone ring. Maybe she slept through it. She smiled, remembering one of Jordan's other quips. He claimed that the only thing better than the sleep of the just was the sleep of the just after. Maybe tonight he'd been right.

He usually left a note, but none lay on the stand. Thinking the message might be on the kitchen table, she moved to that room.

On the kitchen table lay the folders with the material for her book. Next to the stack lay the note from the publisher, nothing else. She dropped into the chair Jordan must have used to read the folder. She gasped as she gazed at the sheets lying on the table.

"My God!" She thought. "What had he thought when he saw this? Maybe like my old boss, I just used him to get a story. What have I done?" She put her head down and sobbed.

******

Meanwhile across town, as the killer prepared the sacrificial altar, he set the phone on the dresser and started the music. He wanted it loud. The lyrics belted out by the girl band The Bangles.

He took a deep breath. Closed his eyes, recalling the light fading from the girl's eyes as his hands clenched her throat. The only way to end the taunting voices in his head. Perhaps one day he might capture that moment on film. Allow him to capture the moment without killing. But until then he must continue.

Grabbing a can of beer from the ice bucket on the motel desk, he popped the top. Drained it in one long gulp. Tossed it aside, then grabbed another, which he sipped as he admired the naked body displayed before him. Since the light from the motel's bedside table cast a shadow across her, he adjusted the shade. Her smooth, creamy skin glowed in the light. Free now from his haunting images, He smiled, satisfied.

After taking his cell phone from his pocket, he snapped pictures then put it aside. He slid her to the bed's center. Kneeling next to her, he opened the serrated blade on his pocket knife. He wedged the blade beneath her tongue then sawed it off. Taking out a plastic bag from the satchel, he sealed the severed tongue inside. He hummed along with the song as he worked. Then sang the chorus along with the singer. "Wayo Wayo."

He moved the girl's legs together and rolled her on her side. He pulled one arm up to her shoulder, bent it up at the elbow. He then flipped the wrist, so the hand paralleled the upper arm. He poised the other arm to the back, again to shoulder height. Elbow downward. Hand trailed to the rear.

He chuckled as he took a tube of lipstick from her purse. He resumed his humming with the tune as he wrote, "Walks Like an Egyptian," On the mirror above the bed. Adding the phone number, he wiped the lipstick tube with a towel. After making sure he removed all traces he might have left, he exited the room.

*****

Later, Archer strode through the motel parking lot, now filled with police cars and an ambulance. Their light bars flashing. Like beacons, they beckoned him. Another murder. Not unique in Memphis, but special for Archer. A serial killer he chased for years. The first had been with his partner, Jordan. A death that had rocked both their souls to the core.

Inside, the dimly lit corridor smelled of urine, feces, and sex. An open door gave the hallway; it's only light. Entering, Archer shuffled around the uniformed officers and paramedics crowding the room. A uniformed black officer nodded to him. His face grim, he shook his head and then shrugged. "Hey, Jack."

Archer nodded towards the nude body on the bed. "So, what've we got?"

The uniformed officer turned back to the body. "Female. Guessin' thirteen, maybe fourteen. We've rousted her a few times for loiterin'." The uniformed officer shrugged. "What can I say. They keep workin'."

Archer shook his head. "Shit! Another one?"

The uniformed officer shrugged again, gestured with his thumb to the message on the mirror. "Except for checking for signs of life, no one's touched the body. We'll have to wait for the M.E.s folks to check her. Looks like it, though."

Archer glanced at the paramedics. "Everybody's mum on this. Right?" Both nodded then ambled out of the room.

Archer turned to the uniform. "Who found the body?"

"We did. 911 call," the uniformed officer replied.

A man wearing a stained wife-beater undershirt and jeans peered around the corner of the door. One uniformed officer stepped in front of him. Turned the man around and escorted him away from the door. Archer followed them out.

"You, the manager?" Archer growled. The man turned to face him. His eyes open wide as he ran his hand through his greasy brown hair. He nodded. The man's body odor made Archer's stomach churn.

"You call this in?"

The manager shook his head.

"Did you see who she came in with?"

"No, didn't see her come in at all." The man's breath reeked of bourbon and tobacco.

"How about the person that rented the room?"

"Reddish brown hair. Mustache, with a little goatee. Glasses. Muscular, like you. But a white guy. 'Bout my height, maybe little taller."

"What time?"

The manager rubbed the stubble on his chin. As if considering some great mystery. "Nine. Maybe nine-thirty. It might be on the register."

"I see you got a camera by the desk. Can I look at the video?"

"Been busted for a month. Told the owner. Promised to fix `em soon, but..." The man shrugged.

"Shit." Archer turned to the uniformed officer.

"Can you guys check with the places around here? See if they might have something that picked up this place or the area nearby?"

The officer nodded. "No problem."

Archer turned back to the manager. The man's eyes remained riveted on the room's doorway. Archer took him by the arm and led him to the lobby.

After opening the book on the desk, the manager ran his finger down the page. "Guess I forgot to write down the time. Man's name was Dwight Eisenhower."

Archer reached across the desk. Pulled the register to him. His face grim, as he studied the page.

Archer rolled his eyes. Shook his head. "Not, John Smith?"

The man shrugged.

"How'd he pay?"

"Cash."

"Did you get a credit card, though? Just in case?"

The manager held up a finger. "Oh, Yeah. Sorry, Detective."

The man pulled a file box from a drawer. Shuffled through. He pulled a slip out and handed it to Archer.

Reading the card, Archer frowned then shook his head. "Richard Nixon?"

The manager's smile revealed several missing teeth. The ones visible stained and yellow. "Yeah. A lot of our guys use phony names on the register. Guess this guy wasn't too smart. Huh!"

CHAPTER TWO

As Jordan raised the glass to his lips, the plastic token spun into his line of vision. He tossed back the drink, then trapped the spinning chip as he set the glass back on the bar.

"Yeah, asshole! That's the chip I planned on giving you at the next meeting. Six months sobriety. Now, this."

Jordan turned to the muscled man looming at his side. His leather jacket open, showing a sample of his jailhouse tattoos. Hair down to his shoulders, he wore a baseball cap turned backward.

"Nice to see you too, Hector. If you're gonna give me a lecture, let me buy you a round. Not good to drink alone."

Hector pried the chip from Jordan's hand, leaned close.

"I'll have a Dr. Pepper. Diet. You?"

Jordan held up his glass.

"Hey man, hit me again and give my friend here a Diet Dr. Pepper."

Hector dropped on the next barstool. As Jordan studied the big man in the mirror behind the bar, Hector scowled back. Jordan's usual five o'clock shadow now looking more like midnight. Hector's Black Fu Manchu mustache gave his face its normal menacing appearance. The mirror's reflection, the perfect artist's rendering of drunks in a bar.

"Man., I don't know why I even bothered looking for you."

Jordan scoffed. "Then, why? You feel some holy mission to save me? Maybe developed a man-crush from our time together?"

"Fuck you. I felt sorry for your girlfriend."

"Girlfriend? Boy has she got you fooled! Sure as hell fooled me for a long time. She's a user just like her old boss."

Hector scowled. "What the hell you talkin' about, man?"

"She's gonna get herself famous writin' about me and my dead daughter. Wondered why she took such a shine to me right off."

"Oh. So now she's another excuse to get drunk? Oh, poor Bob Jordan. Boo! Hoo! Gotta run home to Mamma Booze."

As the bartender delivered their drinks, Jordan handed the man a five-dollar bill from the currency stacked before him. Turning to face Hector, Jordan wobbled, almost falling from his stool.

He chuckled. "Jesus, Hector. You sound like an AA lesson all the time. Lighten up, man. Let's party."

Hector shrugged. Sipped his Dr. Pepper. "I don't know what that gal sees in you. She's callin' everybody to hunt your ass down. Since you ain't havin' it anymore, might tap it myself since she's got a taste for white meat."

"More power to ya, Hector. Hell, she might take a shine to you. Want to do your story. Hector! The exploits of the former doper and drunk!" Jordan held his glass up as if offering a toast.

"You quittin' the force too?"

Jordan turned to Hector. Scowled. "Nah! Just takin' a little medical leave."

"Medical leave?"

"Heart trouble," Jordan muttered. "Yeah! Heart trouble." Jordan held the glass up again. "This is medicine. General anesthetic. You know what that means, right?"

"Well, I talked to that partner of yours. She said they hadn't heard from you in a week. Sheriff's got his shorts in a knot tryin' to cover cases."

"That worry you? Afraid that crime's gonna start runnin' rampant here in the Delta? Some serial chicken rustler terrorizing the coops?"

"Thanks, Hector. You makin' any headway?"

Jordan turned to the sound of the woman's voice and grinned.

The blond beside him scowled and shook her head. Slightly over five feet tall and petite, she wore skintight blue jeans and a leather jacket. A former boxer, her size fooled a lot of bad guys into putting up a struggle. Deputy Sheriff Christine Urich had no qualms about going toe to toe with anyone.

"Hey, podna." Jordan clapped Hector on the shoulder. "Hector here's worried about the shortage of law enforcement officers around here. Right, Hector?"

"Jesus, Deputy, he's got a real snoot-full."

Jordan held his finger up to Urich's face. Wobbled on his stool. "Quick question, rookie. What's a snoot-full register on the Breathalyzer? Come on, Urich, you should know, girl."

Urich took hold of his arm. "Come on, Bob. Let's get you outta here."

Jordan pulled his arm free. Reached for his glass and fell forward. His head struck the bar as he collapsed on the floor.

Hector shook his head. "I guess that saves you havin' to Taze him."

"Give me a hand, Hector."

They stooped. Lifted the now unconscious Jordan to his feet.

"Let me check his eyes. Make sure he doesn't have a concussion."

Hector propped Jordan on his feet as Urich examined both of Jordan's eyes.

"I think he's okay. Probably passed out before he hit his head."

She put Jordan's other arm over her shoulder, then stashed the cash from the bar in Jordan's pocket. Together they dragged him out. After flopping him into Urich's back seat, she shook hands with the big man and gave him a peck on the cheek. "Thanks, Hector."

"Where you takin' him?"

"My place. He can sleep it off on my couch."

Hector glanced inside at Jordan's unconscious form curled up in Urich's backseat. "Need help?"

"Nah! Maureen and I have company. Between us, we'll get him settled."

Once Hector watched Urich's taillights disappear, he kicked an empty beer can across the parking lot. It clattered into a parked car.

"How does such an asshole rate any friends? For some reason, God must love him."

He stomped off to his motorcycle. Kicked it over and rumbled off into the darkness.

*****

Someone breathed near Jordan's ear. He opened one eye. As he met the small black child's gaze, the boy glanced up. "He ain't dead, Aunt Chrissie!"

"Good, then I'll kill him after you go to school. Now scoot! Go brush your teeth, Joshua. Your Momma's already waitin' out in the car."

"It ain't school! It's day camp!"

"Well, whatever. Get goin'!"

The sound of feet scurrying away pounded in his head. The boy's beaded braids clacked as he ran. Jordan pulled the pillow from under his head. His tongue glued to the roof of his mouth. Desperate, he covered his head with the pillow, blocking light and sound. Urich tugged it away. Reaching to grab it back, he sat up. She shoved a steaming mug under his nose. He blinked, rubbed his eyes, looked around.

"How'd I get here?" His tongue enormous, his words slurred. He shaded his eyes with his hands. "Are you standing in front of that window on purpose?" he groaned as his trembling hand grasped the cup.

"Yeah, sunshine. We got work to do."

"Cattle rustling? Somebody steal a cotton picker?"

"No. Roy lent us out to Tunica County. We're gonna bust pimps."

An olive-skinned man not over five feet tall emerged from the back of the mobile home. Bare-chested, wearing jeans, he cocked an eyebrow and smiled. "So, Sherlock! Are you back among the living?"

Jordan winced and closed his eyes. "God, Paulo! Do you need to shout?"

He grinned while twirling his mustache.

Jordan pointed at him. "That's new. Grow it yourself, or did you have it pasted on."

"Ah, Christine insisted. Makes me look more dashing. Eh?"

The little man put his arm around Urich. Kissed her. She grinned as she scratched her nose then arched her eyebrows. "It tickles."

Both she and Jordan chuckled as if they knew the same joke.

Paulo grinned, glanced at Urich. "Has she told you the news?"

Jordan shook his head. "No. I was gone when she got back. Little medical leave."

Urich scoffed.

"Show the man!" Paulo held out her hand. The enormous diamond sparkled.

Jordan's jaw dropped. "Shit! Is that real?"

Urich blushed. Paulo beamed.

"Helluva big rock. You guys set a date?"

They shared a glance and smiled.

Urich turned back to Jordan. "Paulo has a big match coming up in about six months. So, not before then."

Jordan nodded at Paulo and grinned. "I thought you said there was nothing to that old myth about women sappin' your strength before a big fight."

Paulo arched his eyebrows and grinned. "Not that. In fact, you are right. Practicing for the honeymoon can be good for the back and leg muscles. Plus, it keeps the mind clear. Helps you focus."

"Why wait? Urich think she might get a better offer?"

"God, Jordan, you are a complete asshole!" Urich punched him on the shoulder to emphasize her point.

"No! It is my mother. She would demand too much of my time to plan the wedding." Paulo shrugged. "That kind of woman trouble I do not need before the big fight."

Jordan stood. He wobbled, staggered. "Where's my boots?"

Urich pointed to a chair. As he bent to retrieve them, he flopped forward onto the floor. On his hands and knees, he rubbed his head. "God, my head."

While Urich gave him a hand up, Paulo dashed to the kitchen. He called over his shoulder.

"I have what you need. It kills the hangover. Sit down. I'll fix it in a jiffy."

Jordan's head throbbed. After retrieving the coffee mug, he raised it to his mouth and took a sip. His shaking hands spilled coffee over the side. Paulo stirred something in the kitchen. Soon he emerged with what looked like a glass of orange juice. "Here, drink this up- one gulp. It will get rid of the alcohol. Make you better, pronto."

Jordan did as instructed. The liquid smelled and tasted like orange juice, but had a slimy texture. He burped after he swallowed. "What was that?"

"Orange juice mixed with two raw eggs. You have to be careful to not break the yolk when you stir, so it goes down whole."

Jordan's stomach churned. The vomit rose in his throat. He dashed to the bathroom, dropped on his knees before the commode, and wretched.

Paulo turned to Urich and grinned. "That should clear his head real good, eh?"

She chuckled as she gave Paulo a hug.

*****

The young red-haired Detective poked his head over the edge of Archer's cubicle. He wore a blue polo shirt, like Archer's, it had a gold detective shield embroidered on the breast. He grinned as he held a sheet of paper in his hand. "Hey Jack, I got the report back on that credit card."

Archer tossed his pen on the desk. Stood and took the sheet. "Let me guess. It's bogus, right?"

"That must be why you're such an outstanding detective. It's hard to believe the forces of evil stand a chance here in Memphis. But I guess we coulda been lucky. Most bad guys ain't that smart."

Shaking his head, Archer tossed the sheet on his desk. "Rosco, didn't your Mama teach how to speak gooder English?"

"Hell! Told you Third grade was the toughest four years of my life. Anyway, the M.E. says, cause of death was strangulation. Tongue cut off, postmortem."

"Shit, listen to you. Usin' all them big words. Law School must be payin' off. So, this is just like the rest. The composite from the manager almost identical to the others. Signed in as some dead President. He kills them in sleazy motels with little or no security. Only difference was the pose."

Roscoe nodded. "He must not have much imagination. This was the same as the first one. Must be a repeating series."

"Same pose as Jordan's daughter?"

"Yeah. Jordan know we're lookin' for a serial on her murder?"

Archer sat back down. Leaned his chair back, then put his hands behind his head. "Rosco, I sure as hell can't be the one to tell him. Plus, the boss ain't ready to call it a serial. Scared it'll hit the papers. Upset the politicians. Besides, Jordan's not in the Department anymore. She's dead, and that's all he is entitled to know right now. Hell, down there in Mississippi, I'm not even sure he's still in law enforcement."

"Listen. He made quite a splash solvin' that writer's murder last year."

"Good closer when he worked here too. I just hope that young thing he's been tappin' can straighten his ass out."

Roscoe came from behind the partition. Leaned against Archer's desk. "She still buggin' you about looking at the files?"

"Yeah. Raisin' hell with the boss, too. Wants to keep us humpin' the case. Keeps hollerin' that three years makes it a cold case. Thinks if we can solve it, it'll help Jordan move on."

"You can't tell her nothin' either. Not only is she not family, but she's a reporter or somethin' right?"

Archer shrugged and nodded. "Guess, a part-timer with WKNO. Blogger.

"Now there's a match from Hell. Cop and reporter. Boss claims the press are all Satanists. Would have your ass for even lookin' at `em."

"Well, she's been good for my old partner. I just hope they can keep it together."

*****

As Charmain waited at the pancake house, her cell phone chirped. After checking caller I.D., she put the phone to her ear. "Hey! Did you find him?"

"Hector did. He was in a bar. Real drunk."

"Is he okay?"

"Yeah. Hungover, but he'll live. Paulo did his best to nurse him back to health," Urich chuckled. "Might teach him a lesson."

"Thank you so much for findin' him. Tell Paulo, thanks too. I'll call Hector later."

"Do you want to talk to Bob?"

"I think I should let him call me. I hope I haven't spoiled everything. But..."

"What happened?"

19

"I need to talk to Bob about it first. That was the problem in the first place. He found out the wrong way. He'll give me a chance to explain, but he needs to get over the shock first."

"Jordan's complicated, but he's not stupid. I'm sure he'll come around."

As the call ended, she set the phone aside. It had been over a week since she woke in the night to discover Jordan gone. After three days with no word from him, she worried about his safety. Had reached out to Hector and Urich to find him. Make sure he was safe. At least that had been successful. Now she could only hope for the best.

"Sorry, I'm late."

Jarred from her thoughts, she looked up at Archer standing next to the table. He scanned the room.

With a smile, she beckoned to the vacant chair across from her. "It's alright. Sit down. No one knows me here. If you don't see anybody you know, you're safe. And I sure won't tell."

Still scanning the room, Archer settled into the chair.

A server appeared beside the table. After taking their order, she left them alone. Charmain leaned close, put her hand on his. "What's wrong, Jack. You seemed stressed out. Am I finally gettin' to you? The nag?"

"It's this case I've been working for a while. The boss is real secretive about it. Swore us all to silence. It would be my ass just to be seen talking to the press right now."

"Well, I want you to know that I'm gonna start workin' on the book about her killing big time, kinda like all that stuff on the Black Dahlia. I've got a publisher. He wants to see my manuscript as soon as I'm done. Also, I'm going to start a series on it with my blog and radio show. So, I'm gonna start puttin' the heat on your bosses too."

"I'm not sure that's gonna get you anywhere. But what the hell. If it gets them riled up, that might be for the best. You're gonna have to watch yourself, though."

Charmain scoffed, then scowled. "Why? Free press. They can't stop me. Are the bosses ready to take the heat on it, too?"

"That's not what I meant."

She scowled. "Then what?"

"Shit! What if you spook her killer? Make him think you're on his trail. You ain't protected. He killed once. What would stop him from doin' it again?"

Silent Charmain gazed off, pondering Archer's words.

Archer leaned forward, put his hand on her arm. "Listen. If you do it, might be smart to have Bob take some time off to watch your back. Or you could move in with him down in Davis City. You guys have talked about it. Might be safer for you down there."

A tear formed in Charmain's eye as she hung her head. Archer's brow furrowed. He took her hand in his. "What's wrong? I didn't mean to upset you. I just want you to be careful. I like you. You're the best thing that's happened to my old partner in a long time. Losin' you, would kill him."

Still crying, Charmain shook her head. Archer moved to her side. Put his arm around her. Drawing her head to his shoulder, he stroked her hair. "What's wrong? I mean, you're a tough woman. I was just trying to warn you. I'm sure Bob would say the same thing."

"I don't know what he'd say." She whimpered.

"Whaddaya mean?"

"Oh, Jack, I've made a mess of things. I'm not sure Bob wants anything to do with me right now. I haven't seen him in a week. I've called and texted him, but he's ignorin' me."

"You guys have a fight?"

"No. It's complicated. I need to talk to him about it. But I want to do this thing. Help solve this murder, but I'm afraid it might have already cost me his feelings about me."

"Sounds like you might want to put the case on the back burner. Take care of you and Bob first."

Charmain stopped sobbing. Wiped her nose, grinning. "Did you have to say it like that?"

"What do you mean?"

"Put it on the back burner." She scoffed. "You are aware, I'm hopeless in the kitchen."

Archer grinned. Relieved, he comforted her a little. "Still though. You see my point?"

Charmain nodded while drying her eyes. "You're right. Maybe I should track him down and clear the air. At least then I might find out whether I should go ahead with this project."

Charmain stood. She gave Archer a peck on the cheek and headed for the door.

As she crossed the parking lot, a man trotted to her side. "Excuse me, ma'am. Is that your car?"

Charmain turned to face the reddish-brown haired man with a mustache and goatee, then glanced back to where he pointed.

"Uh, huh. Why?"

"When I pulled in the lot, I might have bumped it. Wanna do the right thing, you know?" He shoved his glasses back on his nose, then laid his hand on her arm. The gentle touch of his hand contrasted with the rippling muscles in his arms.

Charmain turned back to the car. Together, they walked around it, studying the finish. He pointed to the fender. "That's where I hit it. It's a nice car. I'd feel bad if I damaged it."

Charmain peered at the spot, brushed back her hair, and looked up at the man. "I don't see anything. Thanks anyway."

The man smiled and shrugged. He reached in his pocket and handed her a card. "This is my home and cell number. Please call me if you find something later. I feel real bad. Miss uh..."

"Charmain. Charmain Crump. Well, thank you." She glanced at the card. "Uh, Mr. Nixon. But I don't think it's going to be a problem."

CHAPTER THREE

Jordan and Urich sat before the Tunica sheriff's desk. The uniformed man sat with his arms folded across his chest. Lean, not over five feet six inches tall. His gray eyes, incongruent with his chocolate complexion. Balding, his hair a silver fringe around his head. His voice commanding as he briefed them on the operation. "Just like always, we're caught in a migration. Memphis cracks down on the sex trade, and it moves outside town. What better place than here. We got our high roller wannabees with wads of cash. Draws 'em like flies to a cow pie. Now we gotta chase 'em back out. This time we're doin' it different. We're goin' after the pimps and stealin' their product."

"How's it different?" Urich interrupted.

"Know about Operation Cross Country?"

"Yeah. That FBI thing they do once a year. Great idea, but the pimps know it's once a year. Then business as usual," Urich chided.

"Since it was last month, we're gonna do it again right here. We're also gonna try to move not only the kids out of the trade but the ones of legal age. We'll go after 'em all. They want out of the business, we'll get 'em out. They give us their pimp, we vacate the charges."

Urich and Jordan traded looks. Jordan turned back to the Sheriff. "How long are you doin' it like this?"

"That's gonna be how we do it from now on."

Jordan's brow furrowed. "But why us?"

"Locals recognize my people, but not you."

"But Roy said this would only be temporary," Urich protested.

"It is. They'll learn your faces, and then you'll go back. That happens, I'll borrow from another county. I'm hopin' the pimps will finally give up. Stick to West Memphis or stay in Shelby County where they belong."

*****

Later, in the motel room, Urich studied the man in the plaid shirt with a clerical collar seated on the next bed. Even though the room seemed cool, his shaved head beaded with perspiration. The man's short-sleeve shirt exposed arms roped with muscle. They shook hands when they met. His handshake, firm, but not overpowering. It gave Urich the impression that the man must be secure. Not needing to impress with physical strength. Must be strong inside, Urich thought to herself. Excellent for a cleric.

He did not make eye contact with Urich. Instead, focused on some spot behind her on the wall. His face grave as he listened on the headphones attached to the recorder. He glanced at Urich, as they heard the door in the next room open. She started recording. Seeing Urich's actions, the uniformed Deputy seated at the table set his phone aside. Unsnapped his handcuffs and stood as if poised for action. A woman's voice came over the headphones.

"You need a shave, honey," While the woman snapped chewing gum, a Southern accent dripped from her tongue.

"If you want to rub cheeks with me, gotta take care of that. Kinda rugged lookin', but a girl like me can't go runnin' around with whisker burns."

Jordan's voice now came over the headset. "Well, for what I got in mind, we won't be face to face."

"No problem, unless you want it Greek style. That's extra."

"How much?"

"Screwin' the pooch a hundred. Up the Hershey Highway twice that." The woman moaned. "Damn, that feels good and hard. I'll suck it after for nothin'. Ain't had a rod that fine in a long time. You ready to party, honey?"

"Before you take your clothes off, you need to know I'm a Deputy Sheriff."

"Shit! Lookin' like that. You some out-of-town vice or do you always look like you've been on a bender, asshole."

"Ouch. Damn it. Drop the purse ma'am, and back off."

"I'm gonna kick your ass!"

A crash over the headphones prompted Urich to leap to her feet. Jordan moaned. Urich shook her head and chuckled as she tossed off her headset. As she drew the pepper spray canister from her belt, she threw open the door to the adjoining room. Through the opened door, Jordan staggered back before sprawling on the floor, holding his head. Once past Jordan's body, Urich leaped into the next room. Her pepper spray held high. The uniformed Deputy followed, his cuffs in hand.

"Drop the purse!" An aerosol hissing came from the other room. Followed by a scream.

"You are under arrest. You have the right to remain silent..." Urich continued with the Miranda warning as she snapped on the cuffs. She dragged the woman into the room where Jordan and the minister waited. After shoving the woman on the bed, she kicked the woman's purse towards Jordan, still sprawled on the floor. "God, Jordan! Disarm 'em before you flash the badge."

The minister remained on the bed, saying nothing, just watching them wide-eyed.

*****

A few moments later in the stake-out room's bathroom water gushed from the sink's faucet. "Hold still and keep your eyes closed!" Urich commanded as she rinsed the woman's face with a wet rag. "You're damn lucky it didn't get in your eyes."

"I'm sorry. Lost my temper. Havin' a rough week," The woman protested as she bent over the sink. When they finished, Urich escorted the prostitute to one bed before explaining what they wanted.

The woman studied the three, still chewing and cracking her gum. "Can you take the cuffs off? They hurt."

Jordan glanced at Urich. She clutched the pepper spray canister and nodded. Jordan unfastened the cuffs.

The woman shook her hands in front of her. "I'm sorry. I lost it for a minute. I'm cool."

She continued to chew as she ran her fingers through her raven, spiked hair. Squirming on the bed, she tugged at the red skirt's hem. She pulled it down, revealing only half her thigh. "So, if I tell you I want to get out of the life, you're gonna let the Reverend here take care of me. Plus, if I give up my pimp, all the charges are dropped. That's a lot for a girl to consider."

Urich turned to the cleric.

The preacher nodded. "Ma'am, I'm Wayne Belkey with the Shining Light. You are...?"

"Georgia. Georgia McCain. My close friends call me Blondie." She batted her eyes.

Belkey frowned. "Blondie? I don't understand. Your hair is black."

"That's up top. You get to know me well enough; you'll understand."

Belkey tugged at his collar. Urich grinned and winked at Jordan. He shook his head as the minister continued. "Uh. Well. I see. I guess. Our program rescues young people like yourself. We provide housing, meals, and medical services. We also help with job placement or find training. Either will allow you to live a life of dignity."

The young woman scowled. "So, you're deliverin' Heaven on Earth instead of the other kind."

Belkey paused, cocked his head to one side. "I never thought of it that way. But I guess you're right."

"Gee! That sounds peachy! Can I get a smoke out of my purse?"

"This is a no smoking room, ma'am." Urich snapped.

"Oh! That makes all the difference in the world. I'd never wanna break any rules, officer." She snapped her gum again. As she gave Belkey a measuring glance, her tongue played across her lips. Confident she had his attention, she re-crossed her legs, raising the skirt to provide Belkey with a look at her inner thigh. "What you expectin' in return?"

Belkey face flushed, cleared his throat. "Ma'am, I want to feel like I have done something worthwhile. Seeing you happy and out of this situation is enough for me."

"Yeah! Right!" Georgia stared off as if pondering the offer then looked back at Belkey. With her eyes on him, she tipped her head back and sneered. "See, I like this life fine. My man treats me real good. Don't beat on me or nothin'. Makes sure I'm safe. I give him a split off the take for protection. Live in a nice apartment. Get paid to party." She shrugged.

"He did a fine job of keepin' you out of this mess, huh!" Urich chided.

"These busts just part of the business. You haul me in. I call him, and he comes bail me out. Of course, I gotta reimburse him, but it doesn't happen more'n once or twice a year."

"I don't see him here now. We could be hurtin' you really bad," Jordan added.

Georgia reached inside her blouse. She flipped a pendant out and held it up. "If it was like that, I'da pushed this button. He'd have busted the door down. Wasted your sorry ass."

Urich leaped to her feet. She threw open the door and scanned the hallway. Georgia shook her head and chuckled. "Don't bother. He's gone. Push the button on this twice. It means the fuzz. He takes off and waits for the call. Did that while I was holdin' off Dirty Harry here." She nodded towards Jordan. Cackled.

Jordan rose. Retrieved Georgia's purse, searched it. "We got more here, Georgia than solicitin'. You assaulted a police officer. Resisted arrest." He pulled a half brick from the bag. Glanced at Georgia, then dropped it on the floor.

She snapped her gum and grinned. "That's my workin' purse. Girl does what she's gotta do."

He removed a wallet. Glanced inside. Jordan studied the ID then looked at Georgia. She could be this young, but she looked older. Her pale white skin, already wrinkled. The woman looked close to thirty.

"Says you're nineteen. You can be charged as an adult."

Georgia shrugged. "We gotta a good lawyer. He'll plead it down. Doubt I do more'n thirty days. If that."

Jordan turned to Belkey. Belkey arched his eyebrows as he turned back to the woman on the bed. "Georgia. I don't think you understand. At Shining Light, we can offer you a better life. A future."

"Like I need a future? Thanks, but no thanks."

*****

The dark blue van had a lighthouse painted on the side. Its beacon throwing a cone of light along the side. The engine idled as Jordan and Belkey stood beside it. Three young faces peered out of the van's side windows. "Well Reverend, at least your day wasn't wasted."

"I had hoped we'd save them all. But that's just my pride talking. I'm grateful for these three."

"Three out of eleven's not bad. Good batting average in the majors."

"Will you be here tomorrow?"

"Yeah. Me and Urich are here till they get to know us. I guess we go to another casino tomorrow, though. Spread the good work around."

"Then till tomorrow." Belkey climbed into the van and drove off.

Jordan seated himself in the unmarked Sheriff's car next to Urich. "Not too bad for a God Botherer."

Urich shrugged. "He had away with them that's for sure. Hell of a lot more patient than me. I wanted to pop 'em all.

Jordan turned to her. Frowned. "You one of those Spare the Rod, Spoil the Child folks?"

"No. Don't believe in that. I mean I wouldn't hit my best friend just cause they did something I didn't like. It's stupider with a child. Teaches nothing."

"So, you gonna take me to my car?"

"No! Hector said he would."

Jordan's jaw dropped. "Hector?!"

"Yeah. I'll drop you off at the church. He'll be in the meeting. He said you can either wait for him in the parking lot or go inside. He'll drive you to the bar you left your car at then."

Jordan grimaced. "Shit! Just give me the fuckin' keys, and I'll walk or take a cab."

Urich shook her head. "Can't do that."

"Why the hell not?"

"Hector's got 'em."

CHAPTER FOUR

As Urich climbed the steps to the deck outside her trailer, footsteps behind her prompted her to turn. Joshua raced across the street, leading a golden cocker spaniel. The boy's beaded braids, and the dog's ears flopped as they ran. Joshua knocked Urich slightly off balance as he hugged her legs while the dog scampered around them. Its leash tangled their legs, toppling both to the ground. After they landed, the dog pounced on Urich's face and bathed her with her tongue.

Scowling, Urich pushed the dog away. "Eww! Ginger! Your breath smells awful. What have you been eating?"

Joshua looked up and grinned. "I gave her some of that cheese that Mr. Jordan left in the fridge." A slight lisp in his voice caused by the absence of two front teeth recently lost to maturity.

"Oh, my God. Joshua, that wasn't cheese. That was some kinda stink bait he uses for catfishin'."

Wide-eyed, Joshua's eyes shifted to the dog. "Ginger liked it. Ate it right up. Licked the dish clean!"

After they untangled themselves from the leash, they got to their feet.

"Momma's almost got supper done. I gotta finish givin' Ginger her walk."

Joshua took off again at a dead run down the street. The dog trotting at his side on the leash. Urich dusted off her trousers, adjusted her gun belt, and finished climbing the stairs.

Inside, the aroma of chicken made her mouth water. Her housemate, Maureen, still clad in nurse's scrubs, looked up from the skillet, sizzling and bubbling on the range. On the counter beside her stood a plate filled with fried chicken. "I hope you're hungry. Got the urge to cook when I got home. Just gotta finish the gravy, and we're ready."

Urich took off her gun belt. Placed it in the cupboard over the fridge and locked the door. "Damn! I gotta buy a gun safe. I'm not sure this is gonna be a deterrent for that boy much longer. You know he fed Ginger that stink bait that Jordan put in the fridge?"

"What? That boy! Musta done it when I snuck in a nap after work. Thought he was awful quiet."

"Won't hurt her, will it?"

"Don't think so. Jordan said he just uses cornmeal, chicken blood, and hand soap."

"Hand soap?"

Maureen nodded. "My Daddy uses it too. Might make the dog upchuck, but won't hurt her. I mean, she always eatin' dead stuff off the road. Never phases her."

"Let's change the subject. The smell here is makin' me drool. Don't need that damn dog spoilin' my appetite."

"How'd the day go?"

Urich glanced at her watch, then took out her phone. "Oh shit! I promised Charmain I'd update her on Jordan. You can listen while I talk."

Urich smiled as she put the phone to her ear. "Hey, girlfriend. I got you on speakerphone. Maureen's here, cookin' away. She wanted to hear about the day, so I thought I'd catch you up at the same time."

"Thanks, Chris. Hey, Maureen."

"Back at ya!" Maureen called from the kitchen.

"So. Is he all right?"

"Yeah. I think he'll live. Spent the day at the casino bustin' working girls. Your boy got his head smacked, and his pride shattered by one. Good for him, though. Teaches humility."

"Where's he now?"

"I dropped him off at the church in Harmon. Hector was gonna try to hook up with him there. Then take him to his car after the meeting."

"Listen, you guys have been great. And thanks for keepin' me posted."

"You mean he hasn't talked to you?"

Charmain paused. "No. Not a word from him for a week?"

"Have you called him?"

"First coupla days, but he ignored me. Guess he needs some space."

Urich scowled, put her hand on her hip. "Damn, girl. You're the best thing that's happened to him for a long time. You guys have a fight?"

"No. Nothin' like that." Charmain sighed into the phone, a sob in her voice.

"Well, what the hell happened."

"I really can't tell you. I need to talk to Bob about it first. It wouldn't be fair."

"Well, for what it's worth, I'm in your corner. I'll see if I can get him to come around. Call me if you just need to chat. Girl to girl. Anytime."

Charmain sniffed. "Thanks. I will. Say hi to Paulo for me, okay?"

"Sure, girl. Take care."

With a frown, Urich set the phone on the counter. "I'd kill that asshole if it wouldn't hurt her even more."

Maureen removed the pan from the stove. As she poured the gravy into a tureen, she shook her head. "Men!"

The trailer door flew open. Paulo entered, holding his nose. A tall black man trailed him, leading Joshua by the hand. As he led the boy, the big man shook his head, grinning.

Maureen approached the big man leading Joshua, her arms outstretched, a grin on her face. "My men have returned!"

She froze in her tracks, scowled, and stepped back. "Phew! What is that?"

The stink rapidly overpowered the cooking smells, combining into a cacophony of odor that had them all holding their noses.

"Ginger barfed on me!" Joshua pointed to a big yellow splotch in the middle of his shirt.

"How'd it get on you?" Maureen asked as she took the boy by the hand and led him down the hall.

"We ran a long way. Ginger looked tired, so I was carryin' her."

Soon the sounds of running water came from the back of the trailer. Followed by Maureen's voice instructing the boy in how she expected him to clean himself. When the water stopped running, Maureen returned, carrying the boy's clothes at arm's length. She opened the door and tossed them outside. After giving the tall black man a peck on the cheek, Maureen smiled up at him. "Was Ginger all right, Steven?"

The tall man nodded. "Probably feel a lot better after she heaved. Mrs. Lambert laughed when I told her what happened. Said she warned Josh about giving her treats before they walk. Said he might listen better now."

*****

Meanwhile, Jordan squinted as he entered the Church basement from the dark parking lot. People talked among themselves. As he joined the line at the coffee urn, a woman with purple streaks in her shoulder-length black hair turned and smiled. "Bob! I am so happy for you."

"Oh, yeah?"

"Yes. Six months sober. I know you shouldn't feel pride, but I am happy for you."

Jordan ran his fingers through his hair and sighed.

"What's wrong? Are you okay? You look a little pale. Maybe you should skip out after you get your token. I'll tell George. We can work it out, really."

"No, Mary. It's not like that. I didn't make it. Fell off big time. Been on a binge for a week."

She clasped his arm. "It happens to us all. But you're here. Been sober today, right?"

Jordan nodded. She led him by the hand to the coffee urn. After both served themselves, they grabbed folding chairs and carried them to the circle. Two people spread out to make room for them. Mary set her chair on one side of the opening, then beckoned to the space next to her. "Come on, sit by me."

As Jordan glanced around the circle, he recalled the first time he met Hector at one of his first AA meetings. Fortified with liquid courage, Jordan told his story. The screwed up major case that set the tone for the rest of his career in Memphis. The long absences from his home and family, and finally his daughter's murder. Instead of the expected affirmation, it had stunned the group, silent. Except for Hector. The big man clapped, then said: "What a great bunch of excuses to drink!"

As Jordan became more and more committed to sobriety, others in the group encouraged him. Hector remained his nemesis-taunting and challenging. One night, proud after an evening of social drinking with Charmain, he shared this experience with the group. Finished, Jordan declared he might not have a problem with alcohol. He could control it. No one else in the group besides Hector responded.

The big man sat up in his chair and guffawed. "You're just lyin' to yourself, and lyin' is dyin'!"

At that point, Jordan felt the spur of commitment. Sobriety one day at a time. At a later meeting, he introduced himself as an alcoholic. Mary reached over and squeezed his shoulder. Several others smiled and nodded, recognizing the courage he displayed. Hector just shook his head and growled. "So you discovered denial ain't a fuckin river in Egypt. Way to go!"

On the eve of his reaching his first thirty-day token, he realized there would be no one to present it. He needed a sponsor.

That night Mary explained the value of an AA sponsor. "In the program, people that are starting out are most successful if they have a sponsor."

"What's that?"

"It's a person you can call if you sense you may have a relapse. The sponsor can help by talking to you and listening. They have experienced what you're going through now. It's almost like having a portable meeting."

"How do I get a sponsor?"

"You ask them. If they agree, you call them when you have a rough time. Also, anytime they can't help, they guide you to someone who can."

"Are you or George sponsoring anyone?"

"Well, it's best if the two are the same gender. Pairs of the opposite sex just don't work out well. So, I can't. You could talk to George, but he is already sponsoring two others. He'd probably say yes. But he's stretched too thin already. Also, he may not be best suited for you. You're too much alike."

"Anybody you suggest?"

"Not really. Keep it in mind, though. Listen to the others. It works best if the two are not alike. If they are, they tend to enable each other. Find someone who is your polar opposite. One you might not even like. That would be the best person." Mary's words led him to Hector.

Prepared for rejection, Jordan asked Hector to be his sponsor. Hector said nothing at first, scowled as he coldly studied Jordan.

Finally, the big man answered. "As long as you don't drive me to drink."

From that day on, Hector had been there for him. He wondered now if he had fucked this up too. As Jordan sat down in the chair, he spotted Hector setting across from him. He sneered, then flipped Jordan the bird.

*****

After the meeting Hector drove Jordan to his car. Hector turned off the motorcycle. As Jordan climbed off the back, he removed the helmet he'd borrowed from Hector. His teeth chattered as he handed the helmet to Hector. Surveying the parking lot, he spotted his car parked next to the bar. Crickets chirped in the darkness. The sound of music came faintly to them from inside. After tying the spare helmet to the bike, Hector tossed Jordan his keys.

"I'm goin' in for a cup of coffee. Or maybe some tea. They make a nice Russian here. Really warms you up. You comin'?"

"I don't know, Hector."

"I don't care if you drink. Hell, have a brandy or an Irish coffee for all I care. It's up to you."

"I mean I gotta be in Tunica tomorrow real early. Maybe I should pass."

"It's not that late. Hell, barely nine o'clock. Besides you probably haven't eaten. They got great burgers here."

"It's not that. It's..."

"Scared huh?"

Jordan nodded. "Man, I was so close. You know?"

"Yeah. I know. But you're here sober right now. That's what counts. Right? That's the program. Fuck yesterday. Tomorrow ain't here yet."

Jordan shook his head and grinned. "Do you think Bill W. would agree with your interpretation of one day at a time?"

"Fuck him. This is a new century. Man's gotta roll with the times. You comin'?"

Jordan nodded then followed the big man into the bar.

CHAPTER FIVE

Jordan flinched as Urich applied the tape, holding the microphone wire in place. "Can you put that somewhere else? Maybe over the other shoulder?"

Urich pulled the tape loose. She peered at his bare shoulder. "Looks a little red. Let's see if it can go that far."

"The boss said this would be temporary. This is what. Our second week? Fourth Casino?"

"It's just you're such good bait. You attract 'em like honey. Don't know whether it's your rugged good looks or your aura of success," she replied with a sly grin.

"The Feeb oughta take a turn. He's not doin' shit but sit around lookin' important. Let 'em grab his manhood once in a while. If he's got one, that is. Where is he anyway? Gettin' his hair done?"

Urich shook her head. "He has been handy fetchin' Latte' and stuff."

"Good with the press, too. Seen how pissed he got when the Sheriff postponed his press conference. Thought he'd hold his breath till he turned blue."

"Sheriff shoulda known the Feds would step in when we started catchin' all these guys from Memphis. Crossin' state lines makes it Federal." Finished with the wire, Urich turned him around, pinched his cheek. "There, that okay?"

Jordan swung his arms in a circle before putting on his shirt. He glanced over at Belkey perched on a bed reading a Bible. "How you doin', Rev? Have a pleasant weekend?"

Belkey looked up from his Bible, pushed his glasses back on his nose. "Sunday is the busiest day of the week for the clergy."

"So, you did a lotta preachin'?"

"Had an important ritual," He nodded. "Yes."

Jordan smiled. "Any room left at the Shelter?"

"You've succeeded well. We've a dozen underage and eleven more older girls. We've just about maxed out our available shelters."

"What then?" Jordan tucked in his shirt.

"We have four donated houses about ready for occupancy. I toured some others we're considering in the last few days, but they'll need some work."

A knock on the door interrupted their discussion. Both turned as a man wearing a gray pinstriped suit rushed in. The name tag on his jacket identified him as the manager. His face pale. "We've got a problem. I need your help, please." The man glanced from Urich to Jordan.

"Problem?"

The man placed his hand on his forehead. His jaw trembled. "Yes! We found a body."

"A body?" Jordan asked.

"Yes! Upstairs. Maid found her. She looks dead. I've called the paramedics, but our security chief said we need the law here too."

Jordan turned to the uniformed deputy sitting at the table. "This is not part of our assignment, but Urich and I'll go with him. Call your boss. Have him send someone."

Opening the door, he turned to the man. "Lead the way. We're right behind you." Urich trailed them as they rushed down the hallway.

Upstairs, they marched behind the manager. In the first open room they passed, two women clutched each other, seated on a bed. Both wore matching blue T-shirts. One wailed in Spanish, the other stroked the wailing woman's head and rocked her. The manager stopped outside the second open door. Without glancing inside, he beckoned them in.

The naked girl lay on her side with dried pools of blood near her chin and hand. One forearm raised to her shoulder, bent upward at the elbow with the hand pointed forward. The other trailed her in an inverted pattern. Jordan stopped, stepped back. At his heels, Urich collided with him. Frozen in place, his jaw dropped. Urich stepped around him as his eyes remained fixed on the body.

After checking the body for signs of life, Urich glanced around the room. She turned back to Jordan, still frozen near the doorway. "Jordan, what's up, man?"

Jordan said nothing. His eyes glued to the body, he shuffled to a chair near the room's table and collapsed. "Give me a second, okay?"

Urich looked back at the dead girl, then turned to Jordan. "Sure. Do you know her?"

Silent Jordan's eyes roamed the room. His eyes locked on the mirror. "Oh, Shit. No! No!" His head dropped into his hands, and he sobbed.

Urich's head snapped toward the mirror. The message scrawled in lipstick.

"Walks like an Egyptian." A phone number, then a postscript. "Call Archer."

*****

Jordan remained silent in the chair as the local authorities processed the scene.

"We're done with the body," The technician announced as he climbed off the bed. A photographer snapped pictures of the room and the mirror. Next to Urich stood a man wearing a beige blazer and black slacks. A gold badge clipped to his belt. He nodded towards Jordan, still sitting silently in the chair. "What's with him? Never seen a stiff before?"

Urich shrugged.

He turned to the technician. "Whattaya got for me."

"Fourteen maybe fifteen years old. Strangled. Some signs of a struggle. Lookin' at her mouth, Meth user. Tongue and finger cut off post-mortem. Time of death late afternoon yesterday, maybe early evening."

"Rape?"

The technician shrugged. "We'll know more after the autopsy."

The detective nodded. "She was a pro. Security said they'd run her out a few times. Hustlin' customers. Wonder who this Archer is?"

"I think it's Jack Archer. Memphis Homicide." Jordan said, breaking his silence.

The Tunica detective turned. "Oh, it speaks finally. Why do you think they meant him?"

"Because he and I worked a similar case a few years back. Never solved. Cold case, but I'm sure he still works it."

The detective leaned down close to Jordan. "Killer sendin' a message?"

Jordan sighed. "I have no fuckin' idea. Call Archer and find out. In the case before, the phone number was her pimp's. We used it to bust him."

"Huh. Some more Memphis shit dumped in our laps. Boss won't be pleased, but I'll suggest that we do that. You got Archer's number?"

Jordan read off Archer's number from his phone. Once the detective scribbled the number on a pad, read it back aloud to check. Finished, he planted himself before Jordan, both hands on his hips. "This is not your case. It's not even your jurisdiction. Don't be callin' your old buddy yourself. Got me?"

Jordan stood. As he trudged out the door, Urich scurried in his wake. She got beside him as they moved down the hall. "What gives

Jordan? I've never seen you like that. Somethin' special about that old case?"

Jordan stopped. As he reached under his shirt to pull off the wire, he looked her in the eye. "Special? Yeah, you might say so. It was my daughter."

He tossed her the recording equipment. "I'm done for the day. Might be done for good. Call the boss. Tell him I'm on medical leave. If you want to join me, I'll be in the bar."

*****

Urich returned to the room where they had prepared for the sting. Belkey still read his Bible. He looked up when she entered before glancing back at the door as if expecting Jordan to follow.

"I'm sorry, Reverend. I think we're done for the day."

He set the Bible down. "They need you to help with the dead body?"

"No. I'm afraid my partner is indisposed right now. Got called away. A family crisis."

"I'm sorry to hear that. I always felt comfortable around him. Not inhibited by my calling like most people. I hope everything works out for him. I guess I'll head out. Check on our new arrivals. Will you have the Sheriff call me again when they start up again? We made real progress here."

As he reached the doorway, Belkey turned back to Urich. "Do tell Mr. Jordan I'll pray for him."

Urich nodded as she took out her phone.

"This is Sheriff Speck," Roy said as he answered. "Hey, Urich. I just got off the phone with Sheriff Atkins in Tunica. Sounds pleased with the work you guys have been doing over there. What's happenin'?"

Urich told him about the murder and Jordan's reaction. Roy sighed. "Darn, it worried me when I sent you guys over there.

Wondered how it would be with him bustin' the working girls like that."

"Why in the hell didn't anybody tell me about it?" Urich screamed over the phone. "I'm his partner. I should have been told this kind of crap."

"I'm sorry. You've been doin' pretty well together. A real team. As close as you guys seem to be, if figured he told you the whole story."

"Well, he didn't. I knew someone murdered his daughter, but nothin' else. What's the deal?"

"Well, you know things went to hell with Bob when that case against those three teens got tossed. They let 'em walk cause his partner screwed up the chain of evidence on the DNA. After they sat on death row for three years, the press came out enraged. All they seemed interested in was roastin' Jordan alive."

"If his partner screwed up, why'd they go after Jordan?"

"Partner ate his gun. Jordan was around, so they attacked him."

Urich pressed her fingers to her forehead. "Shit!"

"Yeah, they badgered him real bad. Specially that bitch on Fox. I was shocked when he got into that relationship with her protege'. Anyway. Jordan took the hounding real hard. Neglected his family. They started havin' trouble with the daughter. She ran off a lot. Got into drugs. Her supplier got tired of bangin' her for product, so he peddled her ass on the street. Wasn't more'n thirteen."

"Jesus, Roy. And you sent him out on this detail?"

"Well, I thought he might be past it by now. He'd been sober quite a while. Hell, I even trusted him with the Department's vehicles again."

"So, what happened with his daughter?"

"They found her murdered in a motel. Never solved it. But that wasn't the worst of it."

"What could have been worse?"

"The way he found out. There was a killing in Memphis. Nobody knew who the girl was, and Jordan was on call. Found out by walkin' onto the scene."

*****

Jordan pushed the second empty shot glass away. As he raised the third, a hand touched his shoulder. "You look lonesome, detective."

Jordan turned in her direction. His eyes opened wide; his jaw dropped. "Mrs. Marsh."

"Please, just Carla. Okay? Nice seein' you. Expecting someone?"

"No. Not really."

She slid onto the next barstool. The little black dress she wore almost reached her mid-thigh, giving Jordan an excellent view of her shapely legs.

"Okay, if I join you, or do you prefer being by yourself?"

"No. I mean, sure. Buy you a drink?" He waved to the bartender. "Nice seein' you too."

After ordering a scotch and water, she took a cigarette from his pack on the bar. As Jordan lit it for her, she held his hand to steady the flame. Once it glowed, she pursed her lips to blow it out.

While her tongue played over her full lips, she gave him a smile. "I believe I'm making you nervous, detective." She placed her hand on his knee. "Don't be afraid I won't bite."

The heat from her touch radiated up his leg. Her long black hair parted in the middle, partially covered her face. One eye played peek -a- boo behind it. Her startling blue eyes drew him in like pools waiting for a swimmer. Except for a few lines at the eyes, still the face of the young girl growing up in the beauty pageant world.

"Damn! This is like an old home week!" Urich announced her arrival from Jordan's other side.

"Carla, you remember my partner." Jordan nodded toward Urich.

Carla leaned around Jordan and smiled at Urich.

"Mrs. Marsh. Haven't seen you since the trial. Troy, okay?"

Carla brushed her hair back and shrugged. "I wouldn't know. Oh, and by the way, it's not Marsh anymore. It's Clausen. Divorce was final last week."

"I thought you and the rest of the Murder Club were in Hollywood," Urich growled, almost sounding accusatory.

Carla drew on her cigarette, then exhaled smoke in Urich's face. "Well, I came back. Needed a break. Just finished the script for the movie. Needed to do some research for my next book."

"Need anything?" the bartender asked as he joined them.

"Maybe a diet soda. You got Sprite?" Urich said. The bartender nodded. As he walked away, Urich turned back to Carla continuing her interrogation. "So, what's this new book about?"

"Well, I thought I'd branch out a bit. Get away from the Erotica." Beneath the bar, her hand moved up Jordan's leg. "Do a Mystery. You know? Hard-boiled detective solves the crime while finding genuine romance." She brushed his manhood.

She turned to Jordan. "Maybe you could help me? Flesh out the technical details? That is, if you have any spare time."

Urich turned to Jordan. "Well, there you go. Something to do while you take your leave. Jordan knows all about police procedure, right, Boss?"

Jordan could not speak. His mouth dry and thick, his cheeks warm. He nodded. Carla squeezed, he trembled. She took her hand away and reached into her purse.

A sly smile played at her lips as she passed a card to Jordan. "Case you lost my number from before. Listen. I've got to run. Meeting some college friends for a girl's night out. Call me. I'd love to pick your brains. Get some ideas for the book. Okay?"

She slid off the stool. Wiggled as she adjusted the hem on the black spandex skirt, then gave Jordan a peck on the cheek. "Thanks for the drink."

With a finger wave to Urich, she strode away. As she reached the doorway, she glanced back to make sure she still had an audience. Satisfied, she left the bar.

Urich gasped. "Jesus, Jordan! That's all you need. You know the paparazzi trail her everywhere. She rolled her eyes. "I can see the caption now. Hangin' right there next to the checkout counter at Krogers. Carla now seeing Detective who locked up her husband!"

"Yeah. Wouldn't be one of my brighter moves." He downed the third shot glass.

*****

The Rolling Stones played *Sympathy for the Devil.* He liked soft music when he worked out. Not loud. A soft background. Traffic rumbled outside.

With a sharp intake of breath, he raised the bar from his chest. His arms trembled. With a gasp, he set the bar back on the hooks. The bar safe on the stand, he sat up on the bench. Bench presses without a spotter could be dangerous, but he enjoyed living on the edge.

While wiping the sweat from his body, he strode to the refrigerator. He removed the pitcher he prepared earlier and filled a glass. As he sipped, he strolled to the table that occupied the other half of this tiny kitchen. Once he snatched up one photo, he studied it as he settled into his chair. The Stones switched to *Midnight Rambler.*

"Charmain Crump, he said to himself. "Pretty. Smooth chocolate skin, like a Hershey bar. Bet that's how you'd taste. A real Black Beauty. What were you doing with that Detective? Archer tappin' you on the side? Never would have thought. Figured he was a straight arrow, family man."

He hummed and tapped his fingers to the tune as he studied the picture. After pulling the laptop toward himself, he Googled her name.

His eyebrows arched as her image came up on the screen. "Well! Used to be a cheerleader at Memphis University. Nice short skirt. Been a few years, though, but still got that bod. A reporter! Humph. That's interesting. Interesting girl. I remember you. Black Beauty! Yes! That football player assaulted you. Gave up a job at Fox News to Blog. Works part-time for NPR. A little weekly half-hour special on Saturday nights on the radio. Is our boy, Archer, getting a guilty conscience, maybe thinking about blowing the whistle? I wonder. Give his side woman a leg up with a headline? Perhaps I can help." He grinned. "Give you an inside source, Charmain. Real inside."

He pushed the laptop aside. Moved over a stack of magazines. Thumbed through them. As he cut out letters from the magazine, the music switched to the Bangles, *Walks Like an Egyptian*. He crooned the chorus as he snipped.

CHAPTER SIX

Archer and Todd, his partner, followed the uniformed deputy down the hall. The deputy stopped at a closed door and knocked before entering. After stepping back into the hallway, he gestured for the Memphis officers to enter. As the door closed behind them, the two men seated at the table rose. Neither smiled.

The younger brown-haired man nodded. "Thanks for comin' Lieutenant. I'm Detective Collins, lead on this case." He indicated the short, balding black man still seated. The man scowled as he gave both Memphis detectives a measuring glance." This is my boss, Sheriff Atkins."

Archer nodded to Todd. "This is Detective Roscoe Todd. My partner on this case."

After shaking hands all around, the men seated themselves at the table. The Sheriff nodded to Collins as if to proceed. "When we spoke earlier, you said that you have had similar killings in Memphis."

"That's right, four. I brought the case files here with me." As he spoke, Archer set a stack of file folders on the desk. Todd slumped in his chair. Appeared bored, content to let Archer talk.

Collins glanced at Todd, sneered before turning back to Archer. "Victims had their tongues cut out? Posed like some kinda Egyptian Hieroglyphic? Message written in lipstick on the mirror?"

Archer placed his hands on the folders. "That's right—Walk's Like an Egyptian, each time with a phone number of the victim's pimp. I got photos of the message here in the files. Also, we got composites from witnesses at each. They all look pretty much the same."

Collins glanced at his boss, then back at Archer. "It was the same here except this time the message also said to call Archer."

Archer looked to each one in turn. His brows knitted. Half a frown. Puzzled. "And out of that, you figured that it had to be me? You psychic?"

"We got your name from one of the first officers on the scene. Said you and he worked a similar case in Memphis some years back. Jordan.

Archer's jaw dropped. "Shit! I thought he was Jergen County."

"He is. He and his partner were here helping us out with some vice busts at the casino. You know him?"

"Yeah, I do. He started out as lead on the first case and then got moved off."

Collins scoffed. "Why? He fuck up?"

"No. Victim was his daughter."

Collins slumped in his seat. The Sheriff rubbed his brow. Sighed. Turned to Collins. "You know about this?"

Collins shook his head. "Explains a lot."

The Sheriff sighed, hung his head. "Damn, I feel like a heel now. Right after Jordan found our victim, he walked off the bust. I called and chewed out Speck down in Jergen. Guess I have to do a Mea Culpa. I'll leave you to this while I call Roy and make sure he knows what happened."

Collins turned to Archer. "Four of these with the same perp. A serial?"

Archer nodded. "Escalating too. A year between the first two, then six months between the last two. Last was just a week ago. I made a list of the details in each case. Got 'em in a spreadsheet so I could compare columns."

Archer opened his laptop and turned it on. "I can put your case in so we can visualize 'em right here."

"How about you email the file to me? I can print up some copies that way, we can both look at the same time."

"No problem," Archer replied, not looking up from his laptop.

After Collins returned with the printouts, they all studied the sheets. Collins whistled and shook his head as he read. "This is slick. Nice, the way you got these arranged. Damn, even copied the composites right in there. Can't see 'em on the sheet, but they show up nice on the screen."

Archer sighed, leaned back. Studied Collins. "Thanks."

"Our victim had a fingertip removed. Did any of the other victims have pieces cut off?"

"Nothin' but the tongue. Rest is the same." Archer replied.

"All killed at a motel or hotel. You got composites. What about video? Nothin' there?"

"He used real shit holes. Either they didn't have any security cameras or what they had didn't work."

Collins grinned. "We're in luck here. Casino has cameras everywhere but the rooms. Probably would do it there, except the guests would freak out."

"You've checked it, right? Got the guy that rented the room on camera?" Todd interjected. Now sitting up as if energized.

Collins nodded. "Copy of the video is on my desktop. We can check it now."

"How did he check-in? Use a credit card?" Todd now focused.

Collins scoffed and shook his head. "Yeah, just like your case. Name on the card was Herbert Hoover. This guy have somethin' about dead Republican Presidents?"

"Who knows? He started with Reagan and works backward." Archer replied.

"What's the FBI think?"

"FBI? Shit! I had to get special permission from the Chief to come and talk to you guys about it," Archer protested. "They haven't spread the word on this perp, but I guess they might not have a choice now."

"You mean they've been sitting on it? That ain't gonna set well with my boss." Collins growled.

"Doesn't sit well with me either. I pushed for it, but the brass didn't want it. Why? I don't know. I figured if we went public, we might get some leads: Crime Stoppers and shit. Maybe warn the working girls. Might save a few lives."

"Jesus, what a fucking mess! Come on, let's watch the video. Might see something I missed."

After entering Collin's cubicle, they seated themselves in front of the monitor on his desk.

He narrated as he clicked the mouse. "I started with registration, then tracked him in and out of the Casino. If nothing else, we can make some good pictures. Might even be better than your composites."

"That would be too easy. I mean, if they go public on this, the picture alone on TV or in the papers might lead us right to him. Somebody has to know this asshole," Todd added.

The video started. A man wearing a baseball cap, t-shirt, and jeans strolled to the hotel desk. As he filled out the registration card, he removed his hat, exposing neatly trimmed reddish-brown hair. He also had a mustache and beard matching the face in the composites. Archer guessed the man to be in his late twenties or early thirty's. The man held the pen in his left hand as he wrote.

Archer noted that on his legal pad. "Stop it for a second, okay?"

Collins paused the video.

Archer pointed at the screen. "See? There on the right forearm. Tattoo? Can you zoom in?"

"Shit! How could we get so damn lucky?" Collins said as he used the mouse to enlarge the image. "Kinda grainy, but I think I can just make it out."

Archer leaned close as he peered at the screen. "Maybe we can have the tech guys clean it up."

"Memphis can do that?"

"Worth a try. Maybe run it by the local parlors. Somebody might remember it. Nothin' else, it's another way to spot the guy. Let's keep runnin' it." Todd nodded his head in agreement.

They watched as the man strolled down the hallway to the room where they found the body.

Todd shook his head. "Cocky. Shit, he's got headphones on and is struttin'. Hell, he's doin' the Moonwalk right in front of the door."

Collins nodded. "Wonder what he listens to, to get him in the mood?"

Archer shrugged. "Not sure. He leaves that message about *Walks like an Egyptian.* Maybe that. Oughta listen to it. It's not dark or anything. Just nonsense. But maybe I listen to too much Hip-Hop."

"You sayin' a cracker like me might have a different take?" Collins scoffed.

"Like they say in our Sensitivity Trainin'. It helps to tap into other worldviews," Archer retorted without smiling.

In the video, the man entered the room. They fast-forwarded until the girl arrived. She knocked, stood on tip-toe to the peephole, and the door opened. After she entered, the man shot a glance down the hallway before closing the door. Again, they fast-forwarded the tape. After a half-hour elapsed, the door opened. The man again glanced both directions down the hallway. Slipped the "Do Not Disturb" sign on the door before he strode away. They switched to the lobby to watch him exit the building. The video faded.

Archer turned to Collins. "What about the parking lot? Cameras there, right? Get lucky with a car?"

Collins shook his head and chuckled. "I'll show ya how he made his getaway."

The screen changed to the parking lot. The killer strolled to a tree where a bike stood chained. After unlocking the chain, the man mounted the bike and rode away.

"I asked one of our guys about the bike. Says, it's a brand they sell a dime a dozen at Wal-Mart and Toys R Us."

*****

Stopped before the mailbox bank in her hallway, Charmain set her grocery bag down before unlocking hers. As she grabbed the mail, she tossed it in the bag before proceeding up the stairs. Outside her door stood a short young man with tight dark black curls. He grinned as she approached. "Hey, girlfriend! Just stopped by to see how ya doin'. Those groceries?"

Charmain rolled her eyes and grinned. "Yes, Tony."

Tony took out his cell phone. "Before you start, girl. Let me call the Fire Department. Give `em a heads up."

She nudged him with her shoulder. "Don't start. It's just some TV dinners and odds and ends."

"Good. I thought you might be goin' back on your vow not to cook unless supervised by an adult."

"You mean you or Glenn?" Charmain poked him playfully in the chest.

Tony arched his eyebrows and winked. "Well, that hunky boyfriend of yours counts too. That barbecue he fixed last month was to die for. Has he left the recipe yet for the rub?"

Charmain's smile evaporated. A tear formed in her eye. She brushed her long black hair away from her face. "No, he hasn't," she whimpered.

Tony stepped forward, put his arm around her shoulder. "Girl, are you okay?"

She nodded, wiping her nose with her wrist.

"Wanna cup of tea? Or maybe something stronger? Listen. I brought home a bottle of wine to try from the restaurant. Let me run up and get it, and I'll be right back. I think we need a heart to heart."

As Tony rushed off, Charmain opened her door and carried the bags inside. After she finished putting the food away, Tony returned, wine bottle in hand. "Salesman left it for us to sample. Assured us that even though it was a new label from California, we'd love it. We can try it together. Get your opinion."

Charmain smiled, gave him a hug and a peck on the cheek as she tossed the mail on the table. Tony grinned, then retrieved a corkscrew from one of her kitchen drawers. As he twisted it in the bottle, he turned to Charmain. "What's goin' on? I haven't seen that hunk of yours for almost two weeks. You two have a fallin' out?"

"Oh, Tony. It's that damn book."

"The one about his daughter's murder? He didn't like it?"

After removing the cork, Tony filled two glasses with the red wine and set them on the table before joining her.

"Yes, that one. Bob got up in the night. Was rummaging around and found the folder. It had all the pictures, plus my notes and articles about it. I think he freaked. He didn't say anything, just got dressed and left."

"You never told him about it?"

Silent Charmain gazed off, chewing her lip before replying. "There never seemed to be the right time," she whined in protest.

"When was this?"

"About two weeks ago."

Tony took a sip of his wine, placed his hand on hers. "Have you talked to him?"

"No. I've called, texted, heard nothing except he didn't go to work. It was like he fell off the earth. I finally called that sponsor of his. Hector."

"You mean that lout with all the tattoos and the potty mouth?"

Charmain sniffled, then giggled. "Oh, Tony, You're so judgmental. He's quite gentle and sweet." She sipped her wine.

"Whaddaya think? Is it palatable?" Tony pointed to the wineglass.

Charmain shrugged. "Kinda sweet, but okay."

"So, did Hector find your boy?"

"Yeah, he went on a bender. He and Christine found him in a little bar in Jergen County. Christine took him home and got him back to work. I guess he's okay. But Hector said he's furious with me."

"Well, remember his experience with the Wicked Witch of the West. You used to be among her flying monkeys."

Charmain nodded. "When I worked for Fox? That's true. She even tried to use me to ruin him. I never considered that."

"Anyway, I'm sure he'll come around."

Tony pointed to the stack of mail setting in front of Charmain. "Lotsa bills and junk, like mine."

Charmain glanced down at the stack and flipped through until she came to a large padded envelope. "Hmm. No return address, wonder what it is?"

After undoing the clasp, she pulled out a sheet of paper with pasted letters on it. A puzzled crown crossed her face as she glanced at the sheet before setting it aside. Reaching into the envelope again, she pulled out two photos. The top one showed her and Archer having lunch. She gasped as she glanced at the second snapshot.

"Oh, my God!" She shrieked as the photo slipped from her hand.

Tony leaned forward. Glanced at the picture. His jaw dropped. The photo showed the body of a naked young girl lying on a bed—a pool of blood by her mouth and one hand.

Charmain snatched up the letter. Eyes wide, she reread it.

Hello Black Beauty,

I hope you don't mind if I call you that. It seems that I'm not the only one who feels that way. I am surprised. I never thought Detective Archer would be one who strays. But I guess I'm wrong. Anyway. I'm glad he has such good taste. I'll bet you're as yummy as you look. We'll save that for later. Right now, I just want to become your muse....

"Oh, My! God!" Her jaw dropped. Her hand covered her mouth, stifling a scream.

"What's it say?" Tony asked. As he picked up the envelope, a severed finger slid out and landed on the table.

*****

After setting his coffee mug on the desk, Reverend Belkey pulled the unopened envelope from his in-tray. Running the opener beneath the flap, he pulled the letter out. A picture dropped out as he unfolded it. He glanced at the photo of the young girl, no older than fourteen. Dressed provocatively, she appeared to invite solicitation or proposition. After setting the picture aside, he picked up the letter. As he read, he chewed his lower lip. His hand trembled. He shifted in his chair, then cleared his throat. He gazed off for a moment, then resumed reading the page of cut-out letters pasted to form a message.

Your Holiness,

I use this greeting with all due respect. I have long admired your work rescuing these unfortunates from their chores of iniquity. The long hours you face. The grinding poverty you endure, so the work can continue. The frustration that comes with the failures along the way.

God looks kindly on your efforts. But that seems a meager reward for such noble and heart-rendering work. I am sure, at times, you find your spirit flagging. The ache from the futility. The seeming endlessness of the evil you fight. I am confident you come close to surrendering. To walk away. To say you've done enough. I hope this letter serves to energize your flagging spirit. Motivate you to new heights. Give you a reason to press on.

You see, I too remove these girls from the profession, but differently. Like the Grim Reaper, I harvest these wayward souls. Perhaps you learned of my work at the casino while you were assisting the police. I am efficient in what I do. While the outcome for the girls is different, I argue that my works produce a better result—no relapses and cost-effective. But let's save that discussion for a later time. I'll get right to the point.

I am preparing to harvest the girl in the picture. I propose to give you three weeks to find and save her before I move on her. If you can get her into your shelter, she is safe. If not, I will let you and the police know where you can pick up the finished package.

Doesn't this sound like fun? A challenge? Can you feel your fatigue falling away, energized with a new purpose? I do hope so. I look forward to our little contest and sportingly wish you the best. Also, if you make the police aware of our little game, I will move on the girl immediately. Make no mistake. They will never get ahead of me.

Affectionately,

The Gingerbread Man.

Belkey set the letter down. Picked up the picture. Three weeks. Twenty-one days. He rubbed his forehead and sighed as he looked at his calendar.

CHAPTER SEVEN

Archer sat in the interview room with Charmain. He frowned as he studied the letter.

"God, Jack! He must have been right next to us at the restaurant. Why? What was he doin' there?"

"I suspect he followed me. Might have some fascination with the guy workin' the case."

"What case? You said this girl was murdered in Tunica. Why would this creep be followin' you?"

Archer sighed. "The one in Tunica was not the first. There've been others."

"Others? Where? Here?"

"It's all part of an ongoing investigation. I can't talk about it yet."

She frowned, crossed her arms, and leaned back in her chair. As she peered at Archer, her eyes narrowed. "Humph!"

"Yeah, and what he saw made him think you and I were an item. Don't know if he'll use that somehow. I've already told my wife about it. So, at least it's cool where I live. Here it's a different story."

Charmain shook her head. Her eyebrows arched. "What do you mean?"

Archer said nothing. Sighed. "Like I said..."

"Jack, I am really getting fed up with all this." She struck the table with her fist. "Does it have anything to do with Bob's daughter's murder?"

Silent, unable to meet her eyes, he hung his head as if studying the killer's note.

"Alright, what can you tell me? What about the finger? Is it for real?"

"We don't have the DNA back on it, but everything else seems to match. So, I'm pretty confident it is."

"And that's her in the picture."

Archer nodded, still staring at the note. "We had this stuff he sent checked for prints. Nada! Zilch. Guy ain't idiotic."

"But why? Why did he send this to me?"

"Profiler says he's wantin' attention. Unhappy with the fact that we've not gone with this to the press. Matter of pride."

"Jack, what are you talking about? Profiler? Not gone to the press with it sooner? That makes it sound like he's done this before."

Collins entered the room carrying a stack of papers. He handed them to Archer. Nodded to Charmain and joined them at the table.

"This is Detective Collins, Tunica County. Bill, this is Charmain Crump. She's the lucky lady who got the letter with the finger." Archer turned back to Charmain. "He's the lead investigator for the Tunica victim. Bill's been workin' with the Profiler. What's the word today from his majesty."

"Actually, it's her majesty," Collins turned to Charmain. "We had been communicating with her through texts and emails. She'll be in shortly after she gets through pressing the flesh with the brass."

They all turned as the door opened. Collins and Archer stood as a stout, balding man led a tall, thin woman into the room. Her brown hair trimmed to just below her ears. She studied them silently behind her glasses. Unsmiling, she glanced at each in turn as Archer made the introductions. She smiled and extended her hand to Charmain. Charmain stood to shake her hand as Archer introduced his boss, Captain Johnson.

"I'm Dr. Holly Maynard. I've studied the material on your cases." She turned to Charmain. "Are you okay? It's not every day a person gets a fan letter from Jack the Ripper."

Charmain frowned, gave Archer a withering glance.

After shaking hands with Charmain, Captain Johnson turned to Archer. "What exactly does she know about this?"

Charmain stepped between the Captain and Archer, nearly toe to toe with Archer's boss. "She knows that there's more goin' on than some of you big-wheels will admit," As she spoke, she shook her finger under the man's nose. "I'm a reporter, and I want you to know that right now, this is all on record. I'm sure my audience is as eager to discover the truth as I am!"

"I understand you're the young lady hounding my bosses and this officer about Bob Jordan's daughter," Captain Johnson replied, "Demanding we work the case."

Charmain placed her hands on her hips, continued her stare down with the Captain. "That's right. I also have a publisher interested in a book about that case. Also, as I told Jack, I intend to start a series on the murder in my blog and my radio show."

Johnson turned to Archer. "Tell her."

Archer placed his hand on Charmain's shoulder. She turned to face him. "Jordan's daughter was the first. This girl is the fifth victim."

✳✳✳✳✳

After hearing the approaching roar, Jordan dropped his cigarette in the street and stepped on it. As he walked towards the driveway, Hector's cycle swerved in and stopped next to him. After he removed his helmet, he turned to Jordan. "Not sure what you want me here for. Scared of your ex-old lady? Think I might hold her off or somethin'?"

"Nah. Nothin' like that. She and I are cool. She's gettin' married. Nice guy. She's happy."

"So, what gives?"

"She's sellin' the house. Wanted me to go through and get the rest of my stuff out or anything else I might need."

Hector shook his head. "So, you want me to help haul shit. You got a truck comin'?"

"I doubt there's much here. I want to make sure there's nothin' here I might regret losin' forever, you know? We lived here for a long time. Probably stuff from when I was a kid. Know all my fishin' stuff's still here. Probably in the garage."

"How long you live here?" Hector scanned the living room as they passed through the front door.

"Fourteen years. Bought it when we found out the baby was on the way. Got to spend a while gettin' it ready for her." Jordan smiled as he recalled the time. The joy they both felt. The planning. The anticipation. His wife insisted on finding out the sex of the child. Claimed she needed to know how to decorate the nursery. How he made a habit of saying, "Ah! He won't care." She would rap him on the arm. They would wrestle. Not enough to harm the child inside her, but enough to start a little physical contact- a prelude to hot sex.

Jesus, he lusted after that woman. It only faded when he met Charmain. But right now, that too seemed beyond his grasp. Maybe like the song said. He was destined to be the King of Pain. He opened and closed closets on the first floor.

"While you take this walk down memory lane. I'll go look around the rest of the house." Hector climbed the stairs to the second floor.

The house, hollow and empty now. Silent. A chill in the air. Jordan's footsteps echoed. The closing doors sounded like gunshots. As he scanned the barren kitchen, the only sound, the clomp of Hector's boots upstairs. No aroma of food cooking. Instead, a mustiness hung in the air. Like his life, abandoned, alone.

Past the kitchen, he entered the garage. Empty except for two tackle boxes in the middle of the floor. A collection of fishing rods lay next to them. He picked one up. His favorite fly rod. It had been years since he held it. The line looked good. The reel, coated with oil, looked perfect. Fishing had been his passion at one time. Learning to tie the proper flies, then how to place them to lure the fish. He wished he could go back to those times. He might never learn the skill well, but his daughter had the knack.

When the sonogram confirmed the baby would be a girl, Jordan felt disappointed. Then he held her in his arms at the delivery, gazing into his eyes, the infant captured his heart. As soon as she could walk, she became his shadow. His wife laughed, claimed Jordan had to be careful when he walked not to make sudden stops. If he did, the girl's nose would be right up his butt.

Whenever he was home, she hovered around him. Demanded to go with him. Even had her first tantrum when Jordan couldn't take her with him to work. As she got older, she still loved hangin' with her Dad. They spent every day off together—especially fishing trips.

Then the case against the teenagers went sour. As he worked long hours, his home life suffered. Sometimes not coming home at all. He missed her school events. Then planned outings canceled or missed without notice. She drifted away. Got into drugs and ran away. Finally disappeared, found dead in a motel.

Jordan turned away from the fishing gear. Strolled to a cardboard barrel near his old workbench. Inside, on top of the discards, he saw it. Her pink fishing rod, broken in pieces. His wife would not have done that. It had to be her. He had broken her heart, so she had broken the rod. His heart ached. His eyes filled with tears.

"Is this why you wanted me here?"

Jordan turned to Hector. The big man stood holding a liquor bottle in each hand. As he held the bottles up, water dripped from them.

Jordan shook his head. "I forgot all about them."

"Yeah, right. Toilet tank stash. Man, you had it down pat. I did the same thing myself. Always had a good supply around in little hidie places. Good place to hide it from the old lady, too. I mean, how many women look in there? Found one in each of the bathrooms. Shit, man. You okay?" Hector peered in his face as Jordan wiped a tear from his eye.

"Actually, Hector, I wanted you here cause I figured I'd walk away after this and get loaded. Figured if you and I could talk, it might help. I figured I couldn't make it to a meeting."

"Well then, if it's alright with you, I'll dump these babies down the kitchen sink. After that, we can talk out on the front porch. If you're done in here."

Jordan glanced around the garage. Picked up his fishing gear, then followed the big man to the kitchen. After they dumped the bottles, they sat on the porch and talked. Finally, Hector checked his watch. "Listen, I gotta head out. You gonna be okay?"

Jordan nodded. "Just gotta lock up."

He trailed the big man with his eyes as Hector mounted his bike and rode away. As the bike's roar faded, Jordan returned to the house. After opening the door beneath the stairs, he entered the half bath.

"You missed this one, Hector. Most people do."

Jordan raised the cover on the toilet tank. Reached inside and retrieved the dripping bottle. Twisted off the cap, then took a long drink. After replacing the tank lid, Jordan strolled to his car with the bottle in his hand.

As he dropped into the car seat, he muttered to himself. "I tried."

*****

Meanwhile at the Memphis Police station, Charmain stood eye to eye with Archer. "You mean you knew this all along and never said a word?" Charmain snapped at Archer. Archer turned to the Captain, a pained look on his face.

Archer's boss placed his hand on Charmain's arm, stepped between her and Archer. "Please. Ms. Crump. Lieutenant Archer and all the other officers have been under strict orders. Total silence about this investigation. That included not only regular officers and technicians but the paramedics as well."

"Some nut job has been murdering young girls for three years, and you've been coverin' it up?" Charmain stared daggers.

"Please!" Dr. Maynard interrupted. Her voice soft, trying to de-escalate by example. "Ms. Crump. Let me explain what is going on. Perhaps you'll see why we kept this quiet."

Charmain turned to Dr. Maynard. She took a deep breath—a tear formed in her eye. "I'm sorry. This has all been a shock. It's affected me personally and professionally. I just want to get some answers. Also, if I can help bring this demon to justice."

"After examining what you received," Dr. Maynard replied, "We might have just the means to do that."

Charmain wheeled around to her. "How?"

Dr. Maynard put her hand on Charmain's arm. "If you help, we can give him attention and possibly open a line of communication that might lead us to him."

Charmain shook her head. "I'm a journalist, not a cop. My job is to report the truth, not cover it up."

Dr. Maynard made a wry face. "So, in a crowded theater, you would feel compelled to scream fire if you smelled smoke?"

Charmain shook her head. "No, I would do it in such a way that informs people, so they could be safe, not start a massive panic that might get people killed."

Dr. Maynard nodded. "Then let's talk further. Perhaps you can help without compromising what you consider your professional responsibilities."

Silent, the group seated themselves around the table. Dr. Maynard turned to Charmain. "In a case like this identifying it as a serial takes time. It usually takes at least three victims to be sure.

Charmain nodded, glanced at the others before turning back to Dr. Maynard. "But now there've been five."

Dr. Maynard nodded. "But there are other reasons for not making it public."

Charmain made a circular gesture as if to say continue. "And these are?"

"Others might want attention in the same way. They even go as far as committing similar crimes. While it gets them attention, it also gives rise to more killings. Plus, the more details are known about the case, the harder it is to catch the original killer."

Charmain frowned. "Copy cats?"

Dr. Maynard nodded. "That's right. Not knowing the details of the killings, we can rule out copy cats and false confessions. Find the true killer. Withholding details is an important investigation tool."

Captain Johnson held his hand up. Everyone turned to him. "A lot of the guys working this case have been bitchin' about the brass's failure to release details." His glance towards Archer made the detective squirm. "These cases create quite a stir. Not only is there a public outcry about it, but vigilantism also rears its ugly head. People that are different, unpopular, or just a bit odd get targeted. Look what happened in the Son of Sam case. The public has a right to know, but it needs to be done responsibly."

Charmain glanced around the table. "I guess I understand." She turned to Archer. Put his hand on his arm. "I'm sorry I bit your head off."

Archer nodded, placed his hand on hers.

Maynard turned to Archer. "Obviously, the killer is upset because he has not gotten the attention, he feels he deserves. At the same time, he is curious about the investigation. I believe that is why he followed Lieutenant Archer. He saw you with him on at least one occasion. Once he discovered your profession, he hopes to use you to force the issue."

Charmain scanned the faces around the table. "This all sounds so crazy. Even this name he picked. The Gingerbread man? Hardly calls up any sinister image."

"That's not the point," Dr. Maynard replied. "He thinks he's brilliant. Taunts us. Do you remember the story of the Gingerbread man?"

Charmain shrugged. "Just that people chase him."

Archer pointed to the line. "Yeah. He taunts them just like he does here in the letter. See?"

"Run, Run, Run. As fast as you can. But you can't catch me. I'm the Gingerbread man," Charmain read aloud. "I guess I hear the taunt. I can imagine him looking over his shoulder and sticking out his tongue when he finishes." After setting the note aside, Charmain glanced around the table. "Do you know what this guy looks like or anything?"

Archer reached into the folder and set a composite and a still from the casino tape in front of her.

She gasped as glanced at the photo.

"You recognize him?" Archer asked.

"Oh, God, I think so." She snatched up her purse. After rummaging inside she held up a card. "I met him in the parking lot at the place we met."

Archer snatched the card from her hand his brow furrowed as he examined it as she continued. "As I was leaving, he came up and said he hit my car. Seemed nice. Gave me his card and told me to call him if I discovered any damage later. I didn't, So I just kinda forgot about it. Said his name was Nixon. Thought it was funny. So close to an old president and all. Said nothing, cause I figured he'd probably got enough grief about it."

Collins pointed at the picture. "And that's him in the photo?"

Charmain's eyes drifted once more to the picture and nodded.

My God!" she buried her face in her hands and shivered. She leaped to her feet, paced while hugging herself.

Archer stood, put his arms around her. "Nixon is an alias, he's been usin'. Well, now we know how he found out who you were. Come on, sit down. If he got that close, we'd have to make sure you're protected. Okay?"

She nodded. "So, what do I do? What do I write? I know nothing more than what you told me."

Dr. Maynard pointed at the note. "You have the details he wrote about here. I guess he did it to establish his Bonafede's. So, we wouldn't write it off as a hoax."

"But what if I say something in my broadcast that makes him angry? He might start killing again. Will he come after me?"

"Dr. Maynard believes you're safe for now," Collins replied. Dr. Maynard nodded in agreement. "Thinks he might be in love with you from afar. Or at least lusting from afar. He's relying on you to spread his message."

Charmain continued studying the photo. She shook her head as if in disbelief. "Oh, God! You say I'm safe now. Will that change?"

Dr. Maynard shot a glance at the others. She turned back to Charmain. "I can't say for certain."

Captain Johnson turned to Archer. "Jack! We can do a protection and surveillance detail on her. Okay?"

Archer looked at Charmain. "You cool with that?"

"What would that mean?"

"I'll talk about it with you later. We can work somethin' out that keeps you safe and doesn't cramp your style. Okay?"

She nodded. Turned to Dr. Maynard. "What if I put out something that makes him angry? Makes him wanna go out and kill."

"Charmain, that is out of your control," Dr. Maynard replied. Her tone, soft and reassuring. "He will kill again, no matter what you do. It's just with this communication link we might use it. Might help identify him or even persuade him to give himself up."

Captain Johnson turned to Charmain. "You'll be a part of the team. See everything we see." He looked to the others before continuing. "In that spot, you will also serve as our conscience. You think we're not releasing enough. You can blow the whistle. It's up to you."

Charmain nodded. "So, what is the plan?"

Captain glanced at Archer. "If Jack agrees, the group should meet regularly. The police will investigate, share their results with you, and together you could put out regular press releases. I would hope Dr. Maynard could help compose them, so they meet our goals, plus Ms. Crump will make sure they meet with certain journalistic standards." He turned to Charmain. "I feel, and I am certain that Dr. Maynard would agree, that it be important that you be the public face. So, you would also lead any press briefings and deliver any announcements."

Dr. Maynard nodded. "Yes, the Gingerbread man chose you. I'm not sure of all his reasons, but it is a line of communication we should exploit."

Charmain sighed. She glanced around at the faces turned her way. "Okay." She wished now with all her heart, she could discuss this with Jordan. Perhaps soon, she hoped. Very soon.

*****

Urich glanced at the phone's screen as it vibrated. "Thanks for callin' me back, Hector."

"No problem. Was ridin', so I had to wait to call back after I pulled over. Can't ride one of these and use the phone, you know?"

She told him about finding the body at the casino and Jordan's exodus.

"Huh. Just comin' back from meetin' with him when you called. I was with him at his old house, cleaning out some old stuff before his ex-wife put it on the market."

"He wanted you to haul stuff. Hector, you must be a saint."

"Nothin' like that. Just sponsor stuff. Holdin' his hand while he raked through some old shit."

Urich chuckled. "I'm havin' a real hard time picturin' that."

"Anyway, when I left, he seemed okay. But shit. Losin', a kid. Specially that way. I don't think a guy can ever get over somethin' like that. You might suggest he get some counselin' too. I don't think AA is enough for him." Urich's phone buzzed. She glanced at the screen then put the phone back to her ear.

"Listen, Hector, thanks for keepin' me in the loop."

"No problem, sister. Say hi to the Champ for me."

Urich switched calls. "You comin' back?"

"Nah! Goin' fishin'. S'pose Maureen might be up to cookin' catfish again?"

Urich could almost smell the booze over the phone that accompanied his slurred speech. "Aren't you with Hector?"

"That was a couple hours ago. Now I'm on the bank drownin' some worms. Whaddaya say? You guys up for that?"

"I'll check with Maureen and call you back."

Setting the phone on her desk, she placed her head in her hands. She recalled what Hector told her. Decided this might be the chance to talk him into getting some help besides AA. Getting Maureen's blessing, she called Jordan back.

"Damn Urich. You oughta seen the son of a bitch I landed. Makes the last one look like a midget. Oh, shit!"

Followed by a clattering sound came over the phone as if dropped.

Alarmed, Urich shouted into her phone, "Jordan! Jordan! You okay? Can you hear me? Damn!"

The only reply a moan before the call cut off.

She called back, but it went straight to voicemail.

*****

That evening Belkey cruised Lamar in the mission's pickup, searching for the street girls plying their trade. A group stood at the corner of Knight Arnold. One had a bushy Afro, while two had shoulder-length straight black hair. The fourth had long, beaded blond hair that hung down to the middle of her back. All wore skirts that barely reached their thighs. After he pulled to the curb, the blond moved from the group. As his window came down, she leaned over, exposing ample cleavage.

"You lookin' for a little sugar tonight, honey?" She cooed, then stepped back. Her eyes opened wide. "Oh, it's you!" She turned to the other girls. "Anyone here wantin' to retire?" Two shook their heads. One giggled behind her hand.

"Rose. I need some help," Belkey pleaded.

The woman turned back to the car. "I've been tellin' you that for a long time, Reverend. You needs to get you some sweet thing once in a while. Take that holy edge off you."

The heat rose in his cheeks as he picked up the photo from the seat beside him. He passed it to her. "I need to find this girl."

"Ooh, that's tender. That what you up for? Us mature gals ain't enough for you?"

"No. She's in danger. I need to get her to the shelter. Do you know her?"

"Yeah, right. Girl is in danger? From what; gettin' old? Maybe startin' her period? Shoot! I mighta seen her around. Not down here. Closer to downtown. Lemme ask the other girls. Okay?"

Rose strutted back to the group. They passed the picture around. The woman with the bushy Afro carried the photo back to the car. "Hey, Rev, Wassup?"

"I need to find that girl. She might be in danger. Ever seen her?"

"Yeah. Used to run with my little sister. Real mover and a shaker, I hear. Primo pussy. Do anything you want. Loves it."

"Do you know where she is? Where I could find her?"

"Nah. Ain't seen her for a while. Not since my sister got took."

"Your sister?"

"Yeah, some creep strangled her in a motel near here. Never caught him, though. Cops don't care about us workin' girls. Specially, the black ones."

"The same guy that killed your sister might be getting ready to kill this one."

"You got some kinda crystal ball? Girl's here all thought you had no balls at all." She cackled, staring at the picture. "All I know, she like the rest of the young tender stuff. They don't do the streets. It all go through the pimps. A girl that young, dressin' like she askin' for it? She gonna be scooped up right now by the Po-Po."

She handed the photo back to Belkey. "Her pimp, Lester. Lester LaRoyce. Ask around. Somebody put you in touch."

As the woman strolled away, Belkey pulled away from the curb. At least he now had a lead.

CHAPTER EIGHT

Archer handed the photo across the counter. The man, wearing a black tank-top, chomped on a short cigar as he studied the picture. His exposed, muscular shoulders displayed a myriad of tattoos up to his chin. As the man studied the photo, Archer's eyes roamed the room. Bare brick covered with posters depicting devils, skulls, angels, dragons, and unicorns.

"Samples of my work." The man behind the counter mumbled, still engrossed in the picture. "That Dragon over there is my masterpiece. Drew it up for Madonna, but she changed her mind. Musta been her post-Sean Penn period."

A brunette with spiked hair joined the man at the counter. Her short skirt displayed her slim legs. The tattoos there resembled a bird's legs. Archer guessed her feet probably had talon tattoos.

"How ya comin'?" The man asked, not bothering to look away from the photo.

"Havin' a hard time with this latest change. That skull and crossbones are hard to transform to some flower," the woman replied.

"Jesus, Donna. Dumb bitch shoulda known better than to put something like that on her ass, anyway."

"Well, her husband thought it was sexy. But now her daughter is all up in her face. Why's your ass poison, Mommy? The kid asks. Told her Sunday school class about it too."

"She might have to go to a plastic surgeon. Told her that, but she figured we could make it look like a sunflower or somethin'."

Donna leaned close, studying the picture over the man's shoulder. "Phases of the moon. Not many of those around."

Archer liked what he heard. He might be in luck. He stepped close to the counter. "You guys do that? Or is it somebody else's specialty?"

"We don't. I doubt this is local."

"Really? How can you tell?"

After setting down the picture, the man pulled a laptop out from under the counter. His fingers flew over the keyboard before he spun it around, allowing Archer to view the screen.

The man pointed at the image. "'Cause it's made by this company here. Seen 'em before. Crappy. But for the guy that wants a temp tattoo, it works. Not terrible quality for a temp. They claim it'll last a week if ya don't fuck with it. But it cleans off real easy."

"This is fake?"

"Yep. Nice, but phony as hell."

"Who sells 'em?"

"Some piercing shops might. But most buy 'em online. Get a nice discount if you buy enough of 'em."

*****

Meanwhile at the television studio, Charmain took a deep breath, then recited from the teleprompter beside the camera. "At a press conference today, Memphis police officials and the Sheriff of Tunica County announced the formation of a special task force. In the last three years, five teenage sex workers have been murdered. These killings occurred in Memphis Motels and a Tunica Casino. Evidence suggests that the same person or persons committed these crimes. The task force led by Detective Lieutenant Jack Archer of the Memphis Police Department and Detective Bill Collins from Tunica will bring these persons to justice."

The screen switched from a closeup of Charmain to a tall black man standing before a microphone. His blue uniform had five silver stars on the epaulets. "Any murder in our jurisdiction is a serious matter. Rest assured, we will hunt down the person or persons involved in these killings."

One by one, images of each victim appeared on a screen behind the Memphis Police Director as he talked. The pictures, taken from school yearbooks or family portraits, selected to portray their unblemished innocence. Reverend Belkey stood next to the Director and the Tunica Sheriff. A tear glistened in his eye as he listened to the Sheriff add his own rallying cry.

The Sheriff then turned to Belkey. "On my right is Reverend Wayne Belkey, from the Shining Light Mission. They specialize in rescuing sex workers from the life. Move them into decent living and working conditions in the area. Reverend, would you like to say a few words?"

"Thank you, Sheriff. Yes, I want to say to everyone listening and watching out there that I am afraid. There's a monster out there on the loose, preying on the young. Never mind that these young women have fallen into lives that some here might consider sinful. Most, if given a chance, would want to be out of this life. Free to do what all normal kids do at this age." Belkey gazed into the camera momentarily before returning to his written statement. "Shining light works with sex workers of all ages. We are a small organization, but I have enlisted the help of other clergy in the area. We will turn no one away. With this in mind, if you are a sex worker living in this area and want out of the life, call us. Our hotline, they tell me, is displayed on the screen. Operators will be on duty twenty-four hours a day to take your calls. Call us. We will come and get you. Take you to a place of safety. Make sure you are healthy and comfortable. Then we will do our best to find you a job or the training you need to live the kind of life that affords you both safety and dignity. The police may catch this monster now, but there are others out there. Believe me, the life you're living is not your only choice. Again, the number is listed on the screen. Right?"

Finished, he glanced up at the camera. A man standing beside the camera gave him the thumbs up. "So, call us. No hassles, no judgments, no sermons. We only want you safe." As he stepped away from the microphone, the usually cynical media applauded.

The screen now switched back to Charmain. She repeated the Reverend's hotline number. She then suggested people could also call the station. If they wanted, they would be forwarded to the people at Shining Light.

At the end of the broadcast, Charmain stood next to Dr. Maynard at her desk.

"I'll be willing to bet our boy contacts you in the next twenty-four hours."

Charmain looked up, her eyes open wide. "Why do you say that?"

Dr. Maynard smiled before replying. "You ignored all the juicy little things he fed you. The inside scoop. He might be a bit miffed."

A puzzled frown crossed Chairman's face. "Will he be mad?"

Dr. Maynard shrugged. "Could be. Might use it to get him to talk. If he does, tell him you wanted to put those juicy tidbits in, but they wouldn't let you. Said that they might even charge you with obstruction if you did or aiding and abetting. Who cares."

"But that's not true?" Charmain replied, still looking puzzled.

"No. But he'll sympathize with that. Might be a chance to get him to open up a bit. Draw you closer together. The more he talks or contacts, the greater the chance he'll slip up. Then we can get him."

"So, I should lie to him?"

Dr. Maynard scoffed. "Unethical to lie to a killer?"

"Excuse me. Thank you for the help you and your station is giving us."

Startled, both turned to find Reverend Belkey standing next to them. "I'm sorry, I hope I didn't mean to frighten you. I guess we all might be a little afraid right now," He said as he saw the looks on the women's faces and how both jumped when he spoke.

Charmain smiled, took his hand. "Dr. Maynard, have you met Reverend Belkey?"

Dr. Maynard smiled and extended her hand as Charmain continued. "Dr. Maynard is with the FBI."

Belkey smiled, took Dr. Maynard's hand. "Are you part of this task force too?"

"Yes, just giving them some advice."

Belkey cocked his head. "Local Office?"

"Oh, no. I work out of Quantico."

Belkey gave a slight smile. "Beautiful country out there. My Dad was stationed at Quantico before going to Kuwait."

"A Marine?"

"Yes, Ma'am. Recon. A lifer."

Belkey turned to Charmain. "Listen, thank you for the outstanding job you did covering the conference today."

"Why, thank you. It's what we do."

"Yeah, but to get the station behind promoting our mission. That's above and beyond." Belkey replied.

"Well, you're doin' important work. It's the least I could do."

He smiled. "Listen, would you like to come out and see our program first-hand? I'd give you a personal tour and, if they're willing, let you talk to some of our girls."

"Hmm! I'll have to check to see what's on for tomorrow. Okay?"

"Sure. Just call me, I know you got my number."

As he walked away, Dr. Maynard turned to Charmain. "Handsome. Looks to be in good shape, too. I think you've got an admirer."

*****

That evening he replaced the carpet over the cellar door. With the sofa in place, no one would suspect its presence. He fell in love with the house at first sight. Tiny. Only one bedroom, but the basement. A rarity in Memphis. A perfect prison, just in case.

In sad shape, when he got it. The house took three years to get it the way he wanted it. Now it would serve his purpose perfectly. He strolled through the house, admiring his handiwork. Open space except for the small divider between the bedroom from the entryway. The living room. Perfect for setting the occasion. Get them in the mood. Maybe libations to enhance the experience. Then on to the bedroom. Queen-size bed. Satin sheets. Restraints, built into the bedposts at each corner. The mattress covered in rubber in case someone bled there. Then instead of a kitchen, the killing room. The operating table he'd purchased from the medical supply company. No questions asked cash sale from a remodel they had done. Saws, knives in the cupboard, even a drain in the floor to catch the blood if needed. He moved the tripod-mounted camera next to the table. Peered through the viewfinder. "Perfect," he said aloud to himself, "Catching their eyes as they die would be the perfect trophy." He rubbed his hands together. "Can't wait!"

He liked to strangle them now. Watch the life disappear from their eyes. But one never knows. He might shift styles. Keep the police guessing-give himself some variety.

He strolled into the dining room he also used as an office. Seated at the computer desk, he clicked the mouse, starting the live news stream. Ah! There she is.

"You made them admit it." He said aloud. He smiled as he listened to her broadcast. "You may not know it yet, but I will make you a star. The other media will beat down your door. You will not only report the news, Black Beauty. You will become the news. Enjoy the ride. I know I will. See you soon." He switched to another news report. Dazzling. His handiwork finally recognized.

From the refrigerator, he retrieved a beer. He raised the can as if offering a toast to the house. After popping the top, he took a long drink.

"I can't wait for the contest. We need to christen the house." He rubbed his crotch as he talked. Aroused, he took out his cell phone. He scrolled through the images as he pleasured himself. He groaned as he came. He tossed the beer into a trash can. He rubbed his hands together as he reached for a second beer. "Let's go hunting!"

*****

In Jordan's hospital room, Paulo looked back over his shoulder as Urich slammed the door behind her. He turned around to Jordan and shook his head. "You lucky she don't kill you, man. I have never seen a woman so pissed!"

Jordan raised the head of the bed. He looked down at the cast on his leg, then back up at Paulo. "That wouldn't make much sense. I mean comin' all that way to find me, then damage me? I think she's mad cause she cares."

Paulo shrugged, then leered. "I am no expert on women. I only know what I like about them. You know?" He arched his eyebrows.

"How'd'you guys find me?"

"Chris remembered you mentioned a farmer you worked a case on over in that part of the county. He gave you permission to fish on his pond. She went through your old case files and found the man's name in that area that matched what you told her. She called many times before she finally got the farmer at home. He told her where the pond was."

Jordan propped his head up with his arm. "Humph, I'll have to tell Roy I was right. She's gonna be one helluva detective."

The door swung open, and Urich stomped in. Paulo turned to her and grinned. "Hey baby, Roberto says, you have become a brilliant detective for finding him. Gonna give you lots of praise to your boss."

She turned to Jordan, her face flushed. "Yeah, right. You gonna write a nice little note on it for my file. I can see it now. Got drunker than shit. Stepped in a hole while fishing and broke a leg. Cellphone dropped in the pond and unable to summon help. Meanwhile, my partner used all her well-honed police skills, tracked me down, and rescued my sorry drunken ass."

Paulo shrugged, turned back to Jordan. "Like I said, hombre. You in deep shit!" He turned around to Urich. "Are we takin' him home?"

"No, the hospital says, they can't discharge him until he's stable. Apparently, you didn't thrill anybody with your mental status in Emergency. A shrink has to come by and see you in the morning to make sure you're not a danger to yourself or others. At the rate you're goin', you won't ever get out."

"Did you guys get my fishin' stuff? Just got it back would be a shame to lose it. Paramedics said they couldn't bring it along."

Paulo nodded. "Steve and Joshua packed it in your car. Then they took your car to the trailer. Call when you get ready to leave here. We come and pick you up."

Jordan glanced around the room. "Shit! Where's my phone?"

"Remember, you dropped it in the pond. I couldn't find it," Urich snarled. She turned to Paulo. "You really gonna pick him up?"

Paulo shrugged. Avoided looking her in the eye.

"If that is alright?" He muttered, watching her reaction from the corner of his eye.

"Fine! Here, just write your number on this sheet of paper. When he finds somebody who'll let him call, you can meet up then. Okay? Now, are you comin' with me, or do you want to stay here a little longer? Maybe hold his hand or sleep under his bed."

Paulo rose to his feet. "I see you later, Amigo. Don't worry. I get in trouble all the time. Usually, end up sleeping on the couch. Until I get better at taking orders." He shrugged. "I am afraid my training goes poorly. Ah! But she is so feisty. Eh?" Paulo glanced back over his shoulder. He leered and arched his eyebrows as he followed her out.

*****

That evening as he opened the motel door, she slipped inside. Like the others, she blinked up at him. Anxious, wondering what tonight's work might involve. Pain, pleasure, a mixture of both. Perhaps a little fear. Did she get wet thinking about what might lay ahead? He asked himself.

This one clutched her cell phone. Her pimp's number probably on speed dial if things got out of hand. Careless, he watched the man drop her off. Probably off to score some fried chicken. Figure nothing hot and heavy would come down right away.

He had to move fast. He put his hand under her chin. Stroked her cheek. Gentle, he trailed his hand through her long blond tresses. He smiled. Could feel the arousal coming with the game.

He whispered. "Listen, I'm sorry, but I really am hungry right now. How 'bout you? Wanna go grab something quick. Might not even have time for anything else. You see, I'm diabetic. If I don't eat now, I might get sick."

Her eyes opened wide. She glanced over her shoulder as if she could see through the door. "Gosh. I don't know. Lester said I should never leave."

"Well. Don't want to get you in trouble. Here," he passed her some cash. "This is what Lester said it would be. Sorry. Like I said, if you wanna get something to eat, you can come along. I'll bring you back."

She chewed on her lower lip. "I guess it'll be okay. Lester said he wouldn't come 'less I call." Her cornflower-blue eyes sparkling and innocent.

"Alright, then." He smiled, rubbed his hands together. "I'm parked in back, let's go!" He took her hand and led her out the door.

CHAPTER NINE

Charmain turned off her phone as she entered Belkey's office. As the receptionist showed her in, he rose from behind his desk. Taking her hand, he smiled into her eyes. "I'm pleased you could make it so soon. I talked to several of the girls, and they said they'd be happy to talk to you after I show you around. The only thing I ask is that you do not use pictures or divulge their names. Is that a problem?"

He beckoned her to a chair across from his desk.

As she sat, she took out a notepad. "No, Reverend, that's not an issue at all."

"Please, call me Wayne. I don't care for all that ecclesiastical nonsense, Ms. Crump."

"Okay, on the same note, my friends call me Charmain or just Char."

"Then Charmain it is. Pretty name."

"I'd like to know more about you, Reverend. Or I mean, Wayne. You said you didn't have much time for what you call the ecclesiastical nonsense. What denomination do you associate with?"

Belkey gazed off, pondering his answer. "Originally, I received my ordination from a Non-denominational seminary in West Virginia. But I've never served a congregation. I've spent most of my time as a social activist. Do services here on Sunday for the people we serve. But other than that?" He shrugged.

"Is that why you wear those plaid and striped dress shirts with the clerical collar? Kinda like an in-your-face rejection of tradition?"

Belkey rubbed his chin. "I guess so. I like them. Announces me, I think, as a strong believer with an open mind, I guess. But that's just when I'm dressed up. Out hunting for funds or supporters."

"Or appearing on television."

He smiled. "Well, that too. Gotta make sure the donors think I'm not a complete radical, right? Merely the nicest one you'll meet."

"I remember you said you grew up in Virginia."

"Quantico? That's hardly Virginia. Ever been on a military base?"

"Just out to Millington for the air show."

"Life on a Marine base is different. You've heard of Army Brats, I'm sure. Well, no brats in my father's beloved Corps. Don't get me wrong. He loved us, but we knew how to behave. He'd take us on outings on weekends. Instead of hiking or fishing, he preferred survival training and forced marches. Wanted to make men out of us." Belkey chuckled and shook his head. "Jarhead, all the way."

"Where's your family now?"

Belkey gulped, hung his head. "Dad died. Car wreck. Hit by a drunk. Brother died when I was nine. Mom's not around. Ended up raised by an aunt and uncle in West Virginia. They're the ones who got me interested in preachin'."

"I'm sorry. I didn't mean to dredge up a lot of bad stuff."

He gave her a half-smile. "It's okay. I guess that's what gives me the desire to help these young ones. Hadn't been for my aunt and uncle, I could've ended up on the streets just like these girls. Ain't no different for the boys. Maybe worse. When they get caught in the life, they either fight 'em or fuck' em. Either way, it's bad." He frowned. "Like animals. Sorry for my language."

"Hey, let's get some positive vibes goin' again, okay? Tell me about your program."

He nodded. "Yeah, sure."

"How many does your program currently serve?"

"Right now, it's at peak capacity. We have thirty-five in our regular program. Another dozen housed by other people from local congregations. They've been helpful with the recent influx of teenagers sparked by this killer thing. Since they're all school age, it doesn't weigh down our vocational program. But we have to get them all in schools."

*****

Boiling inside, Archer stomped down the hospital corridor. Archer wanted to choke somebody for their stupidity. "This is not how you treat next of kin!" He had screamed at the press officer. The man's feeble contrition fueled Archer's anger. Now he needed to make this right. At Jordan's door, he collided with a short olive-skinned man coming out. "Excuse me, are you a Doctor?"

"No, Señor. He's got one with him right now." Paulo's eyes rolled up as if he could read his own mind, then shrugged. "Como se dice? How you say, uh, Head Doctor? Por Favor?"

"Psychiatrist?"

Paulo grinned and nodded. "Si! Psychiatrist. Fine lookin' woman. Seems real smart. Said she wanted to talk to him alone."

Archer rolled his eyes. Slapped his hand on the wall. "Damn!" He turned to Paulo. "Is he upset? Angry?"

Paulo scowled, shook his head. "No. Nothin' like that. She wanted to make sure he's all right, for they let him go. You a friend of Jordan's?"

"Yeah. Used to be his partner when he worked in Memphis. Detective Lieutenant Jack Archer. You?"

"Paulo Manuelito."

Archer grinned in recognition. "The boxer?"

"Si!"

"Jordan's told me a lot about you. Champion boxer and ballet dancer. Quite a combination."

Paulo beamed. "Yes, Chris got me involved with the dance to improve my footwork, and I love it. Just got back from doin' an off-Broadway show. Hated to leave the big city, but I have a match in a few months to get ready for. First title defense. Need to be ready."

The door behind them opened. Jordan rolled out in a wheelchair holding a pair of crutches. A tall, middle-aged, blond woman in a white lab coat pushed the chair.

Archer stepped up to them. "Excuse me, ma'am. I'm Detective Lieutenant Archer MPD."

The woman blinked, glanced at Jordan. "I'm Dr. Johnson, can I help you?"

"I need to speak with this man." Archer nodded at Jordan. "Could you stick around?"

"Jack!" Jordan exclaimed, looking up. He looked back and forth between Paulo and Archer. His brows knitted with concern. "Somethin' wrong? What is it? Is it Charmain?"

"No! We gotta talk, man. It's about your daughter."

Jordan's eyes opened wide. He leaned back in the wheelchair. "Jennifer? What about her?"

Archer turned to the Psychiatrist. "Please, Dr. Johnson, can you stay while I talk to him?"

She nodded and pulled Jordan back into the room. Paulo and Archer trailed her inside. Archer sat down on the bed, and she turned Jordan to face him. Jordan's brow still knitted in a frown, glanced back and forth between Archer and the Doctor.

The Doctor broke the silence. "Has his daughter had an accident?"

Archer shook his head. "No. She died over three years ago." He now turned to Jordan. "Bob, Jennifer was killed by a serial. She was the first. Since then, there have been five more just like it, including the one you found at the Casino."

"And you're just tellin' me now?"

"Second one happened a year after Jennifer. No one paid attention to the similarities at the time. Then the third and fourth came along within six months of each other. All with the same things. Tongue-cutting, a message including the pimp's number. Brass sat on it. Didn't want to alarm the public. Give the asshole attention. Hell, I'm not sure why. You know the drill. Told us not even to inform next of kin."

"Why now? What's different?"

"Killer forced our hand with the one in Tunica. Took his message straight to the press through Charmain."

Jordan sat up straight. "Charmain? What the hell, Jack? Why her?"

"She's been leanin' real hard on everybody to solve Jennifer's case. Callin' and harassin' me and the boss for months. Threatenin' to write a book to draw attention to the case. Whatever. To calm her down, I met with her to fill her in on the details of the case coupla weeks ago. She not tell you?"

Jordan said nothing for a moment, massaging his forehead. He swallowed. His stomach churned while his mind processed the news. "No. We're kinda havin' a rough patch. So, why is the killer going through her?"

"I guess he's stalkin' me. I never realized, honest. He saw us together. Thought she might be my side piece or somthin', I guess. Sent her a picture of us together. He also included a letter about how he wants to keep her informed. Make sure the cops quit hidin' this thing."

"So, now he's stalkin' her?"

"Could be. Got security on her, though, twenty-four-seven. They'll keep her safe."

"Yeah, right. Know how that shit works. After two days, the killer'll start deliverin' 'em donuts with sleepin' powder in 'em.

Shit, you know what kinda assholes get that kinda assignment. So, why are you tellin' me this today?"

"Had to do a press conference yesterday. Announce all the victims. They were supposed to notify next of kin before the conference. They called your ex-wife, and I guess they assumed she would tell ya. I just found out about that this mornin'. Figured that wouldn't happen, so I came to tell you myself. You didn't see the press conference?"

"I never watch the news. Never anything good there."

"Tried to find you. Your partner, Urich, told me where you were. What the hell happened?"

"Fishin' accident. Shit! I need a smoke. Let's go, Paulo, before I have any more good news arrive."

Dr. Johnson reached out. She grabbed the handle of the wheelchair, stopping Jordan from moving. "Are you going down to the dock?"

Jordan glanced over at Archer. He nodded.

"Let me join you, okay?"

Jordan turned to Paulo. "You okay with this, man."

"Sure. Also, until we know you can drive, Chris say you can sleep on our couch. That way, I am safe, eh?" He leered as he arched his eyebrows.

*****

Once on the hospital's loading dock, Paulo locked the brakes on Jordan's wheelchair. After Archer passed him a cigarette, he lit it. "Damn! So, the killer has been in contact with Charmain? Fuck!" Jordan's hand trembled before taking a drag on the cigarette.

Archer nodded as he lit one himself. "Like I said, he must have been followin' me around. Spotted her and me meetin' and thought he would get at me by contactin' her. Least, that's what the profiler thinks."

Paulo did his best to dance around the two men's smoke while fanning the surrounding air. Finally, he gave up. "Listen. I gotta stay away from these fumes, man. I'll just wait outside. You come get me when you're ready."

Jordan acknowledged him with a wave before turning back to Archer. "Profiler?"

"Yeah. FBI Shrink. Tunica Sheriff insisted on bringin' in the FBI when he found out what we been sittin' on. He don't care about embarrassin' the MPD and Memphis City Hall."

At that moment, Dr. Johnson joined them. "Mr. Jordan. When you and I first spoke, you didn't mention your daughter."

"Would that have made a difference?"

She turned to Archer. "Can you excuse us for a minute?"

Archer glanced at Jordan, then walked a short distance away. The doctor shoved a box over next to Jordan and sat down.

She leaned close as if sharing a secret. "Ten years ago, my daughter was run over by a drunk driver. I am not sure I still handle it well."

As Jordan gave her a puzzled frown. "Why you tellin' me this, Doc?"

She took a deep breath before continuing. "I don't know all the details of your daughter's death. But being a parent and a mental health professional, I know one thing. No matter what, you blame yourself."

Jordan gazed off, avoiding eye contact.

She continued. "I wasn't there when my daughter got run over. Instead, I was here working. She was walking home from school, and the car left the road and hit her. To this day, I blame myself for working those hours. Not being there when she got out of school. For not driving her home that day. For not telling her, I loved her enough when I went off to work that morning. You name it. I can find a reason to feel guilty about it." A tear formed in her eye.

"So, what do you do?"

"I get a lot of counseling. Over time, it has helped. Let's me see that I need to forgive myself. Someday I might. Maybe not. But you need to give yourself a chance. Find a counselor. Talk to them." She handed him a card. "This is the guy I see. Talk to him. If he's not right for you, I'm sure he'll find someone who is. But do that. You owe it to yourself. You owe it to your daughter. Would she want you to feel the way you do now?" She paused. "I doubt it."

She squeezed his shoulder and stood. She dried her eye as she turned to walk away.

*****

After concluding the interview, Charmain and Belkey toured the residences. As they parked near one, a muscular red-haired man carrying a toolbox marched down the driveway. A young black woman burst out the door, scowling as she charged after the red-haired man. She intercepted him as he loaded his toolbox in a red pickup truck. After emerging from the Mission's van, Belkey and Charmain approached the pair. Silent, the man stood with his hands on his hips, while the young woman shook a finger under his nose. At this distance, her words couldn't be heard, but she appeared to be scolding him. As Charmain drew closer, the young lady's tirade drifted to her ears.

"I don't care what kinda emergency you think you have! You don't go bargin' into those bathrooms! You wait for me to go in there and make sure the girls are out! One more time, and I tell the Reverend!"

Still silent, with an insolent grin, he nodded in Belkey's direction. This gesture triggered the woman to turn. Her scowl deepened as she tossed her hands in the air before marching toward them. Belkey turned to Charmain. "Can you give us a moment?"

Charmain nodded, then waited as Belkey met the woman a short way ahead. Meanwhile, the red-haired man leaned against the truck. His arms folded, he studied Charmain. His appraising glance made her skin crawl. Belkey put his arm around the black woman's shoulder. Murmured in her ear. Finally, the woman rolled her eyes, shook her head, then approached Charmain while Belkey strode to the man.

The young woman extended her hand. "Sorry 'bout my yellin'. I'm Doris Williams, home manager here. Mr. Wayne asked me if I would show you around the house while he deals with a problem we been havin'."

Charmain smiled as she took the home manager's hand. "I'm Charmain Crump. No problem. Running a house full of young girls has got to be a chore. You said, Mr. Wayne?"

"Yes! Tha's what all the girls call the Reverend. He don't hold with callin' him Reverend. He say Mr. Belkey's his dad. We uncomfortable callin' him Wayne, so he just has to settle for us callin' him, Mr. Wayne."

"Thanks. You had me confused for a moment."

"You're not from around here, are ya?"

Charmain smiled, shook her head. "I grew up in Chicago."

"Well, come on inside. I'll show you around. Mr. Wayne also said to let you talk to the girls if they willin'."

As they walked up the driveway, Charmain glanced back. Belkey remained with the man, talking. The man leaned on the truck, not making eye contact with Belkey. His body language pure insolence. Instead, his eyes tracked Charmain-a sardonic grin on his face.

As they walked through the house, Doris described the residents. The young woman beamed as she spoke. Her pride in their accomplishments evident. In the kitchen, two teenage girls sat at the kitchen table. As Charmain and Doris approached, both smiled. Doris squeezed one girl's shoulder. "You guys all right?"

"Yes, Miss Doris. We just gettin' ready to start our homework," The one across the table replied. Both girls studied Charmain.

"Girls, this Miss Charmain Crump. She a reporter. Is it okay if she talks to you?" Both girls nodded as Charmain joined them at the table. "I'll get some pie down, and we can have a snack while you chat."

As the girls enjoyed their treat, they jabbered away. Told Charmain about their school, friends, and what they did for fun. When they finished, the two girls left the kitchen. As Doris cleaned the table, she and Charmain continued their discussion.

"If I didn't already know their histories, they would just seem like typical teenagers to me."

Doris grinned. "Those two are my stars. The others have more problems. Not doin' as well. But they all get counselin'. Also, the girls all support each other."

"So how long do they live here?"

A third girl entered. She stood in the doorway behind Doris, listening to the two women talk.

"They can stay as long as they want. Most don't have families they want to return to, and they've had a lot of problems in foster care. Mostly, they seem happy with each other. We're their family now."

"Yeah! Except for Mr. Creep," the new girl interjected.

Startled by the interruption, Doris' head snapped around. "I'm sorry he came in unannounced this morning while you were showerin'. But sometimes we have to put up with his rushin' around."

The girl sneered. "Well, he seems to have a lot of emergencies."

At that moment, Belkey entered. He looked grim but seeing the girl, a smile captured his face.

The girl smiled. "Hey, Mr. Wayne." She rushed to greet him with a hug. Belkey seemed stiff as he accepted the girl's embrace. His face flushed, he stepped back. "How ya doin', Joannie?"

"I saw you out there talkin' to Bert. I told him if he walked in again on me, I'd cut off his little weenie!"

"I'm sure Mr. Wayne made things clear to him," Doris chided. Ain't no need for you to bother with him."

The girl scoffed. Stuck her nose in the air and stomped off.

After finishing the tour, they returned to the main office. Seated in Belkey's office, Charmain reviewed her notes as Belkey talked on the phone.

Finished with his call, he turned to her. "Listen, I'm sorry about that little scene when we arrived. Our maintenance man is not the most sensitive guy. Seems to think nothing takes priority over his work. But he does a good job for the wages we can pay." Belkey shrugged, then glanced at his watch. "Listen, I've got an engagement tonight. I've got to get goin'."

Both stood. Charmain packed up her notes and extended her hand. "Well, thank you, Wayne, for taking the time to show me your program. I hope as we go through this, I can let folks know about you and the job you're doin' here."

He smiled as he took her hand. "Listen. I'd like to know more about you. How about if we have dinner? Maybe this weekend?"

"I appreciate the offer, but I'm seeing someone right now. Otherwise..." She smiled, cocked an eyebrow, then left the office.

*****

Night fell as he entered the house. The capture last night went smoother than he expected. Just squeezed the drops into her milkshake as he handed it to her. She lost consciousness before finishing half of it. She had been breathing when he left. He hoped that still held true, but did not really care. He only practiced now for the main event. The trick would be keeping her alive. Ignore his obsession. Conquer his needs.

He shoved the sofa to the side before lifting the rug off the cellar door. He lifted the door then clicked the remote, turning on the light below. "I'm sorry. I got home later than I expected. I should have that light on a timer. Come on up. I brought food if you're hungry."

Walking away from the trapdoor in the floor, he checked the bolt on the back door. Once again, making sure he latched it tight when he entered. He set the fast-food bag on the coffee table in front of the couch. Her blond head emerged from the opening in the floor. She looked around wide-eyed before she climbed the stairs. Her arms crossed her chest to shield her developing breasts. Her naked skin covered in goosebumps. "I was here? Did we do it? Where's my clothes?"

He ignored her questions. "I wasn't sure what you would like. There's burgers, chicken, and fries there in the bag."

As she moved to the table, her long legs moving her like a fawn across a meadow. She grabbed the bag. Pulled out a burger and greedily devoured it, then pulled a second burger from the sack.

"Did the TV work alright?"

She nodded. "Yeah. After I figured out the remote, it worked fine."

"Was the music, okay?"

"Music was not really my taste. Guess it's okay for older people." She chewed the burger and looked around. "Can I have my clothes? I'm cold."

He smiled. "Want anything to drink? Got some coke. Maybe make you a Fuzzy Navel. It tastes really sweet."

She chuckled, then smiled. "Yeah, I guess. We gonna party now? Lester's gonna be like totally pissed, you know?"

As he mixed her drink, he studied her firm, youthful body. "Don't worry. I'll take care of Lester."

He led her to the sofa. After placing the drink in her hand, he stroked her bare thigh while she drank.

"You're right. That's perfect." She held the empty glass out, inviting a refill.

At the table, he refilled her drink before rejoining her on the sofa. "So how long have you been in the party life?"

"About three months now. Left home. Real drag out in the Gatlinburg boonies, you know?"

"Oh yeah. Dollywood! Hillbilly heaven."

She nodded. "Yeah, nothin' but necks there. Came here on the bus and hooked up with Lester right there in the depot. Almost seemed like he expected me. Like comin' home. Man, what a party. But a girl's gotta pay the bills, you know?"

He cocked his head to the side. His eyes followed her every gesture. "Ever thought about doing' anything else?"

"You want me to come work for you? I mean, this looks like a nice place. God! What a hot car. Is that a Vette?"

He smiled. "Close. Ferrari. Same principle, but made in Italy."

"Yeah, I saw how all those people stared at it. Cool ride. Hookin' for you must pay real good."

He chuckled. "No, what I meant was doin' somethin' other than hooking."

"Hah! Like what! I'm thirteen, man. Can't do nothin' till I get out of school." She tossed her hair over her shoulders and took another drink. "Like that's ever gonna happen. I found out in first grade what I was good at. And it took no formal trainin'. Just soft lips. What is it they say? Find somethin' you like that pays, and you'll never work a day in your life?" She grinned. "Well, I love it, and I get paid. Listen, you got nice arms. Handsome, too. I'm gettin' wet thinkin' about you."

He brushed her breast with the back of his hand. The nipple already erect. He put his arm around her shoulder and drew her close. She wrapped her arms around his neck. Moved her face close to his, inviting a kiss. He could taste her warm breath on his cheek as he stroked her thigh. The peach smell from the schnapps. "Wet, huh?"

She nodded. Her lips parted. Moved her face closer. His hand traveled up her body. His thumb brushed her chin, then dropped to her Adam's apple. As he squeezed, she pushed against his chest. Scratched his cheek before he trapped her hand. Kicked and bucked as he pressed her down on the couch. She wiggled. Squirmed. Gradually her struggles ceased. Her body limps as the light faded in her eyes.

He moaned as his ejaculation exploded inside his pants. As he rolled away from her body, he pulled out his cell phone. He hummed the Bangles tune as he snapped pictures of her naked body. Finished, he carried her to the table in the kitchen. After taking out his knife, he removed her tongue.

CHAPTER TEN

Belkey rubbed his forehead as he studied the page with the clipped-out letters before him.

You're Holiness,

Just a quick note to assure you that I had not forgotten our little contest. You will hear of another one today, but she is outside our arrangement. I just needed a little recreation while I waited. I want you to know though that I thought of you while she and I were together. I even offered her a chance, just like you. Leave the life. Get a job. Go to school—all that fun stuff you offer. You know what she did? She laughed. Said she loved the work. Would never give it up. You wouldn't have been able to save her, anyway. Instead, I arranged her early retirement.

I see you took time away from the hunt to squire around a lovely young reporter. Got the hots for her? Looked like it. Shouldn't waste time with that, though. Already spoken for. You'd have to get in line. Think she likes them married. Probably doesn't like white meat. So, leave it alone.

Well, I didn't want to distract you from your efforts. I wanted to remind you that the clock is still ticking. Got any leads to her yet? Better hurry.

Your Pal

The G-Man*

*cute, huh?

He set the letter on the desk. Massaged the bridge of his nose to relieve the pressure building inside his skull. From a side drawer, he took out a pill bottle. Shook out two pills and popped them in his mouth. He gulped at the soft drink cup to wash them down.

How would this monster find out if he informed the police about this challenge? This animal seemed able to read his mind. He had no choice. He would hunt again tonight. He also had the name of her pimp. He would find him. That would lead him to the girl. He had to do something. He thumbed through his Bible until he came to an appropriate passage. After reading it to himself, he prayed.

*****

As Collins and Archer watched the Crime Scene Technicians search around the body and take pictures, they talked.

"Paramedic says tongues cut out and the finger is missing again."

Collins turned back to the scene. "Yeah, but he dumped her here under this lamp post. No note, no posin'. Just stacked her clothes all nice and neat right beside her. Cell phone on top. I'll check it soon as the Tech's are done with it."

A uniformed officer left a group of women standing nearby and approached Archer. "Girls say she's one of Lester LaRoyce's specials."

Archer nodded towards the women "They call it in?"

"Nah. Dispatch said it was a man's voice. Nobody around when we came. They showed up just before you did. Claim this is their corner."

"Here ya go, Jack. Been dusted and ready." The Technician handed Archer the phone in a bag. Archer turned to Collins. "How 'bout we go notify next of kin?"

"You know her?"

"Nope. Just know her Sugar Daddy."

*****

As Archer stood next to the covered body at the morgue, he studied the man on the opposite side. His braids beaded. A fancy gear outfit with five-hundred-dollar tennis shoes. The baseball cap sideways on his head. He shuffled back and forth on his feet. Handcuffed, two uniformed officers on either side. When Archer nodded, one officer removed the cuffs, then handed the man a cell phone. He glanced at the phone, then thrust his jaw out as he put it in his pocket.

Archer strode to the man's side, put his hand on the man's shoulder. "Lester, my man. Glad you could come in. Give us a hand. Help us clear up some things."

"Yeah, that's me. Got Crime Stoppers on speed dial. What you need to have these boys come down and roust me outta my crib for?"

Archer pointed at the covered body. "Got someone here, you might know."

"Hey, man. I a man of peace now. Don't you be layin' some kinda drive-by on me, bro'? That shit's from another life."

Archer turned to one of the uniformed officers. "He say, man of peace? Sounds appropriate to me. How 'bout you, Phil. You think he likes a little peace?"

The uniformed officer scowled at Lester and shrugged.

"Well, maybe you know this little PIECE right here!" Archer flipped back the sheet. Lester's eyes opened wide as he lunged back. His jaw dropped before he looked away.

"What's her name, Lester? Where she from?"

Lester swallowed. "Her name Charice. Seen her around the hood."

"She got a last name?"

Lester shrugged. "James, I heard some say. Like I said, jus' seen her around."

"Word is she's, one of yours."

Lester's eye's narrowed. "I ain't into shit that young."

Archer held up a cell phone. He pressed a button, and Lester'spocket emitted a buzz. Lester's eyes opened wide. He dug the phone out of his pocket.

"Found this cell phone next to her body. Only number on it was yours. Number one on speed dial. You deliverin' pizzas?"

"Free country. How I supposed to know how she got my number."

"You follow the news? Heard about that creep been snuffin' workin' girls. Specializin' in these young ones? We took her picture around to the local sleaze motels. Manager at the Bellevue said you delivered her there coupla nights ago. Claimed, you came back lookin' for her next day. Real upset when she was gone."

"Cracker must be mistaken. Ask him again, he probably change his mind. You chargin' me with somethin'?"

"Nah. Just thought you might want to do your civic duty is all." Archer nodded to the two officers. "Cut him loose. Thank you, Mr. La Royce, for your assistance."

As Archer and the officers exited the room, Lester trailed them into the hall. "You takin' me back to my crib?"

Without a word, Archer flipped him the bird over his shoulder.

*****

Later Archer sat across from Charmain at the kitchen table, holding the large envelope. Dr. Maynard and Collins on either side. As Archer opened the envelope, she looked up.

"Is it?"

He nodded. Then pulled out the letter. "Do you want me to read it out loud?"

Charmain sat with her head in her hands. She sighed. "I suppose."

Black Beauty,

I hope this day finds you as well as myself. I'm sure you've heard I've been busy. Wanted to give you some details. I kept this one for a while. Kind of a test for myself, I guess. I am sure they told you I did this a little differently this time. Besides keeping her for a while, I didn't leave that droll comment about the Egyptians. I mean, a guy has to have a little variety.

Also tried to talk her into going and seeing that nice Reverend Belkey. Getaway from this life. Learn how to cook, sew, clean. Maybe be an honest woman. She laughed. Oh, well.

I also noticed that the good Reverend might be taking an interest in you. I hope not. You and Archer make a cute couple. I hope our little correspondence gets you a chance to see him more often. I mean, who would guess? You could knock one off over my letters. Might be fun. I'm puzzled why you don't let people know we talk. It would be perfect for your fan base. I won't be sending any more fingers. Just did it this time to let you know it was still me. Only pictures from now on. Promise. Cross my heart.

XOXOXO

The Gingerbread man.

"My God, he must have followed me yesterday. That's when I went to Shining Light."

Maynard scowled. Turned to Archer. "I thought you had security on her."

"We do," Archer snapped as he pulled out his phone. Stepping away from the table, he muttered into the phone as he paced in Charmain's living room.

Collins turned to Charmain. "What did you do, and who did you see there besides the Reverend?"

"Well, I interviewed him in his office. Later, he took me around to some houses they were getting ready."

"Were there workers at the places you visited?"

Charmain chewed her lower lip as she thought. "Yeah. Some guys doin' construction at both houses. He introduced me to 'em— couple retired guys. A local minister and this contractor kinda hovered around everybody. Made everybody nervous."

"Anybody else?" Collins continued.

"Well, there were some girls who lived at the shelter—a few staff people. There was a guy there at the last place. Maintenance man, I guess. Drove a red pickup. I don't think the staff or the girls liked him much."

Archer returned to the room. "Guys watchin' her claimed they didn't spot anybody followin' her. But they probably weren't watchin' for that. Gave `em a heads up, though."

Collins nodded to Charmain. "She mentioned some people she met there. Let's call on the Reverend. Find out who exactly these folks were and talk to `em ourselves. This guy may have tipped his hand."

*****

Dr. Johnson yawned as she scribbled a progress note in the patient's chart. Her cell phone vibrated. After checking the screen, she took the call. "Hey, Carl. What's up?"

"What's up is right. Just got through with a guy you sent me."

"Who?"

"Well, he gave me a release to talk to you in case he needs meds. Robert Jordan. Detective with the Jergen County Sheriff's Department."

Dr. Johnson's eyebrows rose. "Oh, yeah?"

"Yeah! Shit! Jenny, you might have at least given me a head's up, you know."

"I'm sorry. I guess I figured he wouldn't follow through. Big macho cop? Usually, don't want to admit they've got a weakness. How did it go??"

"He seems really motivated. Startin' with three sessions a week. Also, goin' to a support group I recommended tomorrow."

"See, Carl. I have faith in you."

"But Jesus, Jenny, all this BS about your dead daughter. Where did that come from?"

She toyed with her hair as she talked. "Well, I thought it might ease his mind about getting help. Knowing, a big strong girl like me needs it once in a while, too. Might get him spurred in. Sounds like it worked."

"But I felt like I was lying to him the whole time. I mean, you don't have any kids."

"So? Why does that matter? I think it helped get him in. Was that so wrong?"

"He kept asking about you and your daughter. All I could say is I can't discuss other patients with him. Seemed like it satisfied him... But still. It just didn't sit right."

"Just be satisfied we got him in for some help. It'll balance out in the end. Remember what Professor Langford always said."

"Oh, shit! Of course." Carl chuckled. "Sincerity is the key to successful therapy. Our patients need to sense your sincerity to thrive and get healthy. The sooner you learn to fake it, the better."

CHAPTER ELEVEN

Archer entered the interrogation room while Collins and Dr. Maynard watched through the one-way mirror.

"He has the right build. Tint his hair. Put a fake mustache and goatee on him with a baseball cap he'd fit the composite." Collins muttered.

Archer set a folder on the table, then joined the man. He flipped open the folder and looked across at the man. "Bert. Bert. Bert. Tsk, tsk. You're causing the Reverend a lot of grief."

The man shrugged. "Not my fault he didn't do his job."

"Yeah, but you know better. Shouldn't have been anywhere near Shining Light, let alone work there. Shit, man, you're still on probation. Nasty scratch on your cheek."

Bert touched his face. "Bumped into a pipe on one of the jobs."

Archer laid a picture on the table in front of the man.

Bert glanced down and smiled. "Pretty. But older than I like."

"That's right. You like 'em just outta diapers I forgot."

Bert scoffed. "She say I did it?"

"She didn't say anything. She's dead."

Bert smirked. Pointed at the picture. "Shame. That might account for that faraway look in her eyes. Huh?"

Archer trembled as he struggled with the urge to launch himself across the table. Grab this asshole by the neck. Beat his head into a bloody pulp on the floor. "Mind tellin' me where you were night before last?"

The man placed his hand on his chin. "Gosh! Let me see. I really should call my secretary. Have her check my appointment calendar. Wouldn't want to mislead you or anything. Oh, by the way, are you thinkin' about charging me with anything?"

"How about probation violation for a starter?"

Bert shook his head. "Good luck with that. Been off probation for a month."

"How about violating the Sex Offender Law?"

The man shrugged again. "You should let me talk to my lawyer."

"You gotta lawyer? Damn. I didn't know I was sittin' across from such a high-powered dude."

"Whatever. Don't need to say nothin' to you till I talk to my lawyer." The man reached into his pocket and pulled out a card, which he passed to Archer. Archer stood and left the room. He came around to where Collins and Dr. Maynard waited. Inside the interrogation room, the man pulled the picture in front of him. He picked it up and studied it.

Archer turned to Dr. Maynard. "Whattaya think?"

She shrugged. "Next to Sociopath in the dictionary, you'll probably find his picture. But..."

Archer turned to Collins, "Is he off probation like he said?"

"If it had been that recent, it might not be in the file yet. Those PO's got a lot to do. Paperwork can't be their biggest priority. The fact that his bein' at Shining Light might violate the Sex Offender Statutes didn't seem to bother him either."

Archer nodded at Collins. "How about you check up on his status? I'll see what we can do to get his attorney in here. After that, you and I can go kick Belkey's ass. I mean, the guy should have known better."

*****

Later, as Archer and Collins drove to Shining Light, Archer's phone vibrated. "Archer."

"Hey man. This Lester. Me and my boys got yo Chicken Hawk!"

"Whaddaya mean Lester."

"Dude come sniffin' around here. Lookin' for another one. Damn man. We got him. You wanna come by, take him off our hands or

105

you just wants us take care of it ourselves? Make no difference to me."

"Where you at?"

Lester gave him the address. He cut off the call, kicked on the siren and the lights then floored the black car's accelerator as it roared down the street.

"What's goin' on?" Collins asked.

"Lester says he's got the guy. Guess he and some of his homies are keepin' him company while they wait for us?"

"What the hell? How'd they do it?"

"Lester says the guy come around askin' about another one of his girls. Says he made him somehow and will hold him for us. Good citizen that he is. I better call in for back up. They may change their minds. Dispense some hood justice. If we don't hurry, we might not find our boy in one piece."

*****

The patrol car's flashing red lights lit up the scene.

"Come on, boys, back off!" one uniformed officer barked. His partner shoved his way through the towering black men. Inside the circle, a man huddled on the ground at the base of the lamppost. He helped the man to his feet.

"Hey man, we gotta teach this cracker mother fucker a lesson." One snarled as he lunged at Belkey.

Belkey ducked as the fist brushed his cheek. "It's not what it seems. Let me explain. I just want to save her!"

One patrolman held a flashlight up to Belkey's face. He grimaced when he saw the bruise already forming under the Reverend's eye. Belkey shielded his eyes from the light with his hand. "Honest Officer. I meant no harm."

The officer turned to the men who loomed in a menacing circle. Turning to Lester, the policeman pointed at Belkey. "Lester! Do you know who this man is?"

Lester tapped his own chest with a fist. "Yeah. He some Peckerwood come down here try to hurt the girls. Come askin' about another young one. Said her name, Bonnie."

Belkey turned to the policeman. "Officer, that's not true," he pleaded. "I need to get her to the shelter."

As the black cruiser carrying Collins and Archer arrived, the discussion ended.

Archer and Collins approached the group. "Lester! You said you got a package for us?" Archer called out.

Lester pointed over his shoulder with his thumb. "Tha's right, man. Over here by the pole. Mighta bruised him up a bit. Boy's had a tussle subduin' him, you know?"

Archer stepped through the crowd to Belkey's side. "Hey, Reverend. Doin' a little recruitin'?"

Lester stepped forward next to Archer. "Called me. I thought he sounded familiar. Asked about a girl named Bonnie. She, a friend of Charise. Tole him, meet me here. Me and the boys arranged a little welcome committee. You gonna take him, or can we just have him?"

Archer shook his head. "Listen, I'll put you on honorable mention for Crime Stoppers. But me and Detective Collins will take it from here. Okay?" He turned to Belkey. "Where's your car?"

Belkey pointed across the street to the dark blue van with a lighthouse painted on the side. Archer turned to one of the uniformed officers. "Travis. Get that vehicle over there towed to impound. We leave, it'll get torn up worse than it is."

He took Belkey by the arm and beckoned Collins to follow him. The three strolled to the idling black cruiser and left the scene.

*****

Collins and Archer sat in the hospital waiting area while the staff attended to Belkey's injuries. Collins nodded to the emergency room door. "Lester seemed confident Belkey was the man. Plus, Lester said he recognized the voice."

Archer shook his head. "From when? Lester already denied knowing the last victim. Which time should we believe him?"

"But he also said Belkey asked for his girl by name. What about that?"

Archer shrugged, "Got somethin' there. We'll have to ask him about it."

"Also, he coulda been the one sent that letter to Charmain."

Archer shook his head. "You're makin' him into some real criminal mastermind man. Then he does what? Calls the pimp who ran his last victim and asks for the girl by name? Does he go from genius to moron in a heartbeat? I mean, the guy has no street smarts, or else he wouldn't have agreed to meet Lester out there in the hood. Sound like some criminal mastermind?"

Collins shrugged. "Well, just sayin'. Wouldn't be the first one of these holy Joe's to be in sympathy with the devil."

The door opened, and a man in a long white coat stepped out carrying a clipboard. "Your man's done."

Archer stopped the man. "How's he doin', Doc?"

The doctor held up his hand, palm out as if holding them back, shook his head. "Sorry, patient confidentiality. Ask him."

After knocking on the door, Archer and Collins entered the room. Belkey tucked his shirt in his pants before seating himself to pull on his socks and shoes.

"What the Doc say? You gonna live?"

Belkey looked up at Archer. His left eye already swollen shut and purple. "Nothing broken. Might have a cracked rib. Other than that, I guess I'm okay."

"You're lucky uniform got there when they did from what I heard. Lester's buddies wanted some payback."

Belkey made a wry face. "I tried to explain to him. Tell him why I wanted the girl, but he wouldn't listen."

Archer put his hands on his hips. "Well, the last one was one of Lester's. Figure he had a fondness for her."

Collins put his hands in his pockets, leaned against the wall. "Lester said he recognized your voice. Claimed, you asked for her by name!"

Belkey stared at him. Shook his head. "You don't understand. You've gotta believe me. I came down to find this particular girl. She's in danger."

Collins rolled his eyes. "In danger? Only her or all the girls?"

Belkey said nothing. He stared off as if considering his answer. "I don't know. I got her name from some girls I talked to the other night. See, when I don't have other things to do in the evening, like fundraisers or meetings. I go out and talk to the girls on the streets. See if I can convince them to come into the mission. The girls I spoke to the other night mentioned her by name. Thought she might want to get out of the life. Away from Lester."

Collins shot a glance at Archer, then turned back to Belkey. "So, Lester's wrong. You're not the guy that's been out here killin' those young things."

"Yeah! I mean, no. Lester's wrong. If she wants out of the life, then she's in danger from Lester. That's what I meant."

Collins scoffed. "So, these other pros thought she might want to come in from the cold, as they say?"

"Yeah! That's it. Listen. I'll take you to the one that gave me her name. She'll tell you."

Collins sneered. Turned to Archer. "Whattaya think? Suppose we oughta go with the Reverend here. Find that girl. See if she wants to follow through on her civic duty?"

Archer placed a hand on Collins' shoulder. "Easy man. Let's make it easy on the Rev. I mean, he seems to have a good heart. Been tryin' real hard to save these girls from the life. He's respected in the community and all. Let's help out a bit here, brother."

Collins ran his fingers through his hair. Shook his head. "What do you mean, Jack?"

"Let's take him out. Find the one that gave him the name. Got nothin' else. If we can't rule him out, we got a suspect."

Collins glanced over Archer's shoulder at Belkey. Belkey looked away. Pursed his lips, then turned back to the detectives. "I know where these girls usually are. Please!"

Collins shrugged. "Why not?"

Archer turned to Belkey. "One thing before we go. Where were you the night before last?"

Belkey leaned back in the chair. His jaw dropped. "I... I was at home."

"Alone?"

"Yes."

Collins got into Belkey's face. "What were you doin'?"

"Had a trying day. Splitting headache. Came home, studied my Bible for a while, then went to bed."

Collins stomped out with Archer on his heels. Outside, Collins turned to Archer. "See? There you go. Now, all we gotta do is check with God, and the Sky Pilot here is off the hook. Shit! Wish that had occurred to me!"

Archer shook his head. "Yeah, like I said, he's sure some criminal mastermind. Bet he makes Moriarty jealous."

*****

Jordan swung on his crutches to reach the church doorway before it closed. "Damn!" Jordan cursed as the crutch hit the door frame. The woman ahead of him turned and frowned.

Jordan hung his head. "Sorry. Not used to these things yet."

She patted him on the shoulder. "Listen! Why don't you head on over to the circle? I'll bring you a chair. Okay?"

"Yeah! Thanks." As she entered, the woman stepped aside, while Jordan hobbled by.

The woman called after him. "You want coffee too? I think I always see you with a cup. We'll bring that too."

"Ah yeah. Sure, thanks. Just black okay?"

After he settled, he studied the group. Mary sat next to a balding, thin man with glasses. Tiny almost frail looking. The brown fringe surrounding his shiny pate contained streaks of gray. Mary pointed to Jordan, and the man turned and smiled. Leaving his chair, he walked to Jordan's side.

Jordan extended his hand to the man who barely stood five feet tall. "George. How's it goin'?"

"Looking at you I think I need to count my blessings. What happened?" George's voice high pitched almost shrill.

"Uh! Fishin' accident."

"Yeah right! Catfish jump out of the pond and bite ya?"

Jordan turned. Hector loomed at his side. "Urich already filled me in. So, don't give me any bullshit. You try lyin' in here, and I'll call out your ass. Bet on it!"

George smiled as Hector stomped off. "Sounds like he takes your sponsorship real serious." He nodded. "Made me proud to hear him say that. I'm his sponsor, you know. Said pretty much the same thing to him on several occasions. Don't swear like him, though. He's an artist."

Jordan chuckled as he imagined George in Hector's face, red faced, shaking his finger under Hector's nose. God! The little guy must have some balls, he thought to himself.

All bowed their heads as George recited the Serenity Prayer.

*****

After the meeting, Jordan and Hector went to a bar for supper. Hector took a bite of his burger. After he swallowed, he took a long drink from the Dr. Pepper can. "Well, you're just damn lucky. Were you sober by the time Urich found ya?"

"Pretty much. Hell of a lot of pain, though. Got a nice shot from the paramedics."

"Left leg too. Means you can drive. Now what?"

He told Hector about counseling and the support group.

"Huh! Well, that shit's way above my pay grade. Think it might help, though?"

Jordan nodded. Picked up his burger. "Yeah. Not sure how much chattin' about it will help, but the shrink I saw at the hospital said it did wonders for her. So, what the hell!"

"So, what's this support group?"

"It's a group of people who've lost children. St. Jude's sponsors it. Guess that makes sense. So, most are parents of kids dying from cancer, but some have had violent ends. Kids killed in wrecks or drive-bys. That kind of shit."

"Jesus. Ya, forget that there's a lot of nasty shit in this world. How much the innocents get snagged in it."

Jordan felt surprised at Hector's sensitive comment. Seemed out of character. But he said nothing as he bit into his burger. After he swallowed, he wiped ketchup from his chin. "You were right. These burgers are great. Love the grilled onions."

"So, what about your girlfriend?"

"I don't know Hector. It's all real confusin' right now. Learned some new stuff about her in the last few days. I need to talk to her. Plus, she's in the middle of a real dangerous mess."

"Can't tell me about it?"

"I know it may be a surprise, but I guess I've kinda been an ass."

Hector slapped his forehead. His jaw dropped. "Shit, that really surprises me. I mean, you always seem to have yourself so squared away."

Jordan shook his head and chuckled. He took a sip of his soda.

Hector tipped his soda can at Jordan. "So, maybe you oughta be with her."

"I don't know. The whole reason she's in it is 'cause of me. If I show up, it may not help at all."

"When you first split on her, it was her that called out the troops."

Jordan cocked his head. His eyebrow rose. "You and Urich?"

"Yeah. Said she figured you didn't want her around, but you needed somebody."

Jordan ran his fingers through his hair. Sighed. *Had this been what he did with his daughter? Pushed her aside while he felt sorry for himself? Was he doing it again? Would he allow that monster to touch his life again?*"

When Hector belched, he tapped his chest. "Not sayin' you should rush out to rescue her now or anything. Last time you started all this managin' and rescuin', you ended up drunker than shit and worthless to the world. I mean it says right in the steps, man, that you need to Let go and let the Big Fucker in the Sky take care of some of this shit once in a while. But, for yourself, you might want to be there for her."

"God, Hector! Sometimes the shit you say must have Bill W. rollin' over in his grave."

Hector shrugged. "Ah, what did he know? It was him and another drunk in the last Century made all this shit up. They'd be happy we're still around."

Jordan raised his pop can in a toast. "I guess I'll drink to that."

CHAPTER TWELVE

Captain Johnson sat at the head of the table. He rubbed his finger at a tight black curl above his ear as he read the sheet in front of him. Dr. Maynard said nothing, just looked from Collins to Archer. The Captain set the paper aside. He sneered at the group. "Busy day yesterday. You went from no leads to two suspects in just a few hours." His glance switched to Collins. "I'm sure your boss'll be proud."

"The file said he was on parole. Convicted offender workin' in that shelter?" Collins nodded at Dr. Maynard. "Doc even thought he looked hinky."

"That's right, Captain. Warranted a hard look. Plus, the way he taunted the detectives..." She shrugged.

Johnson's scowl deepened. "Well, he might be our guy. All you did is rattle his cage a bit-make him think he could lie low. Startup again after the heat blows over. Meanwhile, if we go near him again, his attorney will scream harassment."

Archer sighed, shook his head. "How were we supposed to know he appealed his conviction even though he was on parole? Even better, no one bothered to inform us that his charges got shit canned. Then his name struck from the register because somebody else copped to the crime. You know he had to have done others. Just got pinched for the wrong one."

The Captain shot him a glance. His eyes narrowed. "Now, if this Bert's the one, he knows we're on to him. He might just stop. Or worse yet, move somewhere else and start up again. Nothin', we can do about it."

Collins leaned forward. "What about the Reverend?" He glanced at Archer. "I don't think Archer will agree with me. But I see him as a prime suspect. I mean, the working girls see him all the time. He probably could get one to come with him or trust him. Also, he would know all that stuff he put in Charmain's letter since he was with her."

Archer shook his head. Leaned towards the table as he talked. "Don't forget, he took us out to find the woman that gave him the girl's name. She confirmed what Belkey said. Also, the other guy. This Bert clown. He spotted her with Belkey on at least one of their stops. Coulda spotted Belkey making moon eyes at her. After that, put two and two together."

"Archer's right," Dr. Maynard added. "I noted Belkey's attraction to Charmain at the first press conference."

"But Lester was sure he recognized Belkey's voice, and again he asked for the girl by name. Plus, he has no alibi for the night of the last murder." Collins rapped the table as if pounding home his words.

The Captain scanned the group. "Well, we need a lot more than that to get even close to charging either with anything. At least I hope you didn't spook him. That way, we might keep an eye on him."

He turned his attention to Archer. "Follow up on both subjects. Examine all the murders again. We might get a rule out. Also, have some of our people follow both of them a little. Can't hurt. Okay? What about Crime Stoppers? Any citizens come forward."

Archer shook his head. "We got several calls about a Calculus teacher at M.U.S."

Collin's head snapped around to him. He frowned. "M.U.S.?"

Archer chuckled. "Yeah. It's a snooty male prep school here in town. Callers claimed the composite matched him to a 'T.' Also, the callers that made the report sounded like kids. We followed up; he was alibied by his pastor. Says he'll be raising the curve on the final. Other than that, nothing."

*****

Belkey set the ice pack on the desk as he opened the envelope in front of him. His mouth felt dry as he unfolded the page of cut-out letters before him.

Your Holiness,

You are tougher than I thought. A nice touch going to her pimp. Might have paid off if I hadn't got there first. His other girl was tasty. Figured you'd go to him. Lucky he didn't hurt you more. God, you are such a good person. Risking so much for so little. Especially, the way some, you try to save, treat you. Also, you surprised me again. I thought that once the police had you that you would fold up like a little sissy. Tell about our contest. Force me to harvest her early. But you didn't. If you had, they would have been watching her. Hoping to catch me. Use her as bait. God, they are so predictable.

But they didn't. I watched Lester take her to school today. That's right school. Middle School right there on American Way. He drove that bright and shiny `57 Chevy Pimpmobile from his crib on Lamar right up to the door. Does it every day. Picks her up in the afternoon. Believe that? He makes her go to school. Must be special that one. You might try to talk to her there. Also, there's a dance Saturday night at the school. She likes those. You might get lucky. Oh well. Like I said nice job. But the clock is ticking. You need to find her. Save her.

Your Doppelganger

Ginger b.

He set the letter down. Could it be this easy? Did the fiend mean to tell him that much? Maybe he figured he would be too frightened at this point to even try. Just give up. Let it happen. I guess we'll see.

*****

Jordan leaned on the crutch as he knocked on the door. He reached down and pulled the handful of Daisies from the bag that hung from his neck. The door opened to the length of the security chain. All he could see were her brown eyes with the gold flecks peering at him. The door slammed shut. The opening had not been broad enough to reveal her expression, only her eyes. *Did he see affection? Lust? Hate? Rage?* His heart leaped in his chest. His breathing stopped. He heard a clatter inside. The door flew open. She rushed to his arms, shoving him back against the railing behind him. They nearly toppled over to the parking lot below.

"Oh, my God! Oh, my God! Oh, my God!" she squealed as she pressed against him. He dropped one crutch as he drew her close and kissed her. Then groaned as she bumped his cast. The flowers slipped from his hand and scattered on the balcony. His hand now moved down her back. Clutched her firm bottom. He wanted to step inside her body.

She placed her hands on his chest and stepped back to study his face. "Oh, Bob. I am so sorry."

"Sorry? What for?"

"Not telling you about the book? I was afraid of what you might say or think."

"Let's not talk about that right now. Shit! Where's the flowers?"

They looked around at the scattered blooms on the balcony, then grinned into each other's eyes.

"How'd 'you know Daisies are my favorite?"

Jordan shrugged, still grinning. "You might have said somethin' in your sleep. Not sure, lucky guess, maybe."

She retrieved his crutch, then gathered the flowers. "Come on. Let me put these in a vase and get you all comfortable."

He hobbled in her wake as they went to the kitchen. He looked around as she filled a vase with water. "Everything okay?"

She grinned back over her shoulder. "Now it is."

After placing the vase on the kitchen table, she wrapped her arms around him. As she moved against his arousal, she whispered in his ear. "Now it is. Let's get you off your feet before you break those sticks you're usin'. I'll clear a path for ya."

As he trailed her, carefully placing his crutches. Not wanting to create havoc in his excitement, she quickly gathered up throw rugs in his path. "Wanna give you a clear shot. Don't want you hurtin' your back yet."

"Sounds like you got plans."

"You bet I do." She tossed the rugs to one corner of her bedroom before moving to the bed. She turned to face him as she slipped off her slacks. "You best get ready, yourself. Get out of those, or I'll ravage you where you stand."

Jordan chuckled and shook his head as he leaned the crutches against the wall. "Sounds like you mean to take advantage of me in my weakened condition."

"Don't talk about weakened to me. Way your tents up that muscle looks like it's fine."

"Damn girl, didn't you pay attention in your biology class? That's a gland. It's not a muscle."

Dropping her slacks to the floor, she unbuttoned her blouse. "Gland. Muscle! Never you mind. I intend to give it a good work out. So, you best be ready."

He dropped his slacks, then struggled to get them free from his cast. He wobbled as he balanced himself on his right leg, still trapped in the pants.

Seated on the bed, she drew him close. Tugged his shorts to his knees. Cupped his manhood, running her fingers up the shaft. She crooned to it. "Oh baby, thanks for bringin' your life support along. He talks nice sometimes."

He ran his fingers through her hair. "Ooh! Damn! Whattaya mean sometimes?"

*****

Later, Jordan ran his hand over her bare shoulder. "God! Your skin feels like silk."

Charmain kissed him on the cheek. "I'm glad you like it, only skin I got."

In the light from the hallway, a tear glistened her eye. "What's wrong?"

"Nothing, just happy you're here."

"So, you cry. Humph. Makes no sense."

She grinned. "Men don't understand. There are good cries, and there are bad cries."

"Yeah, and Eskimo's have about a million labels for snow."

She poked him in the ribs.

"Ouch, damn. I'm just sayin'."

She chuckled. "Hector's right. He doesn't know what I see in you."

"Well, I am learning that it might not be wise to discount what Hector says."

She sat up. A puzzled frown crossed her face. "Why? What do you mean?"

"He told me I was bein' stupid. I needed to come see you. Make things right."

"I gotta give that big lug a huge hug next time I see him."

"But don't offer to cook him dinner."

Pouncing on him, Charmain tickled him savagely. "You are awful. You have no right to belittle my culinary skills."

Breathless from laughing, Jordan could only croak a weak reply as he wrestled with her. "What? I mean, your prowess in the kitchen is a Memphis Fire Department legend. I'm just restating the obvious."

She stopped tickling, poked her nose in the air. "Humph!" Then giggled as she snuggled close. Her hand trailed down his chest, brushing his manhood. He swelled at her touch.

She kissed his bare chest as she inched down in the bed. "Well, thanks for keepin' me company while your better part rested up."

Jordan moaned, then protested. "Whattaya mean better part?"

Their passion stated, for now, Jordan slipped on his slacks before trudging to the kitchen. Once there, he fumbled in the refrigerator. "Gee, you got some eggs. If you had anything else, I could make an omelet or somethin'."

Clad in a robe, Charmain wrapped her arms around his waist and gave him a peck on the cheek. "Yeah, Tony came down and made a cake. Those were left over. He took everything else, so I wouldn't be tempted to cook."

"Suppose I could go up there and find out if they had anything I could use. They trust me in your kitchen, or we could go out and grab somethin'."

"No way. I got you here. I might want to ravage you again, and then what?"

He put his arms around her. Gazed into her eyes. "I know some places here in town where no one would notice."

"My Daddy says you're way too worldly for his little girl."

"That's Daddy talk. The Pope would be too worldly for most Dads."

He fell silent, gazed off into space. A tear glistened in his eye. She took him in her arms, rocked him as he sobbed. Finally, he drew back. "Jesus, I'm a mess."

She took his hands in hers. Looked up into his eyes. "No, one of the worst things that can happen to a person happened to you. You didn't deserve it. You didn't cause it. It's that fiend out there, and we're gonna catch him. He'll pay here on Earth, and then he'll have to face God. He will pay for all eternity for what he did. Believe me."

Jordan rubbed his eyes. "Archer told me about what's goin' on. The bastard contacted you?"

"Yeah. Wanna see it?"

"They didn't take it for evidence. That's sloppy."

"No. They took the originals. I made copies and took pictures of the fingers."

He sighed, "Oh, shit, baby. Why did you get into this?"

"I thought it would give me an excuse to hound them about the case. At first, I considered getting with those folks from the Memphis Writer's Group. Maybe get them to help in the hunt. But before I approached them about it, it got out of hand. The guy spotted me meetin' with Archer to nag him. I guess he thought we were an item."

Grim, Jordan shook his head. "So, he looped you in as a way of gettin' at Archer?"

"That's what the profiler says."

Jordan frowned. "Profiler? FBI?"

"Yeah."

"Shit! You can take most of what those folks know and roll it up into a little ball. Toss it in a thimble and shake it, it'll sound like a B.B. in an oil drum."

"Oh, Bob. She seems real nice."

"Pfft! FBI and nice is an oxymoron. Usually, they sail in. Stomp all over the locals. Do nothing but steal all the credit, before ridin' off into the sunset."

"Do you wanna see the stuff?"

He winced, ran his hand over his head. "Sure. But first, let's order a pizza at least. I'm starvin'. If I don't get somethin' to eat, my little friend won't be much use."

Charmain giggled. Shoved him away and went to the phone.

After their pizza arrived, Charmain set the folders from the case on the table. Once Jordan set the pizza box on the table, he fetched them both sodas from the fridge. He took a long drink from the soda as he studied the letter in front of him while Charmain helped herself to the pizza.

He snorted out a chuckle. "I'll bet Cindy wanted to carve Jack a new asshole when she heard about this."

"Well, he did say he had to convince her that there was nothin' between us. He said when she heard, I was involved with you; she told him he didn't stand a chance, anyway. You got some history with her?"

Jordan shook his head, recalling a party many years before. Archer's wife, while drunk, had suggested that they swap partners for the evening. It was all Jordan could do to keep his wife at the time from assaulting the woman in a jealous rage. God, those had been the days. "Nah! I just think it's her way of messin' with him. Husbands and wives, do that, you know? Listen. Archer said he had some guys watchin' you for protection. What did you do? Give them a picture of me or somethin' so they wouldn't hassle me?"

Wide-eyed, Charmain's head snapped around to him. She set her pizza slice down. "No, why? Didn't they stop you?"

"No, they did not."

"I mean, it took them a while to get used to Tony and Glenn. Stopped them almost every day. Especially Glenn, cause he messes with his hair color and all."

"Shit!" After leaping to his feet, he snatched his gun belt from the table. Drew the gun, jacking the slide, he chambered a round.

"Listen, bring me my phone, okay?"

After scurrying to the bedroom, Charmain returned with the phone.

"Bob, what's wrong?"

His eyes narrowed as he picked up the phone. "I need to call this in. Something's wrong."

CHAPTER THIRTEEN

"So, who's this Jordan, anyway?" Collins asked as they raced down Winchester.

"You said you met him. Found the body in Tunica."

Collins jaw dropped. "Shit! Same guy? What's the deal?"

"He and Charmain are an item."

"You're kiddin'. I thought he had a thing with that blond he works with. Now there's a piece of work."

Archer's phone vibrated. He put it on the hands-free to take the call.

"Archer this Lester! I got that cracker asshole back here on my patch. You come get him `fore I put a cap in his ass! You hear me, bro?"

"Where you at, Lester. I'll be right there! Don't do nothin' foolish man, okay. Let me handle it."

"You said that the other day when me and the boys had him. Now he back here at the school. Slinkin' around. Tellin' me, she in some kinda danger. You don't take care of this, I'll show him danger."

"Where you at, Lester."

"On American Way. Just East of the school. Got his van pinned against the curb. Like I said, get here fast, or I take care of this myself."

"Lester, he ain't worth it. I'll take care of it. Just hang on. I'm on my way. Plus, I'm sendin' a patrol car. When they get there, shove off, we'll take it from there.

Archer turned to Collins as he flipped on the lights and siren. "Call Jordan back. Tell him we're detained. Who knows, maybe we got our guy."

"He's already pissed. Wonder if the backup we called for over there showed up yet?"

"Hope so!"

As they arrived, they found Lester pacing the street next to an MPD patrol car. It sat behind the Shining Light van. Ahead and at an angle, a Metallic Green `57 Chevrolet Bel Air with over-sized chrome spoke wheels with tiny custom tires had the van wedged to the curb.

Lester peeled off from his pacing as Collins and Archer approached.

"Thought we told you to split when uniform showed up."

He struck his chest with his fist while pointing at the police car. "Man took my Glock man. Shit, I got a permit for it and everything. He harassin' me cause I black. Said I had to wait for you before he give me the gun back."

Archer stopped in front of the man. His hands on his hips. "You got a permit, Lester?"

"Sure! Why not? I'm clean. Got pimpin' charges, but shit, those are misdemeanors. Don't affect my second amendment rights."

Archer shook his head as he walked to the patrol car. Opening the rear door, he slid in next to Belkey. The Reverend hung his head as he slid over to the other side to make room. Collins climbed into the front seat.

Belkey glanced at both Detectives. "I know how this looks. Honest, I am just trying to save this girl. She's in danger. I tried telling him." Belkey nodded at Lester, who now glared through the side window. "He won't listen. But you have to."

"Why? Why her more than the others," Archer growled.

Belkey said nothing at first. He looked down at his shoes. Chewed on his lip. He sighed. "I received a letter from someone claiming to have killed the other girls. Challenged me to find this girl in three weeks, or he would get her. Said if I told the police, he would take her right away. I thought I could do it. I guess I was wrong."

Collins' eyes opened wide. The veins in his neck visible. "You say he contacted YOU?"

Belkey nodded. "Looked like he cut the letters out of something, a newspaper or magazine, then pasted them on paper to make a message."

Archer shot a glance at Collins, turned back to Belkey. "You have these letters?"

Belkey nodded. His eyes shifting back and forth between the two detectives. "Back at my office."

Archer beckoned Collins by tipping his head. They both exited the car. Lester leaped away from the light pole he leaned on and rushed to their side. "Gonna take care of this dude, or do I hafta?"

Archer went toe to toe with the man. "Lester, you've gotta big mouth. Somethin' happens to this guy, you'd be the first one we'd come lookin' for."

Lester stepped back. Closed his mouth. His eyes bugged out as he stared at Archer.

Archer shook his finger in the pimp's face. "What you doin' hangin' around here, anyway? You recruitin'?"

Lester's eyes opened wide. He stepped back, pointed to himself. "No, man. Part of neighborhood watch."

Archer cocked an eye at Collins, then turned back to Lester. "Gosh. Your sense of civic duty has me in awe. Do you know the girl he's talkin' about?"

Lester looked down at the ground. Shuffled his feet, looked up. "What if I did?"

"Man said she's in danger. I believe him. Bring her. I'll make sure she's safe. Okay? No questions, no hassles. After things settle down, she wants to come back to you, it's cool."

Lester's eyes shifted from Collins to Archer. "Good citizen I am, I'll have me and some brothers check out the hood. We find her, I bring her to ya. Okay? Now 'bout my gun."

"I can't just give it back to you here. We'll turn it into the property room. Just bring your permit down and any other proof of ownership you might have there. I'm sure they'll get it right back to you.

"Damn." Lester stomped off to his car. Once its engine roared to life, its tires squealed as he left the scene.

"Think he'll bring her in?" Collins asked as the uniformed officer approached them.

Archer shrugged. "Gotta keep an open mind. But at least if he doesn't, he'll keep a close eye on her. Might be safer for her with him. How 'bout you go with the good Reverend. Check what he's got. I'll go see if I can settle Jordan down."

Archer turned to the uniformed officer. "Hey Bill, can you give the Detective and the Reverend a lift?"

The officer nodded toward Belkey's vehicle. "What about the van?"

Archer shrugged. "No-parking zone, right?"

The uniformed officer nodded.

"Have it towed to impound, but tell them don't charge the owner if I call and release it, okay? Also, turn Lester's gun into the property room at end-of-shift. At least the area will have one less gun tonight."

As the uniformed officer proceeded to his car, he waved back at the two detectives. Archer turned to Collins. "Let me know what you find. We'll hook up after. And watch your ass. He is a suspect."

*****

Meanwhile, Jordan and Charmain watched the door, waiting. He had called 911 and reported the absent security. The dispatcher assured them that a unit would arrive shortly. After that, Jordan phoned Archer. He promised to be there as well. Someone outside beat on the door.

"Memphis Police!" A voice shouted from outside.

Jordan beckoned her away from the door. "Stay here. Let me make sure, okay?"

She nodded. Wide-eyed, she backed into the kitchen. Jordan, his gun held at ready, peered through the peephole. He stepped back from the door. Unfastened the security chain and flipped the deadbolt.

From his back pocket, he pulled out his badge wallet. He then slipped the pistol in the back of his jeans. Opening the door, he held the badge up. "I'm Detective Robert Jordan, Jergen County Sheriff's Department. I'm armed, and I called you."

Once Jordan opened the door, a uniformed officer stepped inside. A young black man, he strolled stiff-legged, like a gunfighter walking the street. He looked from Charmain to Jordan. Still wide-eyed, Charmain clutched her robe at the neck while peeking around the kitchen doorway. Jordan stood barefoot; his shirt untucked.

The officer glanced around; a disapproving scowl directed at Jordan. "I understand you're supposed to have a security detail from our department here."

"That's right." Jordan beckoned to Charmain. She moved to Jordan's side. "This is her apartment."

As she tossed her hair over her shoulder, she nodded. "I don't understand it, officer. Until this evening, they stopped everybody they didn't know on the stairs. Even hassled some folks that live here more than once."

The officer turned to Jordan. "They didn't challenge you?"

"No!"

The officer scowled. "They used to you?"

"I haven't been here since they started the security detail."

The officer shoved his cap back on his head. "Maybe they just missed you. Wouldn't be the first time. Just a glitch." He turned to Charmain. "How they keep track of who's comin' around?"

Charmain stepped out on the balcony and pointed to the camera. "Supposed to be another on the steps. I'm sure they saw you show up."

The uniformed officer sighed. "Who they s'posed to be protectin' you from?"

"A killer. The guy that's been killing those teenage prostitutes."

"Shit!" The officer pulled his portable to his lips. "This is two-niner-Savoy. Checkin' out this missin' security detail. Request back up, my location."

"Roger, car ten is two blocks from your location, dispatching now."

"Roger. Where's this detail stationed?"

"They're assigned to Detective Archer. I'll find out from him and let you know." As the first officer called for instruction, the sound of boots clomping on the stairway announced the backup' arrival.

A young black female officer appeared at the door. She strode in with the same stiff-legged gait as her colleague-her hand rested on her gun's handle as she scanned the room. Paused, she turned to the other officer. "What's happenin', Randy?"

"Got a missin' security detail. This here's a..." He nodded at Jordan.

"Detective Jordan, Jergen County Sheriffs"

She glanced at Jordan, smiled. "You used to work Homicide?"

Jordan nodded. "Yeah. Been a while."

"My Daddy worked homicide. Retired last year."

Jordan peered at her name tag. "You're Reggie's kid, Montrese?"

"Yeah. Met you a long time ago. I was in Grade school. Daddy always liked you. Said you got screwed over."

"Listen, 'fore we have this family reunion, we need to find our missin' officers." the first officer interrupted. "You say they were guardin' you from a killer, ma'am?"

Charmain nodded. The two officers exchanged a glance. Just then, Randy's portable radio squawked. "Dispatch to two-niner-Savoy."

"Two-niner-Savoy here."

"Lieutenant Archer en route to your location. Says security detail in apartment ten right below you."

As he signed off and turned to his backup as he drew his gun. "C'mon, Montrese, we better find out what happened to the boys."

He turned back to Jordan. "You're armed?"

Jordan nodded. Slipped the gun out of his waistband and held it up.

"You stay here. Guard the home front. Hard tellin' what's goin' down."

$$*****$$

The ambulance light bar's lights cut through the air above the darkened parking lot. Its diesel engine rumbled as the paramedics stepped inside, closing the door behind them. Jordan turned to Archer on the balcony as both men watched the vehicle drive away. "Any idea what happened?"

"Montrese said both were loopy as hell when she got inside. From what they could tell her, a guy brought 'em a pizza. Said it came from your girlfriend here. Musta spiked it with some kinda drug. Hallucinogenic. They was dancin' and singin'. Just havin' themselves a good ole time."

"They get a look at the guy brought the pizza?"

Archer shook his head. "I suppose. But it might be hours, maybe even days for they get right enough to give us details."

Beside them, Charmain clutched the robe tighter. A worried frown on her face. "They gonna be all right?"

Archer shook his head. "Paramedics thought they'd live. Said the emergency room guys would be the ones that would know. They'd need blood tests to figure out what the hell it was. Might have to pump their stomachs. What's left of the pizza they'll test at the lab. They'll have more answers."

Once inside, Jordan locked the door behind them. As they sat at the kitchen table, Archer dropped into the chair across from Jordan.

He shrugged. "Sorry, man. This kinda shit ain't supposed to happen. They shoulda checked with Char. Made sure the treat was for real." Glanced at Jordan before he continued. "You told me there'd be screw-ups assigned to the detail."

Jordan scowled. "Captain Johnson okay with this?"

"No, and I ain't either. Listen, you got any coffee?"

"Sure, Jack!" Charmain leaped up and went to the coffeepot. Archer followed her with his eyes.

Jordan shook his head and chuckled. "Don't worry, I made it," he whispered.

Archer leaned back and smiled. "Thanks," He nodded at the killer's note on the table. "She's been sharing with you."

"Sounds like a sick fuck."

Archer leaned close to Jordan. "Remember, this is out of your jurisdiction. Even though you're next of kin, you got no business pokin' your nose in it."

Jordan nodded towards Charmain. "Yeah, but she's part of it now."

Archer put his hands up as if surrendering. "I understand. Whatever she learns, she's gonna tell you, anyway. I might as well just tell you both at the same time, be more efficient." Charmain set the coffee mug in front of him. "Thanks, Char. Listen, Cindy said you and her oughta go over and take a class at that gourmet cooking school."

A grin spread on her face. "She talkin' about L'École Culinaire? Sounds like fun. I'll call her later."

Archer's phone vibrated. After checking the screen, he turned to Jordan. "May have a fresh development." He spoke into the phone. "What ya find out?" Archer listened. He rolled his eyes, gave Charmain's address. "Have the uniform drop you here, then have him take the Reverend back to impound. I'll call and have `em release his van."

After ending the call, he called impound. Finished, he put down his phone. "Okay, catch this. You know that, Reverend Belkey. Runs that shelter?"

Charmain nodded.

"Wait a minute," Jordan interjected. "Bout your height. Shaved head. Wears those plaid shirts with clerical collars. Buff guy for a priest or minister."

Archer frowned. "Sounds like him. You met him?"

"He was with us when we were doin' those busts at the Casino. Offered the girls a way out of the life when we arrested `em. Got a bunch out and into his program. Really good with the girls."

Charmain nodded. "That's him. Somethin' happen to him?"

Archer told them about the events with Belkey in the last few days. "I mean, this guy writin' Charmain either had to be someone close to the Belkey or him. Several on the task force put him at the head of the list. Then Belkey shows up huntin' some young thing on his own. Of course, I'm comin' after him. Anyway, the reason he's been out prowlin' is because this dude, doin' the killin', wrote to him."

Jordan and Charmain exchanged glances before he turned back to Archer. "Wrote to him?"

"Yeah. Same kinda letters he sent Charmain. Even used the same name. The Gingerbread Man. Cap'n wanted a rule out." Archer shrugged. "Guess we got one. Anyway, this guy challenged Belkey to a contest. Sent him a picture of a young one and told him if he could get the girl into Shining Light within three weeks, she'd be safe. Otherwise... and to quote the asshole, he would 'harvest' her. Also said if Belkey told the cops, he'd get her right away."

*****

Paulo moved in time to the music. His hand rested on the top ringside rope as he moved from flat-footed to his toes. With his arms held above his head, he leaped across the ring. The boxer throwing punches into the corner jumped aside. "Come on, Manuelito. Man, I got ten more minutes," he whined as he nudged his boxing helmet back in place. "I don't care if you are the champ. I'll bitch to the boss, and he'll make you go train somewhere else."

"I am so sorry. I only wanted to warm up while you cool down. I did not mean to disturb your concentration."

"What the hell you doin', anyway. You look like some kinda fruit prancin' around like that."

"It is part of my routine. Dancing helps me control my feet. Allows me to do many things with my hands without sending messages with my stance. You should try it. Might get you past these little bouts."

The man watched Paulo move around the ring. Rubbed his nose with his glove and snorted. "Yeah, right. I dance around like that, I'd get more fights. They'd be outside the ring instead of in, though. I ain't got a big sidekick like you do to handle the action."

"It is true. Esteban keeps the hecklers in line, but he is, in fact, a pussycat. Merely scares them with his size. Right, Amigo?"

Steven set his book aside. "That's me alright-all lover, no fighter. I am a creature of nonviolence. All I need is lovin'."

Joshua sitting next to Steven, looked up from his comic book and grinned. "That's right. I saw this mornin'. Mama had you pinned down. She jumpin' all over you!"

Steven chuckled and ran his fingers through the boy's hair. "Better believe that little man. Your Mama one mean mammer-jammer. She love you to death, but if you disrespect her, she gonna whip you no matter how big you get."

Urich and Maureen strolled into the Gym. Urich wore sweats and a t-shirt and talked on her phone, while Maureen wore her nursing scrubs. Maureen hugged Joshua, then kissed Steven on the cheek. "You boys behavin'?"

Joshua held up his book. His smile beamed. "I'm readin'. Steven bought me this comic book. Cool, huh?"

She glanced at the cover. "Let me see? That's one a them Marvel things, right?"

Steven nodded. "Figure readin' anything over the summer better for him than messin' with video games."

Joshua nodded. "Don't get mad at him, mom. He treats me real good. Just don't hurt him."

Maureen's frowned, puzzled. Steve shrugged. "The boy seen us fightin'. You know?" Winked. "This mornin'." He turned back to Joshua. "It was just in fun, Josh. We just playin'. See, she didn't hurt me a bit. Just had me down and sat on me."

Maureen smiled behind her hand, leaned close, and whispered. "Guess I gotta remember to lock the door."

Steven grinned and nodded.

She turned back to the boy. "Don't worry, little man. Steven learned his lesson."

Urich put the phone in her pocket. "That was Jordan. He's gonna be stayin' with Charmain for a while. Said he'd be by the office, might need some help."

Paulo leaned over the ropes. Urich ran her fingers through his hair, then pinched his cheek. "That means the couch is open again, so you best behave."

Paulo grinned. "I might need a rest, anyway." He turned to the other boxer still in the ring. "You think you could go a round with a fairy dancer like me? I promise the big boys won't laugh at you when you are done."

The big man scoffed. "Shit. You? You ain't even close to my class. You're no bigger than a rat turd. I'd have to use a telescope just to find you."

Paulo scowled at the taunt. "If you like. After we spar, I can spank you too if you like. Eh?"

"Get the gloves, asshole!" the other man growled.

Urich glanced over at the big boxer glowering from his corner.

"He sounds like he means it," she chuckled. She bent down to retrieve Paulo's gloves from the bag next to the ring.

The big man glared at her. "Bet your ass, little lady. I saw last time. He went five rounds with you. That scared me to death."

Urich said nothing but a tear formed in her eye as she recalled that bout that ended her career. Merely a sparring match. How she and Paulo met. The next day she collapsed. At the emergency room, they warned her. One more concussion might kill or cripple her. She missed the sport she loved all her life. The boxer's taunt angered her as well. She looked up.

Paulo glimpsed the fire in her eyes. "Ah. You know those doctors could be wrong. Maybe you could take one more blow to the head." He nodded towards the other boxer. "That guy couldn't lay a glove on you before you kicked his ass outta the ring," Paulo whispered as she laced the glove. He cocked one eyebrow. She heard the fury in his voice. After giving him a wink, she placed the helmet on his head.

As she held up his mouthpiece, Paulo stopped her. Gave her a quick kiss, whispered. "Don't need it. He won't land a punch."

Urich seated herself next to the bell. "When you boys are ready, I'll do the time. Three minutes, right?" she called across the ring.

As the two warmed up, they leered at each other. While shadow boxing to warm up, Paulo danced around on his toes. "You ready, Gringo?"

After nodding, the other boxer assumed his stance. When Urich rang the bell, the two fighters moved to the ring's center. As they closed, Paulo's opponent threw a right, which Paulo evaded. Before the man could pull back his fist, Paulo landed a punch to his jaw and another to the gut. A grunt exploded from Paulo's opponent as he staggered backward. Next, Paulo landed a barrage of jabs to the man's solar plexus. Stunned, the man's eyes glazed as Paulo nailed him with a savage uppercut to his chin.

"That should help you stay on your feet until the end of the round, Eh?" Paulo taunted.

"Hey, man, back off!" A man wearing a baseball cap shouted as he rushed into the room. "He's got a big bout this weekend."

"Oh yeah? Who wit? The Easter Bunny?"

Paulo danced to his opponent's side as the big man swung without power as if batting at flies. Paulo landed another series of jabs to the side of the man's head that chattered like a machine-gun burst. The big man tottered, stumbled, and then collapsed. While dancing around his fallen opponent, he peered down at the man, smiled. "What's a matter we got two more minutes to go? You tired or sumpthin'?"

The man in the baseball cap tossed a towel into the ring. "Stay down, Jackie. Listen, Beaner! Back off!"

CHAPTER FOURTEEN

"Here, Detective, let me find you a chair." Belkey leaped to his feet, exited. While leaning on his crutches, Jordan studied the photos and certificates hanging on the wall. Belkey returned with a folding chair.

"What happened to you? Is this why they stopped the sting down in Tunica?" Belkey asked as he set the chair behind Jordan.

"No, other things came up."

Jordan eased himself into the chair and placed the crutches at his feet. The leg with the cast straight out in front. He studied Belkey's face. "What happened to you? That's quite a shiner you got there, Reverend."

Belkey's hand shot up to his face. "Just an accident. I was in the wrong place. Nothing major."

Jordan smiled. Shook his head. "What about the other guy? Damage him much?"

"Oh no, it wasn't like that. Simply a misunderstanding."

Jordan nodded. "They gonna start up the sting again?"

"I'm not sure. We're short on space, but if they did, I'm confident we could make accommodations. Possibly send them to other programs in the area. I feel you did some excellent work. I wish we could have done more. Are you here about police work?"

Jordan leaned forward in the chair. "No, Reverend, I'm here for myself."

A puzzled frown crossed Belkey's face. "I'm sorry. I don't understand."

A wave of sorrow washed over Jordan as his smile disappeared. He sighed. "It's hard to talk about it."

Jordan swallowed. His lips trembled as he described his daughter's murder. He omitted her relationship to the serial killings. After he finished, he leaned back. Waited for Belkey's response.

"This was four years ago?"

Jordan nodded. "Yeah. About that."

Belkey shook his head. Silent, his hand rested on his chin as he studied Jordan's face. As he sat up, he folded his hands in his lap. "I am sorry for your loss, but I'm still unsure what I can do for you?"

"I'm gettin' counseling and attendin' a support group. That doesn't seem to be enough. Counselor suggested I come here. Volunteer."

"That this might help you somehow?"

Jordan nodded, sighed. "Yeah! I was a real shitty father. Got all tied up in my own crap. Buried myself in my work. Wasn't there when she needed me. I guess that if I help somebody else's daughter, it might make up for what I didn't do."

"I see. What do you think you could do for us?"

"Not sure. I'm just a cop. Had a little college, just some things for the job. I'm good with tools and such. Also, I might take the girls on outings. I know about fishing. Take a bunch out, show 'em how to drown worms. Tell fish stories. I don't know. I'd be willin' to do about anything. But for now, it can't involve a lot of standin' or walkin'."

"Let me think about it, okay? It's unusual. Most of our volunteers are women. I assume because of your leg, you can't work right now. I mean as a police officer," He added hastily. "Does that mean after your leg is better, you wouldn't be here?"

"No. I would still come. Maybe not as much, but I mean it. I feel doing this would be the best thing for me."

"I see!" Belkey rose. "As I said, let me think about it. I'm sure there are things around here that you could do. Do you live here in Memphis?"

"No, I live in Jergen County. Davis City, you know it?"

Belkey shook his head. "No. I'm afraid not. How far is it?"

"'Bout an hour's drive from here, but mostly four-lane. While I'm off work, though, I'm stayin' with a friend here in town. Here's my card. Call me on my cell. Okay?"

Belkey glanced at the card, then placed it in his pocket. He extended his hand to Jordan. "I'm confident we can use you. It'll take a few days to set it up. Okay?"

*****

After returning to Davis City, Jordan leaned the crutches against his office wall, he shuffled behind his desk. Sheriff Roy Speck entered carrying two steaming mugs. His gold badge gleamed on the breast of his khaki shirt. After setting one in front of Jordan, he settled his six-foot-plus frame in the vacant chair across from Jordan. "Here. Need anything else?"

"Yeah, maybe an ounce of brains. Might keep me outta trouble."

Roy shook his head and chuckled. "Then the rest of us would be bored to death. How long you in the cast?"

"They're not sure. Might be three months."

Roy rubbed his chin. "Shit! You realize since it didn't happen on duty, my hands are tied. You have some leave. I'll check with Legal. See if I can approve Light Duty."

Jordan scoffed. "It was my own damn fault. Don't sweat it, Roy. No matter what, anything in the field would be out. Somethin' happen, and Urich couldn't handle it, I couldn't provide backup for her or anybody else you might put me with."

Roy sighed and ran his fingers through his thick black hair. Jordan liked Roy. Even though a politician, he always had his back. "Listen, I've got savings. Plus, my ex-wife is finally sellin' the house. I should be able to cash out on that. Also, my credit's okay if I need a loan."

Roy sighed. "So, whaddya you gonna do? Sit around? Twiddle your thumbs?"

"Well, believe it or not, I might volunteer."

Roy arched his eyebrows, leaned forward. "Oh, yeah? Where?"

"At the Shining Light program."

"You mean that place that specializes in gettin' prostitutes outta the life?"

"Yeah, that one. Also, I might get some money helpin' a writer."

Roy's eyes opened wide. "Who?"

"Remember Carla Marsh?"

"Jesus. Doin' what? She need a new stud since you locked up her old man?"

Jordan chuckled. "Nah! Nothin' like that. Last time I talked to her, she said she needed some help with a new book she's workin' on. She needs an expert on Police Procedure."

Roy leaned back, smiled. "My wife reads her stuff. I love comin' home to find out she's been readin' that woman's books. She gets to talkin' about the story. Gets that faraway look in her eyes. Next thing, I'm missin' supper, but really glad to be home."

A knock at the door interrupted them. Urich slipped in. "Am I Interrupting some male bonding? Or is this a conversation that's okay for mixed company?"

"Nah! Roy's enlightening me on how to spice up a relationship."

Roy turned to her. "That's right, married thirty years, and I think she might say yes if I asked her again."

Urich leaned against the wall and crossed her arms. A smug look on her face. "Do you really want to know how to keep a woman happy?"

"Yeah, Urich, fill me in," Roy chuckled.

"Learn how to say 'Yes Dear' no matter what. And remember that no man was murdered while vacuuming or washing dishes."

Jordan chuckled, and Roy snorted.

Urich shook her finger at Roy, scowled. "And if you ever ask her how she feels, and she says 'Fine!' Freeze. Don't move. Don't even let her hear you breathe until she says something else. Then slowly back out of the room."

"You're in rare form this morning. What gives?" Jordan asked.

"I was about to ask you the same thing. You called, said you wanted to talk."

Jordan glanced over at Roy, then back to her. "I need a favor. Kinda personal."

Roy looked over at Jordan. "I get the hint. But before I go, I have one more thing to say. Keep in touch. Okay? I might have stuff I need you to do here in the office while you mend. Plus, even if I don't have stuff here, I would appreciate you comin' round and keepin' up with what's happenin'. That way, you'll get back to speed quicker when you can go back on duty. Okay?"

"You mean, make sure we're not lettin' the chicken rustlin' get out a hand and stuff?"

Roy grinned, nodded. "Exactly!"

After the Sheriff left, Urich took the seat he vacated. "I understand you been goin' real regular to AA."

Jordan chuckled. "What else Hector gossipin' about."

"He doesn't talk about stuff from the meetings. He's only keepin' me up to date. Knows I worry about you. Besides AA, have you ever thought about seein' a counselor? Talk to them about grief and stuff?"

Jordan leaned towards Urich. Scowled. "You think I'm nuts too?"

"Shit, Jordan. You know what I mean. Death of a kid is the worst thing that can happen to a parent."

"Well, if it's any comfort, I'm doin' just that. Also got into a support group for parents who've lost kids."

"Is it helpin'?"

Jordan shrugged, then grinned. "Worry about me, huh? I'm touched. Then you'll be thrilled. I'm doin' some volunteer work too. Shining Light. You know that place we sent those girls to from the Tunica busts."

Urich's jaw dropped, her eyes opened wide. "You're kidding."

Jordan leaned back, crossed his arms, a smug grin. "Surprised at my new sense of self-fulfillment?"

Urich scoffed. "Yeah, it's such a switch from the self-destruction you embrace. What's behind this spiritual renewal of the wayward sinner?"

He told her about the serial killer and his contact with Charmain.

"Jesus! So, you gonna sit back and let this task force hunt this freak down? Man, I figured you'd wanna be in on the hunt. I would."

"I might. Do the good work and hunt this asshole."

"How? Sounds like you got enough on your plate."

"Because of Charmain, I got a front-row seat at the investigation. I know everything their workin' on. They had two suspects."

"Really? Who?"

"The first was the good Reverend Belkey himself."

Urich cocked her head. "What? You're kidding. Belkey?"

"Yeah, they found him out huntin' young girls on his own. Sounded real suspicious, but then they discovered the killer wrote to him too. Had some kinda sick contest goin'. Targeted a girl, then challenged Belkey to find her and get her into the program. Told him if he went to the cops, he'd grab her right away. His hunt got him beat up by the girl's pimp and busted by the Task Force."

"Jesus, this killer is somethin' else. I've heard that some of 'em like to play games, but this seems over the top."

"Anyway, it looks like Belkey's in the clear."

"How so?"

"The letters. Unless he wrote 'em himself. But they all came through the mail. His secretary picked 'em up from the post office. Plus, the girl's pimp coulda killed him while he was huntin'."

Urich chewed her lip for a moment. "Hmm! So, who's the other one?"

"This dude that works maintenance for Shining Light. Name's Bert Christian. The task force is lookin' into him. Apparently, he's got a past that put him in their crosshairs. They hauled him in, but it fell apart in a hurry. Guess they had no just cause, and he's got a real ace for an attorney."

"Am I seein' a pattern here?"

Jordan smirked. "See? I wasn't wastin' time trainin' you."

"You're gonna start your own little hunt there in Shining Light."

"Gonna have to be careful. Already warned about jurisdiction, but hell, this fits right into my therapy."

"So, what did you want to talk to me about?"

Jordan glanced at the door. Lowered his voice. "I kinda hoped that in your spare time, you might help me with stuff that needs official inquiries."

She smiled. "Well, nothin' major goin' on right now. They talked about startin' up the prostitute bust again. But none of the local counties could spare anybody."

"Who they got you partnered with?"

"Carl. From Patrol."

"Good cop. Likes patrol. Surprised, he agreed to come over and help."

"Roy gave him a temporary bump up in pay. What about security for Charmain? Word is they kinda fucked up."

"They put SWAT on it. Scared the hell outta the boys upstairs, but at least they won't be sleepin' on the job. And catch this. Hector's gonna watch them. Make sure they don't fall back either."

"Hector? Thought he hated cops."

"Nah! Just me. He kinda likes you. So Whattaya say. You with me on this? Help me out while I hunt this asshole?"

A smile lit up her face. "Sure. Why not?"

*****

Meanwhile in Memphis, Lester stepped into the garage. His cell phone to his ear, he fumbled in his pants pocket for his keys. "Tha's right. I'm pickin' Bonnie up. I want you to stay with her at the house while I go down to the bus depot. Check it out for product. Need to reload after that bastard took Charise. Be here when I get back."

As he ended the call, he punched the remote to open the garage door. From behind, an arm clutched his neck so tight his vision slowly blurred. A burning tingle in his back sent a paralyzing spasm through his body. The phone and the garage door opener dropped from his hand as he sank to the floor. He opened his eyes.

The man wearing the balaclava face hovering above him grinned. "Don't worry. I'll make sure Bonnie gets picked up safe."

Lester could not move. Tazed before, he knew he would be helpless. Paralyzed. The man dragged Lester away from the car to the workbench bolted to the floor. The handcuff snapped on his wrist before his attacker flipped the cuff's chain around the bench's leg and fastened Lester's free hand in the other cuff.

"There. You might miss your little recruiting trip too. But that's just the hazards of doing business."

The man kicked Lester's cell phone across the floor, well out of reach. Then glanced at the car. "I'll leave ya my bike. It's next to the garage. You might need it to find your car."

The attacker ran his hand over the car's finish. "Nice ride. I'll make sure I leave it where no one damages it too much. Consider the bike a trade for your girl." The man chuckled. "Get it? My ride for yours? When Archer gets here, tell him I have a good sense of humor. Okay?"

After picking up Lester's keys, the man hopped in the car. Started the engine and backed out.

The mellow purr of the glass pack mufflers brought a smile to his face as he drove to the school. It had been too easy. Lester never realized what hit him. The Taser worked perfectly. It might take hours before anyone looked for him. Now to get the girl in the car.

At the school, he pulled ahead of the usual pickup spot. Force the girl to approach from behind. The tinted windows would conceal him until she got in. Then it would be too late. The passenger door opened.

"God! What a day! I hope you got some good weed. I'm dyin' for a hit, man." Without looking at him, she slid into the passenger seat. But as the door slammed, she turned.

"What the Hell?" she shrieked. "Who are you?" Her eyes, open wide, rolled back in her head as he hit her with the Taser. His fist slammed down on the door lock as he injected her with the syringe. He tossed her book bag in the back seat. After fastening her seat belt, he leaned her against him as he pulled away from the curb.

The car swap went smoothly. Outside his garage, he surveyed the neighborhood. The street deserted, the only sound, the ticking of the hot engine as it cooled. After opening the passenger door, he lifted her out then nudged the door closed with his foot.

She seemed almost weightless in his arms. He listened to make sure she still breathed, so he guessed right on the dosage. Entering the house through the back door, he set her down on the couch. Even with her weight, he had no problem scooting the sofa to the side so he could remove the carpet. After lifting the cellar door, he carried her down the steps and laid her on the bed.

"God!" he thought, "Girls this age had no fashion sense at all. Scruffy jeans. Baggy t-shirt. Ugly tennis shoes."

While she remained unconscious, he removed the ugly garments. Unsnapped the training bra and tossed it with the rest of her clothes at the foot of the stairs. He chuckled as he pulled down her panties to expose her pubic hair. The girl had chestnut brown hair on her head but had dyed her pubic hair golden blond.

"At least she has a sense of humor," he said aloud as he sniffed the undergarments. "You've been having naughty thoughts today too!" The panties joined the pile of clothes on the floor.

"We'll have fun for a while, I guess."

His knees trembled as he struggled with the desire to touch her. But that might breakdown the control he needed to keep her alive for the rest of the game. He kneeled, closed his eyes. *His step-sister's face appeared before him. She cackled as she stepped back, as if displaying her nakedness. "I saw you peepin' at the window. When yours grows bigger, I might let you have some too!" She mocked him as she slammed the door in his face. He shook his head. No I must not touch this one, yet.*

Still trembling he rose, unfolded the quilt from the bottom of the bed as he spread it over her naked body.

"Can't have you catching a chill."

Once he gathered up her clothes, he climbed the stairs.

CHAPTER FIFTEEN

Archer and Collins talked as they passed the police cruiser parked in the driveway. Its flashing lights lit up the crowd gathered on the sidewalk. Archer narrated what he learned so far. "Lester and his buddies couldn't get the cuffs off. They called the fire department. They find out what's goin' on, and they call in uniform. Lester finally owned up to what happened. Both Lester's buddies and some officers went to the school and no sign of the girl. They called me."

"You told uniform to cut him loose?"

"Nah! I told them he's a person of interest in our case. Said I needed to talk to him. They promised to keep an eye on him. I'm not gonna cut him loose until I feel he's bein' straight with us. Otherwise, he'll take off and try dealin' with this on his own."

Inside the house, Lester sat in the kitchen, his hands cuffed behind his back. A uniformed officer sat at the table next to him.

Lester nodded at the uniformed officer. "How 'bout tellin' the brother here to let me outta these things."

"I only want to make sure you're not a danger to yourself or others first. You cool, Lester? You gonna behave?" Archer snapped.

Lester nodded. "Yeah, man. I'm good."

Archer nodded to the uniformed officer. Once the cuffs snapped off, Lester massaged his wrists as he rose to his feet. Paced, slammed cupboard doors, kicked a kitchen chair across the room. "Mother fuck! Fuck! I'll kill his ass I find him! No matter what! Whatever he do to her, I'll deal it back to him in spades! Fuckin' Cracker!"

"So, you got a look at him?" Archer inquired, then glanced at Collins.

"Fuck, no! Had on one of them ski masks. I come out the door. Next thing I's on the floor. Then he drags me across the flo' and cuffs me to the bench."

Collins stood with his hands on his hips. He turned to Lester. "So, he coulda been a brother."

"No! I seen around his eyes. He white! Sides, this kinda shit is white boy crime. Brothers don't go in for this perverted shit. So, what you gonna do about it?"

Collins shook his head, then shot a glance at Archer. Archer sighed and shrugged before Collins turned once more to Lester. "Listen, you got cute with us. Played like you didn't know about this girl, Bonnie. Then you tried to protect her yourself. Look where that got you, Einstein."

"Man, the dude jumped me right here at my crib. Took the car."

"Probably how he got her," Collins snarled. "We'll go over to the school tomorrow. Maybe somebody saw something. We're not even sure he's the same guy that did the others."

"We put out an Amber Alert," Archer interjected. "Her picture's gonna be out in the papers and TV. Got patrol searchin' for your car. We're doin' everything we can. Now, how about you tellin' us what you know about her?"

*****

Bonnie woke with a start. Clutching the quilt, she glanced around the room. On one wall hung a large TV attached to a cable box. On a shelf above, stood an iPod dock with large speakers. Remotes for both devices lay on a stand by the bed. A desk sat against the opposite wall—her book bag on the chair. A note, propped up there, next to the bag.

While slipping out of bed, she wrapped herself in the quilt. Naked, she shivered as she picked up the note.

I will be back soon. Do anything you like. I am sure you know how to operate the television and the music player. Also, I left your book bag in case you want to keep up with your schoolwork. You will be with me for a while, so I want to make sure you have what you need. Don't worry. You have nothing to fear from me. You might even get to like me after a while. I left snacks for you in the desk drawer, and there is soda in the mini-fridge. The bathroom is through the door under the stairs. It also has a shower. I'll bring you something more to eat later. We can get better acquainted then.

She shuffled around the room, wrapped in the quilt. First, she studied the television, then the iPod dock. While scrolling, she read the playlist on the device then replaced it.

After opening the door beneath the stairs, she peered inside the bath. It looked clean. Maybe unused. Her eyes roamed the room.

Her mouth dry, she shuffled to the black boxy looking mini-fridge next to the desk. Inside sat a varied soda selection.

After picking the one she preferred, she popped the top and gulped it down. She winced as she walked. Seemed raw up between her legs. Had the creep done it to her while she was out? She wondered. What kind of strange mess could she be in now?

*****

Jordan gazed out the pickup's window as it traveled down Lamar. The red-haired man driving wove through the traffic. His t-shirt sleeves rolled to the shoulder, exposed powerful arms with sculpted biceps. As he drove, he grumbled. "Look, I don't know why the Reverend wants you to work with me. I mean, he says he can't afford to pay much over minimum wage, so where does he get off givin' me a helper?"

"I'm a volunteer, Bert. Don't get a dime."

"Volunteer? No shit? You doin' some community service in place of jail?"

"I guess you might say that."

Bert's eyebrows rose. "Whatcha do? Can't be no sex crime or nothin'. They ain't allowed to hire no pussy or ass bandits here."

"No, Just fucked up parenting skills."

Bert's jaw dropped. "No shit? They got laws against that?"

"Don't you think that would be a good idea?"

Bert shrugged. "If they did when I was a kid, my folks woulda been in the pen. Stead of me endin' up in juvie cause I run off. Must be 'cause of all them Liberals in Washington. I tell you the new guy will straighten 'em all out. Hell, even the Klan likes him."

The truck pulled into a driveway of a large two-story house. Two girls who looked to be in their early teens sat on the front steps. They laughed while holding an iPad between them.

"Looks like my pussy posse awaits," Bert announced as he stepped down from the truck. As the girls looked up, both rolled their eyes as they moved off the steps. Jordan followed Bert, doing his best to negotiate the stairs with his crutches. The girls whispered and giggled behind their hands as they watched the men climb the stairs.

After entering the house, Jordan followed Bert to the kitchen. Inside, a middle-aged black woman stood next to a teenage girl. The girl ran a mop over the floor, submerged beneath at least an inch of water. After two swipes with the mop, the girl plopped it into a mop wringer fastened to a wheeled bucket. Noticing the men for the first time, the woman scowled.

Bert held his arm out to block Jordan's entry. "Better not come in here with that cast!" His footsteps splashed as he entered. "Told 'em we needed a drain in this floor! What happened?"

The woman gestured with her thumb over her shoulder—there water cascaded from a cupboard under the sink.

"Damn it! I showed you how to use the shutoff. What the hell's wrong. 'Fraid you'll ruin your nails or somethin'?"

"It broke!" The woman snapped.

Bert stomped out. The woman looked at Jordan and shrugged. Soon, the water stopped. The girl mopping now made progress as Bert returned carrying a water meter wrench.

Bert opened the cupboard and shined a flashlight up inside. "Damn! 'Nother one of these cheap fixtures from that chain store. Guy oughta quit givin' all his money to Rush Limbaugh and buy some decent products."

He came out from under the sink. Looked Jordan up and down. "I'm gonna run get a new fixture. Why don't you just stick around here and keep the ladies' morale up?"

Once the floor dried, the older woman offered Jordan a cup of coffee. They talked as the girl finished cleaning the floor. She touched at her hair as if primping and smiled up into Jordan's face. "You a preacher or somethin'?"

"No, just a guy wantin' to help out."

"I wondered. That's the best behaved I've ever seen, Bert. Thought maybe that might be 'cause you were clergy or somethin'. What do you do when you're not here?"

"Right now, I'm out of work. At least until the leg heals. Then who knows? So, what's he usually like?"

"Oh, just your typical asshole. If you'll pardon my language. Always says something inappropriate to the girls. Kinda like he's flirtin', but without much skill. Targets the younger ones. Scares me. Sometimes he gets one off to the side. Hard tellin' what he's sayin' to 'em."

"Think he might proposition them?"

The woman shrugged. "All I know, the girls complain about him to the Reverend all the time. He's a peeper. Busts in a lot while the girls are in the can. Claims he's havin' plumbing emergencies. Some girls claim he gets a little free with his hands. I worry. These girls are vulnerable. Lots of esteem issues. Not sure they know that they can say no to jerks."

"You think he might take advantage of that?"

The woman shrugged. "Not sure. But he gives me the creeps."

*****

Urich studied the folder in front of her as she talked to Jordan on the phone. "Got nothing back yet on Belkey, but I got some stuff on the other guy."

"Bert?"

"Yeah. You said he calls himself Bert Christian, but that's an alias."

"An alias?"

"I guess that's what you'd call it. His full name is Albert Christian Bell."

"Wonder why he changed his name?"

"We'll get to that. Bell spent most of his childhood in foster homes and juvenile detention. What he did to get into the system, I have no idea."

Jordan nodded as he listened. "They'd seal those. Be tough to find out about it, even if he committed some heavy-duty shit as an adult."

"He worked as a supervisor for that company that does all the janitor work for the Shelby County Schools. He placed cameras in the girl's restrooms at several grade schools. They nailed him for kiddie porn."

"What in the hell is he doin' workin' at Shining Light?" Jordan shouted in her ear. "I mean, he told me himself that they do background checks. That would have shown up."

Urich tapped her pen on the pad and rolled her eyes. "You'd have to ask the Reverend. But maybe this might explain it. His conviction got him time served and probation. During his probation, a man named Roberto Angelino confessed to the crime. Claimed he framed Bell because he didn't like him. Said he was an awful boss."

What made this Angelino change his mind?"

152

"At the time of the discovery, Angelino was working illegally for the cleaning service. The money he made on the kiddie porn allowed him to return to Mexico, a wealthy man. Felt guilty, so he came forward to clear Bell. Federale's in Mexico City taped the confession."

"They extradite him?"

Urich glanced down at her notes. "Note in the file said, as it would be a first offense, all he would get is probation. Cost of the process would be too high. He's just blacklisted. Can't enter the country legally."

"Gee! I'll bet that stung. Wonder how much he made on his end of the thing after Bell got his cut. Must have been a two-part deal to make sure he came through with the confession later. Right?"

Urich grinned. "God, Jordan, next thing you'll start doubting the Warren Commission. Believing in Area 51. You're not gonna start wearin' a tinfoil hat, are ya?"

"Well, I believed in Santa, the Easter Bunny, and the Tooth Fairy at one point. So, I might be susceptible."

"If Bell made a bunch of money with the stuff, he got at the grade school. Why's he workin' for peanuts at this Shelter?"

"Obviously, my mentoring has been wasted on you if you haven't figured it out, Urich."

Urich rolled her eyes. Tapped her pencil on the desk. "That was a Rhetorical question. You know what that is? Right?

"Good. I guess my efforts at educating you have not been wasted."

"Hear that? That's me flippin' you the bird." Jordan's phone beeped. He looked at the screen. He took the call. "Char! Hang on. I'm on another call. How about I call you back? What? Oh Shit! I'll be right there."

He returned to Urich's call.

"Listen, you got anything else on Bell?"

"That's it for now. If you can get some prints off either of them, it might help speed things up. You sound rushed. Everything okay?"

"No. That was Char. She just got another letter."

*****

The door opened at the top of the stairs. A bag containing Bonnie's clothes dropped from above. The voice upstairs called down. "After you put these on, come on up. I got some hot food for you."

She hurried to the bag, slipped on the garments. "Where are my shoes?" She called up the stairs.

"Don't need 'em right now. They're outside. Airin' out. When they smell better, I'll bring them to you. "

After trudging up, Bonnie stopped near the top. With only her head through the opening, her eyes roamed the room. "Why you wearin' that mask?"

The man turned to her. "I guess I'm a little shy."

She finished climbing the stairs. "So, what's goin' on?"

"Let's say I'm taking a particular interest in you."

"Why? You a pimp like Lester? Wanna find out how he runs his business?"

The man shook his head, shrugged. "You think I might be Lester's competition?"

"Well, yeah. I mean, I keep his books and stuff. He says I'm real important to his whole thing. He warned me that others might want to find out how he works his business or take his over. That's why he always picks me up from school and stuff. Don't have to peddle my ass like the others. Just run it for him, plus let him have some if I want it."

"My, you must be special." He beckoned to the table. "Your food is over here on the table. Help yourself. Got soda or sweet tea if you like."

She strolled to the table. Her long legs like a colt. Nice shaped, but long for the rest of her body. Still, she moved gracefully.

"Got either chicken or burgers. You pick. I'll eat what you don't want."

She held her long brown hair back as she peered in the bag.

"Is the chicken fried or grilled?"

"Fried."

She sneered. "I guess the burger. Fried's not good for you."

"Oh! You watch what you eat."

"Yeah. My mom always insisted I stick to healthy food. Makes you feel better. Is this a diet soda?"

"No."

"Can I have some water then?"

He went to the faucet and filled a glass.

"Anything else?" he asked, setting the glass before her.

"That's okay for now."

"What foods do you prefer?"

"Stir fry. Lotsa vegetables. Sometimes, for a treat, I'll have General's Chicken. But it's fried. Not that good for you, even with lots of veggies with it. But what the heck, nobody's perfect. When I was out cold, did we do it? I'm kinda sore down there."

*****

Charmain, Collins, Archer, and Dr. Maynard sat at her kitchen table when Jordan hobbled through the front door. Collins changed seats, giving Jordan the closest chair. After leaning his crutches against the wall, Jordan lowered himself into the chair. While rubbing his knee, he turned to Collins. "Thanks, man."

Collins nodded. "Haven't seen you since the casino. Listen, I wanna apologize. I had no idea about your daughter."

Jordan shrugged. "I understand. I'm usually an asshole myself."

"Now that we're all feelin' warm and fuzzy, how 'bout we get down to business," Archer interjected. "Unless you and Collins feel a need to join hands and sing a few bars of Kumbaya."

Collins frowned as he gave Jordan an appraising glance.

Jordan shrugged.

Archer studied the sheet in front of him. "He says the girl is alive and well. She will remain so as long as we give him a little more attention," Archer looked up as he finished reading. He passed the note to Collins.

"What the hell does that mean? We just guess?" Collins rubbed his chin as he set the letter on the table.

"I guess that's a question we need to run by the profiler," Archer replied. He turned to Dr. Maynard. "We got her picture out on the media. Amber alert. What else?"

"This a copy?" Jordan asked. Archer nodded. Jordan picked up the letter and began reading.

"Did they all come the same way?" Jordan asked as he read. "Any prints. How about DNA? Maybe he screwed up and licked the envelope or the stamps."

Dr. Maynard turned to Jordan. "Excuse me, we haven't met. I'm Dr. Maynard from the FBI. You sound like a cop."

"I'm sorry, Doc," Archer interjected. "This is Detective Bob Jordan. Formerly MPD. Now he's with Jergen County Sheriff."

"And your connection to the case?" She continued looking puzzled.

Jordan said nothing, just blushed. Charmain giggled, took his hand.

"Oh! I see. You and Ms. Crump?" Maynard inquired with a smile.

Jordan glanced at Charmain. She smiled and nodded.

"His daughter was this creep's first victim. Also, part of the team that discovered the girl in Tunica," Archer added. Dr. Maynard turned to Jordan. "In answer to your question, we've checked for prints. None on the letters, both to Charmain or the other person."

"You mean Belkey?"

Dr. Maynard's eyes open wide behind her glasses. She smiled. "My, but you are well informed. Yes. No prints."

"What about DNA?"

Dr. Maynard turned to Archer. "I didn't see results on that. I'll check to see if anyone looked at it." Archer scribbled on his legal pad.

Dr. Maynard turned back to the group. "I'm sure he wants us to give him more limelight. Maybe mention the name he is using. We haven't shared the composite or the picture with the media. Only circulated it in general notices to law enforcement."

"What if you gave him your own name? Instead of this Gingerbread man, he calls himself?" Jordan offered.

"Interesting. It might antagonize him, though. But it could also spur him to contact us again," Dr. Maynard replied. She removed her glasses. She smiled at Jordan. The attention she gave him reminded of praise from one of his favorite grade school teachers.

Encouraged, he continued to speculate. "What if we could find a way to open a dialog with him?"

Collins scoffed. "How would we do that? Call 1-800 Asshole?"

"We only have this creep's word that the girl is alive. How about sharing this with the press? Ask him to supply us with a proof of life every day. Ask for a video or a phone call...", Jordan continued. "Beats the heck out of just sittin' here wishin' and prayin'."

"What Detective Jordan says makes sense," Dr. Maynard glanced at the others as she talked. "We get him talking, we might try things from hostage negotiation."

The others said nothing, just listened as the profiler continued. "We could tell more about this girl through the media. Describe her life, what she's like, what schoolmates or teachers say about her. If you're willing, that would be good for you to work on Charmain."

Charmain said nothing. She glanced at Jordan. "Could I talk to Bob about this before I decide?"

Maynard placed her hand on Charmain's. "I understand. Asking a civilian to get that involved has a risk. How about the rest of us go somewhere? Perhaps grab some coffee while you two chat." Dr. Maynard turned to Archer and Collins, who rose, saying nothing before trailing her out the door.

As soon as the others left, Charmain began. As she talked, she reminded him of a puppy dog begging for a bone. "Bob, the only reason I started this was to make sure Memphis didn't let the case go cold."

"But still, the guy got close enough to you and Archer to take your picture in the restaurant. Archer's a pro. Knows what the guy looks like from the composites, and he didn't make him?"

She put her hand on his knee, leaned close, looked deep into his eyes. The feelings he felt at this moment frightened him even more. He did not think he could stand losing her.

"Honey, this guy scares me to death. He dances around the cops like they're idiots, and they're not. Look how he screwed up the security. If I hadn't been here, he might have just waltzed in and taken you."

"But Jack replaced the usual guys with SWAT. Has a guy stationed at the door. Follows me when I'm out. If we can catch this devil, think about the difference it might make."

"Finding him won't bring Jennifer back."

"No, but if we catch him, he won't hurt more girls like her. This might be the only chance to stop him."

Charmain spoke the truth. Serial killers most often getaway. The ones that do not usually die before they are prosecuted.

"He knows where I am already. If he wants to come after me, he will. He might wait for weeks. Even months. They can't keep the security here forever. Then what?"

Jordan sighed, rubbed his chin. She drew him close and rocked him in her arms. "I promise I'll do what they tell me. I'll be okay."

He leaned back. Stroked her cheek. Nodded. He wondered if Hector would be enough backup. He hoped so.

*****

He rolled the carpet back, exposing the cellar trap door. After opening it, he tossed the clothes down.

"Brought you some food," He shouted down the open door.

After removing the white cardboard containers from the sack, he set them near the table's center. The girl's head emerged from the cellar. She glanced around, then climbed the rest of the way up. Barefoot, she rushed to his side. While shoving her long brown hair behind her ears, she watched him out of the corner of her eye as she reached for one container.

He nodded. "Go ahead! That's right. You said it was your favorite, and I got it at the place you wanted."

She flicked the container open with her finger and glanced inside. She looked up wide-eyed. A smile played at her lips but did not wholly emerge, but she said nothing.

"General's Chicken. That's what you wanted, right?"

She nodded.

"Too sweet and spicy for my taste. Let me get utensils and plates, and we can eat. Okay?"

She nodded. Setting the container near a chair, she seated herself at the table. After setting out plates and utensils, he filled two glasses from a pitcher. "It's Sweet tea. If you'd rather, there's soda in the fridge."

He pulled out the opposite chair and sat down. "Go ahead! Eat up before it gets cold." He poured long brown noodles from the other white box, then set his empty container in hers. Still wearing the balaclava, he twirled the noodles on the fork. He could eat still wearing the ski mask, but it would need washing. "Did you get your schoolwork done?"

The girl nodded; her mouth full.

"I'm surprised most kids your age wouldn't want to do it. Find any excuse to skip it."

After setting her aside, she finally spoke, "How will I be able to keep up?"

"That's a good question. I'm sure we'll figure out a way. But you have to behave. Do as I say no question."

As she scooped a forkful into her mouth, she nodded, chewing, she glanced around the room.

"Did you watch any television today or listen to music?"

She swallowed. "Yeah, There's nice stuff down there. Almost as good as what I had at Lester's. Watched the TV some, but I couldn't get any local channels. Listened to music, like the selection. My Mom loved the Doors. We listened to 'em all the time. Said it helped get her amped up."

"Amped up? Why did she need to get amped up?"

"She was in the Army..."

CHAPTER SIXTEEN

"Her Mom was an Army Ranger?" Charmain exclaimed as she read from the file.

Archer nodded and continued the briefing. "Yes, killed while deployed in Afghanistan. Her dad went to pieces and committed suicide. No other family, so the girl ended up in foster care. Does well in school. Has an IQ in the stratosphere."

"How did she end up peddling sex on the street?"

"Foster father began raping her right after she arrived in his care. The foster mother knew all about it and was afraid to intervene or report it. Overloaded caseworker never followed up, so the girl ran off."

Charmain frowned. "This was in Virginia?"

Archer nodded.

"How'd she get here?"

"Well, she'd learned her body had value. Used it to hitch rides or earn bus fare. Arrived at the Greyhound Depot here in Memphis. That's where she met Lester."

Charmain made a wry face. "The Pimp?"

Archer nodded. "Right. Claims he spends a lot of time there, scoutin' talent. Real good at persuadin' 'em to come work for him."

Charmain shook her head. "How does he do that?"

"He says he buys 'em a meal. Lays this whole empathy thing on them, including putting 'em up at his crib. Don't touch 'em for a while, they just party. The girl hangs with the rest of his stable. They all kinda help with the recruiting. To add to his charm Lester keeps a good supply of drugs. Takes good care of the girls. Makes sure they're safe and comfortable. They just have to do the dirty deed with strangers."

Wide-eyed, Charmain lurched back in her chair, her jaw dropped. "Safe?! What do you mean safe? God, one murdered already, and now this Bonnie..." Charmain glanced down at the file. "Yeah. This Bonnie Richardson is being held hostage by a serial killer."

"Like I said, the girl's smart. Must have some savvy to have made it here safe. Maybe she can charm him like she did with Lester."

"Charmed? Lester?"

Archer's face screwed up in a wry expression. "Yeah, she was his private reserve. Didn't have to peddle her body to make rent. Kept his books, made sure everything ran smooth. Didn't use drugs. The only person she had to ball was Lester."

"How'd he get her into school?"

"Had some phony papers drawn up. Claimed she was an orphan from some foreign country. Beserkastan, Tarakastan, one of the Stans." Archer tossed his hands up and shook his head. "Anyway, a lot of international adoption agencies supply guardianship papers to anyone for a fee. Lester used one of them. After that, all he had to get was a visa. Piece of cake for a man with his kind of cash."

"God, what kind of world do we live in?" She sighed, shook her head. "So, what about Lester?"

"Well, pimping is a misdemeanor, but trafficking kids is a felony. Federal. He's cooperatin', hopin' to make a deal. He knows what happens in jail to folks with this kinda rap."

"So? What else? God, Jack, this all makes me want to barf!"

Archer touched her shoulder and sighed. "I think this should be enough for your first piece. The Commercial Appeal also agreed to run everything you write—front page with a byline. Also, the Doc thought if you moderated all the TV time. Handle the proof of life, and so on, it might spur him to continue using you as the contact."

*****

They finished eating. Now Bonnie sat beside him on the couch. His voice soft and gentle contrasted with his muscular build. The muscles in his arms rippled when he moved. He might even be tougher than Lester she thought. "Are you a pimp like Lester?"

He scoffed. Ignored her question. "What are your teacher's names?"

She told him. "Does that mean you're gonna put me back in school?"

"I wouldn't want you to fall too far behind while you're away. You behave, and I'll get the assignments for you."

Her brows knitted she turned to him. "How will I turn them in?"

"I'll arrange that. Don't worry."

She smiled into his eyes. Leaned close. Placed her hand on his knee. "You're a nice man. What do you look like under that mask? I'll bet you're handsome too. I like your eyes. I see a mustache and a beard. Bet they tickle. Your hair that color too? Can I kiss you?"

"If it makes you happy."

Their lips met. A chaste kiss. She opened her mouth. Tried to encourage him with her tongue, but he pushed back.

"Thanks for the Chinese. It's my favorite." She cooed in his ear. Her hand moved from his knee as she stroked his thigh. As he felt himself become aroused the taunting voice rang in his head. "Little brother, you're a worm." His eyes closed, his sisters face floated before him. His hands moved to Bonnie's neck.

"Do you wanna do it now?" she gasped.

Trembling, he pushed her back. He shook his head, unable to speak then glanced at his watch. "I have to go." he managed to croak.

He stood and beckoned her to the cellar door.

"Can I keep my clothes? It's chilly down there."

He nodded.

*****

As Jordan hobbled into the Shining Light office, Delores, the woman at the desk, motioned him over. She shoved her glasses up her nose and smiled. "Bert's sorry. He got called out early." She handed him a slip of paper. "He headed here. Said you could catch up with him. If you miss him, call his cell. The numbers on the sheet too."

After glancing at the note, he slipped it into his pocket, then made his way back to his car. The traffic to the address in Orange Mound had been a mess. He took almost an hour to reach the address. As he parked in the building's driveway, he saw no sign of Bert's pick up. He pulled out his cell phone and dialed the number the secretary gave him, no answer. After leaving a message, he exited his car. His search for Bert might get him a peek inside, talk to the people he worked around. As he hobbled to the door on his crutches, he scanned the neighborhood. No signs on the house marked it as a Mission property. The two-story house looked out of place in the rundown surroundings—new shingles, fresh paint, storm windows in place, and unbroken. Even the flower beds looked tidy, weed-free. The yard mowed and well edged. He once heard a real estate agent that this sort of house gave them nightmares. The nicest house in the neighborhood. *How could you value a place like that here?*

As he neared the entrance, a black girl in her early twenties opened the door. She wore a baggy top that failed to hide her ample breasts and jeans so tight they looked as if they had been put on with a paintbrush. She smiled. "Can I help you, sir?"

"Yeah, I'm lookin' for Bert."

The girl rolled her eyes. Stepped to the side of the door as if inviting him in. "What's he done now?"

Jordan hopped up the one step then swung himself through the doorway. "I'm not sure what you mean."

"Last guy come around here lookin' for him, wanted to kick his ass."

"What for?"

"Said Bert put hands on his daughter. Guess she called him from here and told him instead of me."

"Are you the manager here?"

The girl said nothing. She looked as if she realized something and stepped back from Jordan. She looked him up and down. "I'm sorry. Who are you?" Her eyes swept her surroundings now as if searching for something. After picking up what seemed like a steel cane, she peered at Jordan. Her free hand fidgeted with a pendant hanging from her neck. Jordan smiled, hoping to reassure this girl who now realized that she'd let a stranger in the house.

"I'm Bob Jordan. I'm supposed to be helpin' Bert out. Told me to meet him here. I'll go back outside if you want to check it out and make sure."

"Oh, God. I saw you out in the driveway, on those crutches. I guess I let my guard down. Not supposed to let anyone I don't know in. 'Specially in this neighborhood."

Jordan nodded to the cane she held in her hand. "Don't be too big a hurry to relax." He leaned back and held a crutch out in each hand. "I got ya outgunned here."

The hand that fidgeted with the pendant moved up to her mouth as she laughed. "Yeah. But never bring a crutch to a cane fight!" She replied with a chuckle, now looking relaxed again. "Come on in, I was just makin' coffee. You can have a seat while I call. But remember, I got you covered."

Jordan followed her to the kitchen, where the aroma of coffee brewing filled the air. She set a steaming mug in front of him. After making her phone call, the girl joined him at the table. "Couldn't reach the Reverend, but Delores at the office described you pretty good. I guess you can relax."

"So, you put up the cane? That all you got?"

The girl shrugged. "Got a can of pepper spray, but forget where I set it down. It'll turn up. I just hope none of the girls think it's some kinda perfume."

Jordan shook his head as he took a sip.

"Now, to answer your question, yes, I am the manager. Got a couple other ladies help out afternoons, and nights when the girls are here."

"Where are the girls now?"

"Two of 'em at work. The other four in school. Got one at Memphis. Freshman!"

"You sound proud."

"I am. These girls all came right from the streets. Wouldn't believe their mouths and how they act." The girl shook her head and rolled her eyes.

"Mine are doin' fabulous." She twirled her hair around a finger and smiled, then held out her hand, "My name's Estelle. Estelle Martin."

Jordan shook her hand. Her hands soft, but the grip firm. "You have some kinda special training to do this work?"

"Yeah, I was on the streets myself for three years. Came into another program like this one, on the Southside a town. After I finished high school, I decided I wanted to give back. You know?"

"Sound like you know what the girls are facing."

"You bet. This new program started up, so I contacted 'em. They hired me right away. Had to take classes on first aid, CPR, and stuff. But that's it."

"Pay pretty well?"

Estelle shrugged. "Minimum wage plus room and board. I got a scholarship at Memphis, so that provides my entertainment. Lotta free fun stuff for students if I get time off. Delores said you were a cop. How come you're helpin' Bert?"

Jordan paused for a moment. He had told no one he had been a policeman. He thought the only one who knew was Belkey. He had not asked Belkey to hide his occupation, so he could not fault the man for sharing Jordan's status. Delores must put the word out, so Belkey must have told her. He wondered if that accounted for Bert being so scarce this morning. He decided he may as well be open with the manager. Admitting it might deflect suspicion. So, he told her what he had told Belkey about his reason for being there.

When he finished, she put her hand on his arm. "I am so sorry for your loss. I think you might be right. I feel like we do a lot of good, and, for me, it makes up for a lot of the other. You know?"

"Did Bert mention where he'd go after here?"

Estelle waved her hand in the air dismissively. "Nah! He says nothin' when he here. If any of the girls are here when he is, I make sure they stay right by me. I've heard he's tried to pull stuff at the other homes. That ain't happenin' here."

"What kind of stuff?"

Estelle chewed her lip for a second before she replied. "Like I said. He's put his hands on some of the girls. Doris, one of the other managers, says he likes to peek. So, I make sure that even if there is a plumbing emergency, he follows me in the door." She folded her arms across her chest. The look on her face suggested she meant business. "He don't come in less, I say so."

"Delores said he had an emergency here. What happened?"

Estelle frowned, looked puzzled. "Emergency? Huh. He just came roarin' in here right after the girls all left. After I let him in, he runs around to all the bathrooms. Flushed the toilets, ran a little water in the sink. Then left."

"Humph! This coffee's great, but I'm afraid it runs right through me. Can I use the restroom?"

"I don't think you can make it up the stairs. You can use Ann's. Her rooms on the first floor. She stood and led him through the living room to a hallway. She pointed ahead. "Second door on the right. Go through her bedroom. Pay no mind to the mess. She's a typical teenager."

Inside the room, Jordan studied the array of obstacles between himself and the bathroom. Books, magazines, papers, stuffed animals, and clothing everywhere. He flicked on the overhead light. He scanned the floor, looking for booby traps in the clutter. Made sure he could navigate through the room, breaking no more bones.

Estelle had been accurate about the condition of this room, but not about all teenage girls. Jennifer had been compulsively neat. Every toy and belonging in a set place. Her room always tidy. If she got something new, the old item, if not broken, she stored neatly in the attic.

"Savin' it for my kids, Dad." She would announce as she came down the stairs from the attic. A dream that died with her. The memory brought a tear to his eye.

Large posters on the wall announced the girl's love of cats and horses. There was even one of a young blond-haired boy Jennifer liked. He failed to recall the singer's name, but he remembered the face that beamed from videos she enjoyed. Way before things went so wrong.

His eye moved to a corner of the room. A blemish in the paint. Circular, no bigger than a dime. He moved closer, then looked up. The surrounding paint appeared darker than the spot. As if the area had been covered by something for a while, allowing the finish beneath to stay clean.

Once in the bathroom, he scanned the corners near the ceiling. In one corner, he found another blemish. Round like the first, but here some paint inside the circle had chipped. On the counter, he spotted a few flecks that looked like paint chips. Even in the room's disarray, the chips looked recent.

Once back in the kitchen, he found Estelle at the kitchen table reading a book. She looked up at him and smiled. "Got some free time. Thought I'd study. Anything else you want to know?"

"Yeah. You said Bert checked all the bathrooms."

"That's right. I didn't go with him. But like I said, he was running water and flushing toilets. Could hear him."

"He have any tools with him?"

Estelle paused, chewed her lower lip, then nodded. "He had his toolbox. Oh yeah! A ladder, too. Little one."

CHAPTER SEVENTEEN

Charmain sat in the center of the microphone cluttered table. The Memphis Safety Director and the Tunica Sheriff flanked her. Doctor Maynard sat next to the Sheriff. Belkey and the Superintendent of the Shelby County Schools sat on the opposite side. All looked grim as Charmain read from her prepared statement. As she described Bonnie's parents and how she came to be orphaned, images flashed on the screen. Bonnie's mother first. Her warm smile and laughing eyes, incongruent with the warrior's mantle she wore. Her father, a fierce look on his face. He glowered in full football pads and a three-point stance, poised to deliver destruction across the scrimmage line. Then the three of them together. Bonnie between them. The picture's background suggested a Christmas Holiday.

As Charmain reappeared on the screen, she paused in her narrative. She looked straight into the camera. "Now she's held captive by a man claiming to have killed several other girls in the last few years. Using this child as a pawn to gain attention."

She paused. Glanced to the two men on either side of her. As if on cue, the two men leaned forward. Their faces portraying all the menace they could muster. Charmain turned back to the camera. "This is a personal message to Bonnie's jailer. We will continue with daily updates about the situation as long as we know Bonnie is alive. That means we expect daily reports from you on her wellbeing. You have twenty-four hours to meet our demands. If you fail, then we stop the coverage. But rest assured, we will hunt you down and bring you to justice."

At that point, the image changed to a dark-haired, heavy-set man sitting behind a desk in a studio. "That was Charmain Crump, a local blogger, and radio show host. She made that announcement today at Memphis Police Headquarters. Local authorities promised daily updates on the hunt for Bonnie and her captor. Police are asking the public to be on the lookout for the girl. She would most likely be in the company of this man."

A grainy enlargement from one of the casino cameras appeared on the screen. The image switched to one composite. "we encourage anyone with information to call either 911 or Crime Stoppers at 528-CASH or 528-2274. Again, the number here on the screen is 528-CASH."

With the remote, Charmain shut off the television. After setting it on the coffee table, she snuggled under Jordan's arm draped over her shoulder. He drew her close and kissed her. She ran her fingers through his hair.

After coming up for air, she smiled. "So, what did you do today? Just sit around watchin' the tube?"

"Nah, spent the day tryin' to volunteer. Belkey has me workin' with that handyman of theirs. I spent all day tryin' to find him."

"Find him?"

"Well, I got there, and he had left on a call. Gave me the address he went to and his cell number. Got there, He'd already gone. Tried to reach him several times. He never answered. I left messages and texts, but never heard a word back."

Charmain sat up. Frowned, "He duckin' out on you? Why didn't you call in your comrades to track him down?"

"Didn't want anyone to forgo their donut break for me. Looks like you marshaled out the troops. After watching, I feel like I oughta be out cruisin' the streets myself. Huntin' that asshole down."

"So, you thought I did okay?"

He kissed her on the nose, then ran his fingers through her long black hair. His lips pursed. Brows knitted as if deep in thought. "Yeah! I think even your Mama would be proud."

A knock on the door interrupted them. Charmain got off the couch. After checking the peephole, she opened the door. Tony marched in, a bottle held high over his head. A tall, thin man with a close-cropped Mohawk carrying a white box trailed him into the room.

Charmain grinned and chuckled. "Tony! Glenn! You boys look ready to party."

Tony gave Jordan a finger wave, then passed the bottle to Charmain. "Brought some sparklin' grape juice and some appetizers. Wanted to toast your new celebrity status!"

Glenn nodded at Jordan as he set the box on the coffee table. "We thought you might need more than the delivered pizza she's been feedin' ya."

Charmain slapped Glenn on the arm. "They're not that bad. We get lots of veggies on 'em." She turned to Jordan with a grin. "Right?"

"If I disagree with her, she'll hide my crutches. What do you mean, her new celebrity status?"

"Well, even the national news picked up your press conference today," Tony announced. "We saw it on CNN. Glenn checked TMZ. That's his big thing, you know. He saw your name mentioned in the press release and everything. Bet the paparazzi will be hangin' at your door soon."

Glenn nodded as Tony continued. "I hope you remember us, little people, as you climb the ladder. Maybe tomorrow you could wear that t-shirt I gave you for Christmas."

Tony looked at Charmain. Arched his eyebrows.

Charmain laughed. "The one with your restaurant's logo?"

"Oh, yes." He turned to Glenn, put a finger to his chin, and nodded. "Now, that would be thoughtful. Right?"

Glenn grinned. Charmain shook her head as Tony raved on. "You should be ecstatic. They'll want you for interviews, invite you on talk shows like Oprah." his arm extended with a limp-wristed wave, he continued. "You are an old Chicago girl. Right?

Charmain nodded, then glanced at Jordan. No smile, his face grim. Glenn opened the box while Tony retrieved wine glasses from the kitchen. As Tony filled the glasses and passed them out, Glenn leaned close to Jordan. "With her looks and appeal. They're gonna be after her. You ready for that? Bein' the Boy Toy on the red carpet?"

Jordan chewed his lip. Said nothing.

Tony raised his glass, offering a toast. "Girl, this is an opportunity most people in your position would die for."

As Jordan sipped from his glass, he hoped Tony's toast did not contain a prophecy.

*****

Bonnie held the newspaper up to the camera. After announcing the date, she turned it around and read the headline story aloud. Finished, she looked into the camera. "I'm not sure what else to say. Except I need to turn in my homework. If you could announce an email address, I could send it to at today's conference that would be like totally awesome. Also, the Gingerbread man wants you to put up a website. That way my teachers can post the work I need to stay caught up. Okay?"

She glanced away from the camera to him. "Anything else?"

He stopped the camera. "Is there any personal message you'd like to send?"

She cocked her head to one side. Stared off and ran her tongue across her lips. Then sighed. "I guess, maybe tell Lester I miss him."

"I'm treating you well. Right?"

She shrugged. Brushed her hair back from her face. "I guess so. But you don't like me as much as Lester."

"What makes you say that?"

"He didn't lock me up like this. He let me have friends and go to school. Plus, he treated me real nice. You know? I miss all that."

"You could have it worse."

She made a wry face. "Yeah, I know. You've been feedin' me real good. And I love that Mexican food you had me try."

She pinched her stomach. "But I need to get exercise. Move around. I'll get fatter'n a pig. I mean you got great stuff down there for me to watch and listen, but I never get to see the sun or the sky."

"I tell you what. You saw my weight set upstairs right?"

She nodded.

"I'll buy a treadmill today, and tonight we'll work out together. Okay?"

"I'll need some more clothes. These are gettin' real rank. Plus, I'd like workout stuff, like shoes and things."

"Okay. Fine." He went to a shelf in the corner of the basement and retrieved a pad and pencil. "Let's make a list, and I'll pick all that up later. Okay?"

She sighed. "Why can't I come with you. I won't run off or nothin'. I promise."

"Do you want me to set this workout up or not?" As he took down the camera from the tripod, she picked up the pencil and wrote on the paper. "Okay," she grumbled.

*****

Urich studied the black box, no larger than a computer memory stick. "I didn't know Jergen County had these kinda toys. Musta cost a bunch."

Jordan's fingers tapped on the laptop's keyboard before him. "Not out of our budget. Roy talked an insurance company into donating 'em. Claimed it would help curb future crime waves. Made a big show of it. In all the papers and on the radio. Let the bad boys know we take farm equipment theft seriously in this County."

"You sure it works?"

Jordan shrugged. "It's been a while since I used `em. Probably just before you got hired. We could test it. I could take it for a ride around the trailer court in my car, and then we could look at how it does on the screen. I put in fresh batteries, so it should be fine."

"I got a better idea. This way, while its bein' tested, you could show me how it works." She turned to the living room. "Joshua! Come here, honey."

The boy lying in front of the television stood. His eyes glued to the screen, he walked backwards to the kitchen, engrossed by the Cookie Monster and his antics.

"Turn that thing off! It's a tape. You can finish it later."

The boy scurried back to the living room. After using the remote to stop the program, he rushed to their side. "Watcha need?"

She held out the little black box. "I need you for an important mission for the Sheriff's Department. See this?" She showed him the tracker.

"What is it?"

"It's a top-secret device that helps us track criminals. Mr. Jordan and I are going to use it in a big case. We need to make sure it works."

The boy's eyes opened wide as he studied the box.

Urich ran her fingers over the boy's head. "It's about time for Ginger's walk, right?"

The boy nodded. His eyes shined as he listened.

"Put this in your pocket. While you walk her, we'll track where you go on the screen here?"

Joshua stepped over to stand by Jordan. His eyes opened wide. "This part of my special deputy duties?"

Jordan nodded. "Exactly. I'll be sure and tell Sheriff Speck how you helped us out on this important case."

"All I gotta do is put this in my pocket. Get Ginger and take her for our walk. Right?"

"That's right. Take her on a good one. Wear her out good. That way, we can make sure it works."

Grinning, the boy stuffed the tracker in his pocket. After grabbing the leash that hung by the door, he raced away on his mission, leaving the outside door wide open. Urich laughed as she moved to close the door. She returned to Jordan's side as he watched on the screen. "See anything yet?"

"Not much. Might be some lag time, and he might have to go a certain distance before it registers. I'll let you know when it shows up. So, you and Paulo really gonna tie the knot?"

Urich nodded. "Met his mom in Vegas at the exhibition fight. She liked me, and I adored her. She calls me at least once a week. Gives me a lot of advice on how to keep the little turd in line."

"Then what? He said he wants to go back to dancing in New York. You gonna follow him?"

"Nah. When he's rehearsin', and in a show, he doesn't get any time off. I'd be hangin' out in some hotel. So, I'll stay here and continue to bust your balls. Just fly out on weekends unless I have to work."

Jordan glanced around the trailer. "He must be rollin' in dough. You gonna still live here?"

"Oh, this is the best part. Paulo's gonna buy the Trailer Park from Mrs. Lambert."

"Where's she gonna go?" Jordan thought about the woman across the way, hobbling behind her walker. Only able to go out when someone drives her. "She goin' to a nursing home?"

Urich shook her head. "She's got no family. She's taken a shine to Paulo, and I think she has a certain lust for Steve. Anyway, she wants to take the money from the trailer court and build a big house next to the trailer court. She says that way she can help Paulo manage it. Plus, she wants it big enough so all of us would live there with her. One big happy family."

"Jesus. You said a big house. You must be talkin' mansion."

I didn't know until now, but she owns the farm ground around here too."

Jordan recalled the first time he met the old woman. Her trailer set on a lot crowded with enough junk and trash to make a junkyard look like a park. The inside had been as bad. Maureen and Urich had tried to keep it up, but working full-time, they could not get it done. Paulo and Steven had pitched in with their open schedules and finally made the place clean and safe. Jordan glanced at the screen. He grinned and turned the laptop to Urich. He slid over next to her and pointed at the screen. "See there he is. At the end of the lane already. Is he cuttin' through the backyards?"

Urich giggled behind her hand. "Oh, My God? That's that asshole Travis's garden. He'll have a fit! Looks like he's makin' a loop now towards the highway. God, I hope he hangs tight to the leash that damn dog loves to chase cars. Drug him right into the street once. Good. It looks like he stopped and is turnin' around."

When the indicator stopped moving, Urich turned to Jordan. He shrugged. "Dog probably has to take a dump with all that runnin'."

Just then, the indicator moved to the highway. Turned and sped off, traveling well beyond the speed of a little boy's legs.

"Shit! He's in a car! Somebody's grabbed him!" Jordan shouted.

"Oh, My God! He knows better than to just jump in a stranger's car."

Jordan stood carrying the laptop. "We'll take this and follow. We don't have lights or siren, but we have this, they won't get far." After slipping it into a bag, he grabbed his crutches and began a wild swing for the door.

Urich raced to the cupboard where she stored her gun. Frantic, she opened the lock and grabbed her gun belt, and followed Jordan out the door.

After jumping into the driver's seat, she started the car. Jordan, in the passenger seat, opened the laptop.

"Fuck, I don't believe this is happening!" she shouted as the starter ground without catching. After what seemed an eternity, the engine finally roared to life. The tires spun, kicking up gravel as she backed up before speeding toward the highway.

"They went to the right?!" Urich shrieked.

"Yeah!"

Both peered down the road as she pulled onto the highway. The tires squealed as they reached the pavement. Jordan glanced down at the screen.

"Shit, the laptop just died! Screen's dead!"

Urich's phone buzzed. She flicked on her hands-free system. Paulo's voice came over the speakers. "Hey, baby. We might be a little late tonight..."

CHAPTER EIGHTEEN

The blue sky contained patches of cotton-ball like cumulus. An earlier rain made the streets glisten, and water vapor rose as the sun dried the pavement. Charmain concentrated on the surrounding traffic. The typically reckless Memphis drivers became kamikazes after these spring rains. As she pulled into the middle school parking lot, she checked her rearview mirror. The SWAT car pulled in behind her.

Tony had not been right. The paparazzi had yet to descend. Jordan told her the security detail might be the reason. Patrolling her balcony, following her car, escorting her to interviews. Their looming presence might be enough.

The killer had come through with a video on YouTube and each day since. Collins, in his usual cynical fashion, claimed it proved she had been alive in the last twenty-four hours. Posted for only a half an hour, it had nearly a half million views. Now the FBI and local Crime Scene experts studied it, looking for any clues in the video that might lead them to the girl.

As instructed, they put up a website. Each day the teachers posted her assignments. When finished, her schoolwork arrived via email, sent from cyber cafes in the city.

After parking in the visitor's slot, Charmain waited next to her car for the uniformed officer. Together they entered the school. After the usual starting time, the halls were quiet. Only a few students rushed by either late for a class or going to the office. A uniformed Deputy Sheriff stood inside, talking to a young black male. When the deputy glanced in their direction, the boy turned.

His eyes opened wide, his jaw dropped. "Man, you called the Po-Po on me? All I did was put bubble bath in Mrs. Ellingson's birdbath."

The deputy smiled and shook his head. "No, Jaron, they're here for somethin' else."

The boy peered at Charmain. "Oh, right. You, the lady I seen on TV! One helpin' find Bonnie!"

"Are we interfering with your duties?" The uniformed officer at her side asked as they approached.

The deputy shook his head. "Nah, just takin' this master criminal to the principal's office. See what kinda hard time he might have earned."

"Oh, man," the boy protested. "We just wanted to give those poor little creatures some pleasure. You know. My mom and my big sister all love their bubble bath. Just figured we share it with all God's creatures. You know?"

The young boy flashed a smile at Charmain. "You find Bonnie yet?"

When Charmain shook her head, the boy's smile vanished. "Damn! Excuse me. I mean darn. I'm worried about her."

Charmain took his hand. "We're all worried about her. Did you know her?"

The boy nodded. "We in the same grade. Got a lot of classes together. Great dancer. We had a lot of fun last Friday night at the dance." When a tear appeared in his eye, he brushed it away with his sleeve and sniffed.

Charmain put her arm around his shoulder and gave him a hug. "We're trying our best okay?"

As the group entered the principal's office, a tall, thin black woman looked up as they entered. She scowled at the boy. Once she removed her large black-rimmed glasses, she let them dangle from the gold chain that looped her neck. She rose to her feet, grasped

Jaron by the ear; he howled. She turned to the group. "Excuse me. I have a small disciplinary matter to attend to."

She led Jaron away, still holding his ear. After she slammed the door behind her. A howl came from behind the door. "Mom. I'm really sorry!"

Then diminished to the drone of angry mumbling.

Soon the principal's door opened. Jaron shuffled out his head down, scowling. The principal, her arm around his shoulder, stopped in the waiting area. She ran her hand over his closely cropped hair, nudged him to the door. The boy glanced over at Charmain. He beamed a smile while pulling out a spiral notebook. He opened it and passed it with a pen to Charmain. "Can I have your autograph?"

She nodded. Scribbled on the page. "Jaron. Right?"

He nodded as she wrote more on the page. She passed it back to him, and he beamed. Then scampered out the door.

The principal shook her head, then turned to Charmain. "Somethin' sure made him happy. What did you write?"

"I wrote that when I saw Bonnie that I would tell her first thing, he missed her."

"What!" The principal put her hand to her chest.

"Well, I think Jaron is kinda sweet on her. I get the feelin' that it might have been mutual."

"But... But... But... She's a ...."

"Child? Is that the word you're lookin' for? "Charmain interrupted. "A scared child. Failed by the system and needs a decent chance? Is that what you meant to say?"

The principal fell silent, hung her head. Finally, she looked up at Charmain. "Bonnie was well liked by her classmates and teachers. We had no idea about her life outside of school. She never talked about it. Even though you never announced it, gossip has already started. The politest term I've heard used is tramp. I've received several calls today from parents. All outraged about having their child even associate with her. You told me when you called what you wanted to do, but I'm afraid a number might not want their kids to have any part in it."

Charmain shrugged. "That's fine. It will only take a few. Maybe only two or three. All I want them to do is go in front of the camera and tell brief stories about their feelings for her. Perhaps talk about the stuff they do together."

The principal frowned. "But why?"

"It's for the man who took her. He'll be watchin'. Readin' the newspapers. They say he wants to bask in all this attention. The FBI people hope that the more he knows about her, the less likely he'll hurt her."

"You think that might work?" The woman asked with a sad frown.

Charmain shrugged. "Already he's doin' stuff to help her keep up with her schoolwork. Would he do that if he just intended to kill her?"

The principal stared after Jaron. She shook her head. "Only two or three?"

"More if they're willing. I'd like to do a couple a day while this goes on. Nothin' elaborate. Just a personal message to her."

The principal set her jaw, stood straight, threw her shoulders back. Nodded. "I know Jaron would do it. Might keep his mind out of mischief. I'll send out a note to all the parents this afternoon. To speed things up, I will tell them we'll let the children decide unless the parents object. If they object, they need to notify our office by the end of the week. In the meantime, there are some I can talk to directly who might go along with it. I believe there are teachers too. If that will help."

*****

182

Archer gave Charmain a hug as she stepped down from the podium. "You did great!"

"Still, it's nerve wracking. Wonderin' if I'm sayin' the right things. Givin' him the attention he wants. Now, this thing with havin' the kids tell stories. I hope they're alright with this."

"Talked to the principal. She said that only a few parents called to opt out. Others are callin' in anxious to get theirs included even though they didn't have to."

Belkey moved next to them. "I agree with the detective. You've done a great job. I'm confident that whoever has that girl must be feeling real smug with all this attention."

"Have you gotten any more letters from him?" Charmain asked.

Belkey said nothing at first then shook his head. "I wish I knew if that was good or bad. I just feel so ashamed right now."

"Why's that?" Archer inquired.

"He has her anyway. I guess I should have just come to you right away instead of trying to do that on my own."

Archer shrugged. "Who knows?"

"I hope no one thinks I did it out of pride. Thinking I could beat this devil on my own. That I could do it better than the police."

Archer turned to Belkey. "Reverend it's hard to say what anybody would have done in your place. He used your care and concern. Damn! He got around Lester. Who knows he might have been able to get around us too."

"Listen to us," Charmain interrupted. "Us out here hurtin'. Worried for the girl. No matter what happens to her that fiend has made victims of us all."

Belkey scowled, hung his head. Charmain placed her hand on his shoulder. He looked up. A tear glistened in his eye. His lips trembled as he spoke. "You're right. Even the girls at the shelter are scared. Worried. I mean it could have been one of them that he'd either killed or held hostage."

Belkey glanced at his watch. "I'm sorry. I have another appointment." He turned to Charmain. "Maybe we could have lunch tomorrow or the next day after the press conference?"

"I'd like that, but right now I'm meeting with the detectives after each conference. Reviewin' what they found each day and plannin' tomorrow's. I can't right now. Give me a rain check?"

Belkey said nothing. Just nodded and walked away.

*****

Meanwhile, Hector and Jordan sat in a diner next to the TV studio holding the press conference. Today's update played on the screen above them on the wall. With the laptop set before them on the counter, both studied the screen. "See, I can track them in real-time or say I want to do something else without watching. I can come back to it later, and it saves the trips."

Hector turned to Jordan. "And the Sheriff uses it?"

"Not right now. We had problems with farm machinery thefts-tractors, Combines, big stuff, costing thousands. We put these trackers on some at a local dealer and then parked them where they'd be easy to steal. Man, we busted thieves right and left. Insurance company was so pleased they paid for the thing. Course they insisted we run a few public stings to discourage the bad guys."

He turned to Hector. "How's trailin' Charmain goin'?"

The big man shrugged. "Had some hairy times in traffic, but with the bike, it was okay. She usually has one cop with her, so I don't worry too much. She's goin' to the cop shop right after this, so I figure I can catch up with her when we're done. You got those on the mission vehicles then?"

"Yeah. One on the van and one on the pickup. Can follow both. Might spot somethin' since that asshole Bert keeps dodgin' me. "

"S'pose we oughta put one of those on Charmain's car in case I lose her."

"Good idea. I'll get one and put it on tonight."

Hector chuckled. "Listen, you gotta tell me about what happened when you tried it out. I talked to Urich, and she didn't say much. Seemed pissed."

"Well, me and Urich are testin' this with the kid. He's runnin' around the trailer court with the dog. He stopped on the screen before moving. Next thing the indicator shows him doin' maybe fifty, sixty miles an hour. Kid's fast, but nowhere near that quick. We're thinkin' someone grabbed him."

Jordan described their pursuit. The mad dash to the car. The chase down the road. Then the screen going dead. Hector's eyes opened wide, hanging on Jordan's every word. Jordan paused in his description to sip his coffee.

Hector leaned forward. "So, what happened next?"

"We're racin' down the road. No lights or sirens, just a fast movin' plain car. I'm surprised the locals, or the State boys didn't bust us."

Hector turned to Jordan. "Shit, if they had s'pose that would have stopped Urich?"

"God, I never thought of that. Hell, with her temper, I wouldn't have tried to stop her. Anyway, Paulo calls. Urich puts it on the hands-free. It's like this big speakerphone in the car. He had no idea that we're concerned or worried. He comes on the phone and starts tellin' Urich he's gonna be late. You know how Paulo is. Mr. Cheerful. Nothin' bothers him unless Urich is mad. Then he gets real tense. I think he's afraid of her."

"Nah! Just the kinda pussy whipped you get when you're in love. Get that way around my girl too!"

Jordan's jaw dropped. He stared wide-eyed at Hector. "You gotta girl?"

Hector shrugged. "Doesn't everybody?" His hand's circular motion urged Jordan to continue. "So, Paulo called."

"Yeah. Says he has to make a quick run to the car wash and wanted to know if she wanted him to pick up something for supper. Guys got a real thing for Asian food, and there's this Thai place he likes near the car wash.

"Urich goes ape shit. Starts screamin' that she doesn't give a fuck. She's got more important things to take care of at the moment. As she is about to cut off the call, Joshua comes on the phone. Says that's no way to talk."

Hector scowled. "What?"

Jordan chuckled as he continued. "Urich swerves to the side of the road and slams on the brakes. I look over. Her face is crimson. She's shakin' all over. I ask Joshua where he is. The kid says, I'm right here with Paulo. Like he said, we gotta go to the car wash. Ginger puked all over the seats and everything. Smells awful. Steven and Paulo are havin' a real bad time with this. You need to say you're sorry, Aunt Chrissie!"

Hector's laughter exploded. He blew coffee from his nose. Only quick action from Jordan kept the spray from reaching the laptop.

CHAPTER NINETEEN

Bonnie sat on the couch, watching him finish assembling the treadmill. "You know, without that mask, you're handsome."

"Well, I thought it might be time we got better acquainted."

"Can we have some tunes to work out by?"

He set the screwdriver down and turned to her. "What works for you?"

She shrugged. Chewed her lower lip. Put her hand to her chin as if pondering a weighty question. "Well, like I said, my mom liked to listen to the Doors when she worked out. Said it helped get her war juices flowin'."

"Okay. Anything else?"

"Oh yeah. Love the Stones. 'Specially the dark stuff."

"Got Midnight Rambler and Sympathy for the Devil."

She smiled. "Ooh! What about Street Fightin' Man?"

"I'll have to check. That dark stuff is good for pumping iron, but I like things a little lighter for aerobics."

"Like what?"

He rose from the floor to walk to his toolbox. "Got a nice mix. Some Dead, Spoonful. Eighties stuff like the Bee Gees and the Bangles."

"You could do the weights thing then while I do the treadmill, but I've never done weights before. You'll have to show me."

"Tell you what. We'll do the weights together. For some, you'll need a spotter."

Bonnie cocked her head, frowned. "A spotter?"

"Yes, the spotter stands close to you while you work out to prevent injury. With strength training, you do the exercise until you can't do it any longer. With free weights, you could fall or drop the weights on yourself at that point. The spotter makes sure you don't."

After starting the music, they went to the weight bench. After setting the weight for each exercise, he showed the proper form, then shadowed her movements. While doing an overhead lift, she tottered on her feet. She shrieked as the bar descended out of control. He stepped in behind her. As he caught the bar, she fell against him. Her firm buttocks pressed against his groin. She grinned at his arousal, wiggled playfully against him. Giggled as he bent with her to set the bar on the table. She nuzzled against him like a kitten clutching his arm. "I guess you might like me as much as Lester!"

He said nothing. Looked away. His face flushed bright crimson. Bonnie pressed her pelvis against him. "It's alright, I like to do it."

His knees trembled as he cupped her tiny breast while gazing into her eyes.

She cocked her head and smiled. "You have a gentle touch."

She wrapped her arms around his waist. Drew him close. He tasted her breath. His hand moved from her breast to her neck. Then he brushed her cheek as he pushed her hair back. Massaging, his hand returned to her neck, his other hand cupped her chin, then too slid to her neck. The taunting voices screamed inside his head. "You're a miserable little worm," echoed in his mind. His lips trembled as he squeezed her throat with his thumbs.

Her eyes bulged as he cut off her air. She tried to knee him in the groin, but he turned her to his side. Raised his leg, the knee struck his thigh. While stepping back, she wrestled with his hands. He stepped with her as if in a dance. A Death Dance in time to the Stones. Overpowered, her face frozen in a silent scream. The life faded in her eyes.

*****

He still trembled while he drove. The voice screamed in his head. Desperate, he hunted. He needed release. The one that only came while watching the light leave their eyes.

"God, what have I done?" he said aloud to himself. "I could have killed her."

It had taken all his will to release her neck. She dropped to the floor at his feet, unconscious, but the rise and fall of her chest showed she lived. While she remained unconscious, he returned her to the basement.

With the voices raging in his head, he pleasured himself with pictures. It failed. His penis now ached from the swelling.

She stood under the streetlight, a caricature of the working girl. Older than most, bleached spiked hair. The dress barely reached the middle of her thighs, yet had a slit, so even more of her leg showed. The plunging tight sweater struggled to contain her ample breasts. She leaned against the post, one spiked heel against it. The bend in her leg opened the slit to maximum exposure. As he slowed, she approached the curb. She leaned into the passenger window as he rolled it down. "Ready to party, honey?"

She grinned when he popped the lock on the door and slid in beside him. As she glanced at his lap, she arched an eyebrow. She reached across and squeezed his tented sweat pants. "Oh, baby! Are you ever."

He hit her with the Taser. The jolt pushed her back against the passenger door. Dropping the Taser on the floor, he grabbed her neck with both hands and squeezed. Immobile from the shock but conscious, her eyes opened wide. His step sister's mocking laughter in his brain fading away. He smelled the fear radiating from her body. In the dim streetlight, he could not see her eyes. As he released his grasp, he flicked on the dome light. Able now to breathe, she screamed.

"There, now I can see!" he gasped. Again, he grabbed her neck, choking her cries to whimpers then silence. Still stunned, she lay there, her eyes locked on his, her tongue protruding from her mouth. As the light dimmed in her eyes and her breathing ceased, he groaned while he spasmed. His pants now warm from his release.

*****

The daily internal briefings with the team evolved into a set pattern. The detectives reported any progress since they last met. Then Charmain described what she had discovered about Bonnie they might use. At this point, Dr. Maynard summarized their findings. Together they would then plan the next steps in the investigation and search.

Dr. Maynard glanced around the table while she spoke. "I think it's a good sign that he's cooperating. We've got the daily proof of life. The girl looks good, not stressed. But I am concerned with her blinking today. It's changed. It seems erratic. People show a lot of emotion in their eyes that way, but usually, there is an increase and then a decrease with a smooth transition between the changes. Hers seemed different. There are brief periods where she blinks fast and then slow. He might be drugging her. I'm having some of my colleagues in Internal Medicine and Pharmacology look at the video. They might have an idea."

Archer raised his hand. "Could she be stressed and having some kinda seizures or strokes?"

"Hmmm! I'll pass that question on. Thank you, Jack." Dr. Maynard made notes on her legal pad.

"Also, he's sending in her school work. Any luck on tracing that, Jack?"

Archer shook his head. "He's using local Internet cafes like Starbucks and taps into email we can't trace. We'll keep on it."

"Since you mentioned differences, she's wearin' different clothes today," Charmain added.

Maynard smiled. "I was about to mention that myself. I guess that's something that would stand out to us women."

"Damn! Let's rerun it, we might notice other things," Collins added.

As Archer worked the laptop on the table, the image of the girl projected on the overhead screen. All turned to watch. As it finished, Collins turned to Archer. "Rerun it. Only this time, slow it down."

Archer ran it again. At the slower pace, the girl's speech could not be understood. Collins pointed at the screen. "There, stop it. See? What's that against the wall?"

Charmain leaned toward the screen and squinted. "Can we enlarge it? I think I might know what it is."

Archer typed on the laptop.

She pointed at the screen. "See? It's a bag but not completely in the picture. It looks like part of the logo for that big sporting goods store."

Archer smiled. "Once again, it's the ladies. Now leading two to nothing. Maybe our boy bought those clothes there. Do you recognize the sweat suit she's wearing? Could it be some kinda designer thing?"

Charmain tapped him on the arm and laughed. "I'm tellin' your wife you're disrespectin' our feminine powers. But I don't know. They're not anything I recognize. Anybody else?"

"We have the sweats, and we have the color. I assume the stores record sales on computer, like everywhere else," Dr. Maynard added with a smile.

Archer rubbed his chin. "It's thin, but we might get lucky. We've narrowed down the haystacks. Now which one has the needle."

Maynard reached over and patted his shoulder. "You weren't planning on doing anything else today. Were you?"

Archer shrugged and restarted the video. It still ran slow. All continued watching, hoping for something else to emerge. Archer's phone buzzed. He murmured into it and listened. He frowned. Ran his hand through his hair. Finished with the call, he set the phone on the table. Buried his face in his hands while the others concentrating on the video failed to notice.

As the video ended, Maynard turned to the others. "Did anyone notice anything else?" Her brow furrowed. "Uh... Jack, are you okay?"

Archer sighed. "I'm not sure if this is related. My regular partner spotted a report from uniform about a body found on Bellevue this morning. Thought we oughta know—one of the older working girls. Uniform patrol found her. Techs guessed she'd been strangled, and her tongue cut out."

Collin's jaw dropped. "Shit! A copycat?"

"We've never released that detail," Archer announced, his face grim.

Dr. Maynard slammed her hand on the table. "I was just about to say another good sign was that he hadn't killed again. If it is our boy, he might be escalating or breaking down, losing control."

Collins raised his hand. "You asked if anyone spotted anything else. I think I figured out the eye blinks. You can play it back. Check for yourselves. I was in the Navy. Signalman. She's sending Morse Code. Quick blinks for dots, slow ones for dashes. She's blinking SOS, the universal distress signal. Means to send help. She's scared!"

CHAPTER TWENTY

Five police cars surrounded a light pole blocking off most of the street. A uniformed officer directed traffic around the bottleneck created. The crime-scene tape ran from adjacent line poles to a chain-link fence that bordered the sidewalk. A crowd, mostly black, gathered outside the tape. All looked grim. Their ominous silence broken by an occasional mutter or shout.

Archer stepped over the crime scene tape draped around the police cars. Inside the circle, Roscoe squatted next to the body. As Archer neared, he stood and shook his head. "One of the locals said she worked this corner. A real regular. Older than the others. Close to retirement."

Archer grimaced, scanned the crowd. "Got a name?"

"Mom! No! No! No!" a black teenager crowding the tape howled.

Roscoe nodded in the youth's direction. "I believe we're gonna get one real soon."

Archer jogged to the young man's side. "You sure it's your mom?"

Tears in his eyes, the boy shrugged, "I think so. Not sure though."

"Do you need to take a closer look?"

The boy glanced around the crowd, nodded.

His eyes fastened on the ground; the boy let Archer lead him to the spot. The boy wiped a tear from his eyes before he slowly raised his head. He peered at the body propped up next to the pole. The front of the woman's blouse soaked in dried blood. Wide-eyed, her eyes bulged out of her face, as if frozen, her mouth hung open. After his brief glance, the boy turned away.

"Is it your mom?"

"No, suh. Isn't my mom. Dress is hers. She...she our neighbor, Miss Rawlins. Always borrowin' mom's stuff. They same size."

"Rawlins?"

The boy nodded.

"She have a first name?"

The boy shook his head. "Cause a what she do, Mom don't want me hangin' around her. Know where she live, though."

Archer nodded to Roscoe. "Could you show this detective where that is?"

"No, suh. I tell him where, though. I can't go ridin' around with no Five-O, man. Gang think I'm snitchin'."

"Okay, stay here until you talk to that officer over there. Then you can go. But don't tell anybody what you saw. 'Specially her family or friends. That's our job."

The boy nodded, and Archer walked to Roscoe's side.

Roscoe nodded to the boy. "Was it his Mom?"

"No. Thank God for that small mercy around here. He says her last name is Rawlins. He'll give you the address. He's worried the gangs might take him for a snitch, so just get the info you need, okay?"

"Hey, ain't I always the sensitive one?"

Archer scoffed.

A crime scene technician stopped beside them. Archer and Roscoe turned to him. "What can you tell us?"

The man shrugged. "Dead maybe four to eight hours. Strangled. Tongue severed. Real messy."

Archer's tongue rolled in his cheek. "Anybody see anything?"

Roscoe nodded towards one car. An older stout black woman sat inside talking with an officer. "Said she saw a pickup stop over there around midnight. Only detail she recalls was that it was red."

"So, she sat out here all that time, and nobody reported until two hours ago?" Archer snarled at the group of uniformed officers clustered around the body.

The crime scene technician said nothing.

Roscoe shrugged. "Jack, if uniform goes down this street and sees 'em they gotta bring 'em in. There was a lot of other activity in the district last night. You can't fault the guys for not enforcing a bunch of pandering misdemeanors and missin' another call out for murder or robbery. No sense jumpin' their asses. Neighbors didn't call it in either."

Archer sighed and turned to the Technician. "How soon can we get a report?"

"If you figure he's your guy, we can rush it. Push 'em to do the autopsy today. Everybody's feelin' the heat on this one."

Archer kicked at a rock by his shoe. It slid under one of the cars. "Good! She's probably one of ours. Listen, make sure you examine her and the scene thoroughly. I want it checked so close you can tell me what kind of bugs live in the ground around here. We got zip on this guy. We need something, anything." The tech nodded and walked away.

"Man, this one's older. Except for the tongue and bein' a working girl, there's nothin' the same." Roscoe protested.

"You sure? Profiler claims we might have destabilized him. If it is, he's gettin' more reckless and more dangerous."

"Shit! Made him crazier? They said all this shit we've been doin' was supposed to de-escalate him, man. Now the profiler said it had the opposite effect? I thought all this scientific shit was meant to help. You know. Get to where we could solve crimes before they even happen. Science! Bull shit!"

"Roscoe, my man, Psychology is one of them soft sciences. Didn't they teach you that in school?"

"Soft science!" Roscoe scoffed. "You mean like a soft dick? You ask anybody, they ain't good for nothin' either. Soft science," he grumbled as he marched off.

Archer's cell buzzed. It was Collins. "We might be in luck. I guessed that he might have made the purchase before he made the video. I took a chance and had the area stores run sales records on the two days before. I think we might have hit the jackpot. It's the one on Winchester. We might even have him on security video."

"Give me a half-hour." After ending the call, he jogged to his car.

*****

As Jordan arrived at Shining Light, Bert's pickup sat in parking lot. He stepped gingerly, not yet confident with his new cast. Delores looked up and smiled as Jordan entered the office. "You're not usin' crutches. Is that good?"

"Got a new cast this morning. Doc says I can walk with it but not run or jump. Better for the back than hobblin' with the crutches. Truck's here, is Bert around?"

"No, he called in sick. The Reverend's still at the news conference, so I'm not sure what there would be for you to do?"

"I thought the truck was Bert's."

She cocked her head to one side. "No, it belongs to the mission. He acts like it's his, though. The Reverend lets him take it home a lot. Says he doesn't like to drive his own car much. Guess it's some kinda classic or special."

Jordan eased himself into a vacant chair across from her. "Anybody calls with problems. Maybe I can take care of some things. I'm handy around my house."

Delores shook her head. "Not so far. I could call you if they do, if there's somewhere else, you need to go."

"How about if I go out and check the houses? Talk to the managers. I haven't been to all the places yet. Might be a chance to get to know the place better. See what else I might do."

Delores said nothing. Just chewed her lip and looked off as if pondering his request. "I guess that would be alright. The Reverend said you wanted to help. If any of them have problems with you, have them call me, and I'll vouch for you. It worked the other day with Estelle, and you charmed her."

"Since I don't know all of them, can you give me a list? I'll go from that, and if an emergency comes up, you can call me. Does Bert have his tools here?"

"No, but there's a toolbox in the back you can take just in case."

After retrieving the toolbox from the storeroom, Jordan loaded it in his car. He opened the laptop on the seat beside him. He called up the tracker on the truck. The screen showed the truck's path and times on the screen. After noting the first stop on the day before, he headed out of the parking lot.

"Okay, Bert, let's see where you've been." He said to himself

*****

Parked at the big box sporting goods store, Archer jogged to the building. Collins and a black man wearing a blue uniform met him at the door. The uniformed man wore a silver badge engraved with a large security firm's logo. He extended his hand as Collins turned to Archer. "Jim Bridger, chief of security for the shopping plaza. He's rounded up tapes from the plaza's cameras. Got real good coverage. If our boy was here, we'd see 'em. Archer shook the man's hand. "Lieutenant Jack Archer MPD. We sure on the purchase?"

Collins held up the charge slip, then read from the receipt. "One blue sweat outfit, like the one she wore in the tape, another red one. Then some socks, underwear, jeans, and four pullover sports shirts. Red, green, yellow, and orange. They sell everything here. And get this—one Livestrong treadmill. The deluxe model, according to the sales manager. All the bells and whistles, including powered incline. Baby raises and lowers one end with the push of a button."

Archer listened and nodded. "Shit. One item matches and you think we got our man?"

Smug, Collins held out the slip. "Charged to one Richard Nixon."

Wide-eyed, Archer snatched the sheet from Collins' hands. Grinned. "'Bout time we caught a break on this."

He turned to the security man. "A treadmill? Damn. If you got any kinda decent security, we can't miss him. Let's go check your tapes."

Seated in the security office, Archer and Collins sat next to the security man's desk. After checking the disk's label, the security officer, Bridger, slipped it into the computer. Soon the image of a man standing at a sales counter appeared on the screen. Archer and Collins, seated on either side of Bridger, leaned close to the screen.

"Shit, there's that damn ballcap again. He's wearin' shades this time, too. Oh man," Collins grumbled.

"Beard and mustache like at the casino the same. He might be a bit scruffier. Like he hasn't shaved for a day. Doc said he might be breakin' down," Archer replied.

The man reached across the counter to sign the charge slip.

"Left-handed. Just like the guy at the casino. You know he does look a lot like the asshole that works at Shining Light." Archer stopped talking. Peered forward again, then pointed at the screen. "Can you back it up a little?"

Bridger clicked the mouse.

"Now, can you zoom in?"

Again, Bridger clicked the mouse.

Archer tapped the screen with his finger. "There it is. See it. That damn fake tattoo!"

Collins grinned. "Gotta be our boy! What the hell's he doin' with a treadmill! Hey. That must be a bitch to load and haul. Did he have it delivered? Lot of folks do, don't they?"

Archer glanced at the bill. "No mention of that here. Can we check with the salespeople about that? Find out if it's separate or something'?"

Collins pulled out his phone. As he talked, he shook his head as he ended the call. "Guy recalled the sale. Said the customer insisted on taking it himself. Said he was good as anybody else with tools, so he could put it together himself. He picked it up on the loading dock."

Archer turned to Bridger. "You got video there?"

Bridger stood. Ran his hand along a rack above the computer. He pulled down a box and flipped it open. After shuffling through the disks, he grasped one and sat down again.

Archer turned to Collins. "Might get his vehicle on this at least if nothin' else."

Bridger fast-forwarded the video to the time right after the sale. Soon a red pickup backed to the loading dock. As a clerk wheeled a hand truck to the vehicle, the man purchasing the treadmill stood by the truck's bed. After the clerk set the box in the truck's bed, the customer closed the truck's gate and returned to the cab. Once he stopped the video Bridger, stood to retrieve another disk. "At least we know what kind of truck it was. I'll check the lot here. Maybe find the plate from there."

Collins glanced at Archer. "Could we be that lucky?"

Archer said nothing, just shrugged as the parking lot now came on the screen. The truck emerged from behind the building. As it turned, the rear of the vehicle came into view. Bridger stopped the image, zoomed in. "Shit! I can make out the first two letters. The rest are blurred. Tennessee plate, but couldn't tell the County."

Archer sighed, a smile crept over his face, "Since we know what he looks like and the vehicle, we can catch him in the lot comin' in."

Bridger nodded. "It's worth a shot."

The Gingerbread Man

CHAPTER TWENTY-ONE

With the tracker, Jordan followed the same path he assumed Bert drove the previous day, hoping this might also reveal the day's logic. He pulled into the driveway of a small house near the freeway. Seated in his car, he studied the home's surroundings.

The grass needed mowing. Weeds grew everywhere. Paper and bottles littered the yard. Both adjacent lots stood vacant. Iron bars covered the windows, the norm for the neighborhood.

Smaller than the rest of the Mission's buildings, it would only house one person at most. A garage, almost as big as the house, stood next to it. Both structures in good repair. Fresh paint, unstained shingles, incongruent with the condition of the yard.

Belkey said they had several donated structures, not in use. This must be one of them.

The track showed the truck had been there twice yesterday. Must be getting it ready for use. An office? Storage? Maybe flip the donated house for funds. He'd ask the Reverend or Delores about it.

The house looked unoccupied. To make sure, he crossed the porch and rapped on the front door. No answer, even when he used his best policeman's knock. He peered through a window on the porch. He saw nothing. After retrieving a flashlight from his car, he shined it into the window. His view, blocked by black-painted plywood. An inspection of the others found them covered the same way.

The back door, secured with a padlocked crossbar. Marks on the paint showed the bar's frequent removal. The sidewalk from the driveway ran straight to this entry. The absence of the same front door path suggested this served as the main entrance. Locked in this fashion, no one could exit.

He examined the mounts for the crossbar. The mounting screws had the rounded heads of a one-way screw only removable by drilling them off. If he did that, it would warn whoever used the building that someone had been inside. Alerted, they might dispose of any clues inside. Jordan examined the padlock. When he worked in the city, he met people who could crack a lock like this with no problem. After he finished running the rest of the route from yesterday, he might call one. Discover if he had any juice left with the locals.

He turned his attention to the garage. Its door seemed new. A padlock like the one on the house's back door kept the door in place. The garage had no windows.

Back inside his car, he checked the tracker screen for the next address. Double-checking, with his GPS, showed it to be a shopping center. Starting his car, he recalled that the center contained a big box hardware store. Probably just picking up supplies for work. He'd stick to his plan, though. Make the trip in this order to capture the driver's thought process.

*****

Jordan had been wrong. As he sat in the mall parking lot studying the surrounding buildings—no hardware store. Instead, a chain sporting goods store anchored the mall. He often browsed there for bargains in fishing gear. No real quality, but sometimes he could find a deal. He cruised, studying the other shops—lots of boutiques and upscale clothing stores, a fudge shop, and a Starbucks.

Archer mentioned the killer used internet cafes for his communication, specifically Starbucks. Inside, the aroma of fresh-brewed coffee and baking rushed to greet him as he opened the door. The store's only patron worked on a laptop at a corner table. Jordan's entrance prompted a greeting from the smiling young Barista behind the counter.

As he clomped to the counter, he studied the shop's interior. Three computers sat on a bar along the back wall to the left of the store—a barstool before each of them. Two video cameras hung from the ceiling. One directed at the front door, the other at the computer station. He might be in luck. He flashed his badge as he stepped up to the counter. The young girl's smile vanished. She looked up at him, wide-eyed.

"I'm Detective Robert Jordan, Jergen County Sheriff's office. We believe someone uses your computers to deal in pornography."

The girl glanced at the computers along the back wall.

"I don't know anything about that," she protested.

"I see you have video surveillance here. Can I view the footage from it?"

"Gee. I'm... I'm not sure." She glanced around as if looking for help. "They never showed me how to run it and all. The mall security does that. Their number is over there on the wall if you want to call them. The manager will be here in a couple hours. Maybe he can help."

Since he could not bluff his way past the security, he took another tack. "How does it work? People just start using them?"

She put her hand to her chest. Again, glanced around the store. Chewed on her lower lip. She pointed to a spiral notebook lying on the counter. "No, they have to sign up over there. They put down the time they sign in and then record when they start. There's supposed to be a thirty-minute limit, then they have to sign in again. That's so there isn't confusion during peak times."

Jordan pulled the spiral notebook to him. Nothing recorded today or the time the truck had been at the center the previous day. "Did you work yesterday?"

The girl nodded.

"Your log here shows nobody used them at the time I'm looking for. Do you think that's right?"

Her eyes rolled up. She sucked on her lower lip. "I think so." She nodded. "Don't have much traffic during the week then. The ones that do come in are regulars like Mr. Johnson over there. They usually bring their own devices. Ours are really slow. I'm pretty sure nobody used them yesterday."

"Humph. Are there other places here close by that offer this service?"

"Gee. I don't know." She leaned across the counter towards the man working alone in the corner. "Mr. Johnson! Do any places close by offers computers like us?"

The man glanced up from his computer. Frowned. "That fancy bread place on the other side of the mall does. But it's worse than here. That's the only one I know of."

Jordan sighed. "Well, I guess I'm going to have to go back to our tech guys. Tell 'em they got it wrong. Thanks, uh..."

"Pamela! I'm sorry. How 'bout I fix you one on the house. Then maybe I have problems in... Where did you say?"

Jordan shook his head and chuckled. "Jergen County. Mississippi."

"Yeah, If I'm in trouble there, I got a get out of jail free card. Whattaya say?"

After returning to his car, Jordan blew on the steaming cup as he studied the tracker screen. The Barista had chattered nonstop while she fixed the drink. A sharp contrast to her talk while he questioned her. Ashamed now for scaring the girl who must be the same age as his daughter would be if she lived. He studied the screen, contemplating his next move.

He remembered the detail they had seen during the test with Joshua and the dog. He experimented with the keyboard until a menu appeared, offering to zoom in or out. He used the touchpad to work it. Quickly the view changed to within the parking lot. The trail went from in front of the big sporting goods store to the back before exiting the lot. He started his car and followed the path.

As he passed the front of the business, Archer and Collins stepped into his path. He hit the brakes to let them pass. Archer talked on his cell phone. Collins glanced in his direction. Neither seemed aware of his presence as they strolled to Archer's car.

He must be getting close to something. He didn't know what. Behind the building, he saw a loading dock. Bert must have picked up something here. He glanced down at the tracker's monitor. The trail from here led back to the house he had just left. He had to get in there. Look. He just needed someone to pick that lock.

*****

Paused at Archer's car, Collins glanced back to the parking lot as Archer ended his call. "Hmm, did you see that SUV almost ran over us?"

Archer glanced around. Turned back to Collins. "No. Why?"

"Driver looked a lot like your old buddy Jordan."

"Really?"

"I think so. I just got a glance, but driver looked like him. He followin' us?"

Archer scanned the area. "I doubt it. If anything he'd be ahead of us. The man's a real bloodhound. Not kiddin' you."

"Still, he's close to the case. Wouldn't be the first time a parent went all vigilante."

Archer shook his head. "Jordan's a pro. He knows dickin' around like that would screw up the case. Hell, he wants the asshole behind bars worse than us. Nah. Musta been somebody looks like him."

*****

After tying her to the bed and gagging her, he started the video. He typed the message on the screen then held the newspaper in front of the camera showing the date. As he tossed the paper aside, she raised one hand from the bed and flipped him the bird. He stopped filming. "That was naughty! But I guess they would see that you're alive and well."

He yanked the gag from her mouth.

"You Asshole! You hurt me!"

He stroked her forehead then trailed his hand through her brown hair. "That was an accident. I couldn't help it."

"I thought you liked me!" she wailed. Tears welled in her eyes. He took a tissue from the stand next to the bed then daubed the drops streaming down her cheeks. "I do. But not in the way you want me to."

"Then why did you use that shocking thing. That hurt too."

"You wouldn't agree to do the video. I needed it done. It was for your own good."

"Yeah. Right!" She grumbled.

"Really. If they don't get one every day, they won't send your school work. You want those don't you?"

"Why are you doin' this? You don't want to fuck. You keep me in this shithole basement. It stinks."

"I've brought you some General's Chicken. It's upstairs. After we're done if you want we can work out okay?"

"You can take your chicken and shove it up your ass. How about if I just starve myself. Then you won't get your little movie. Yeah. That's what I'll do. Won't eat. Won't drink. I'll just stay down here and die. Then you'll be in a mess."

"I'll just wait until you're too weak. Then I can tube feed. Put you on IVs for fluids. Might damage that remarkable brain of yours, but I could still prove you're alive. Wouldn't it be better just to eat and drink? Who knows what might happen next? Maybe I might even let you go back to Lester. That is, if you still want to. How about it?"

He showed her the Taser. Waved it back and forth before her eyes. "You gonna behave? Eat some dinner. Then you have to finish your homework so I can turn it in. All right?"

A tear ran down her cheek. She looked away then nodded.

*****

As he waited for his accomplice, Jordan followed the rest of the trail on the monitor. After leaving the house, the truck cruised the surrounding neighborhood. Up one street, then down another. Even in daylight, the working girls strolled, hoping to get an early start on the work. Had Bert been out looking for another victim? Or just sightseeing. The task force claimed the guy contacted victims by phone. He never arranged targets in person. According to the tracker's timestamp, it had been late when Bert cruised through here. He might come back later. See if something caught his eye that might reveal the drive's logic.

He stopped at a Sonic for dinner. After ordering his food, he called Charmain. She laughed as she came on the phone. "Give me five minutes. I'll call you back."

In the background, Archer commented while others laughed.

As the car hop placed his food on the tray, his phone buzzed.

"My God! I was so embarrassed," she giggled out of breath.

"Why? What happened?"

"Well, when you called, I was sittin' with all the folk's from the task force—my phone's settin' on the table. I forgot to put it on vibrate—your picture flashes on the screen. Then your ringtone plays..." She laughed again, gasped for breath.

"You mean you still have that thing on there? Your Mama warned you. Remember? Said it wasn't appropriate for a proper lady. Right?" In the background, she still roared with laughter.

Deluged by the press when they first met, Charmain linked a personal ring tone to all her contacts. An efficient method for screening calls. Despite her mother's warnings, she linked Jordan to

Love Machine by the Miracles. The recollection brought a smile to his face.

She sniffed as she came back on the phone. "God, you should have seen the look on Dr. Maynard's face when that went off. You'll never hear the end of it from Jack. I'm sorry. I hope it doesn't embarrass you too much."

"Why? I didn't pick it. You did. I'm sure the others envy my prowess. What can I say? I'm an older man, you know. What I used to do all night now takes me all night to do."

"Ooh, and that's what I like." She chuckled before cooing, "You at the apartment?"

"No, I got a few things left to do at Shining Light. Maybe a couple hours. Anything new from the task force?"

"Yeah. Good and bad."

"What's good?"

"Archer and Collins might have a good lead on a suspect. Seems like they spotted a vehicle he drives and might have got a partial on the license plate."

"That sounds good. What's the bad?"

"They found another body this morning, but this one's different."

"How so?"

"Older. Plus, he killed her on the street and dumped her. The killer cut out her tongue, so they think it's him. Dr. Maynard believes he's becoming unstable."

"That is bad."

"That's not all of it either. The proof of life video was scary. He tied and gagged her. At the end of the tape, she flipped him the bird. Dr. Maynard is worried he's mistreating her."

CHAPTER TWENTY-TWO

A dog barked as they walked down the street.

"Sounded like a pit bull," the older black man walking next to Jordan hissed in the dark. "You got yo gun case he runnin' loose?"

"Better, got a Taser!" Jordan held it up for the older man to see. "Got a can of mace too. Use that first. Should run it off."

The man shrugged. "Them dogs tough. Down here, a lot of folk's fight 'em. If they don't do good, owners let 'em go. Folks get attacked by 'em all the time."

"Don't sweat it, Luther, I got your back, man."

"You back with Memphis Five-oh?"

"No. Just doin' some personal work on my own. You been straight?"

The man scowled. "What kinda question that? Jus' gettin' by on gettin' by. You know?"

"How's your daughter?"

The man's smile beamed. "She graduatin' from Vanderbilt. Full honors."

"No, shit?"

The man's chest puffed out, he nodded. "Headin' on to MIT in the fall. Freeride to the Doctorate."

"What in?"

"Mechanical engineerin'. She always been good with her hands. Regular mechanic."

"Like her old man?"

The older man chuckled and nodded. As they neared the house, Jordan extended his hand to stop the other man. He studied the neighborhood. The street appeared empty. Lights came from most of the windows in the surrounding houses. The muffled thump of music provided the only sound other besides the cricket's chirps. Their destination appeared deserted. No vehicles parked nearby.

"I'm not sure if anyone's inside. Windows are covered. I'll go up and check. If I hear nothin', I'll knock. If someone answers the door, I'll show 'em the badge, make some excuse. If not, I'll flash twice with my mag-lite."

The older man nodded. Staying in the shadows, Jordan moved towards the house. He marched across the porch to the front door, making as much noise as possible. Again, he used his best cop knock, then waited. No sound from within. He knocked again. Still nothing. He glanced back. The older man, crouched in the shadows, peered around the neighborhood then glanced back at Jordan. He should have left the Mace with Luther. Probably scared of the dogs.

Jordan strode back off the porch. His boot and cast clomped on the boards-making sure anyone inside knew they had a visitor. He walked around the house to the back. He shined his light on the bar blocking the back door—the lock in place. After returning to the front, he flashed his light twice. Time to check inside.

*****

In the basement Bonnie turned the music down and listened. It came again, like someone knocking. She waited. "What could that asshole be doing now?" she said to herself as she turned off the light. Huddled in the corner furthermost from the stairs. It might be her only chance. *Not make a sound. Draw him down the stairs to check. If he came down in the dark to find her, she might be able to get by him and out before he caught her. What did she have to lose? The guy seemed to be losing it anyway.*

*****

Outside the house, while Jordan held the light, Luther studied the lock. "Thas' a good one. S'posed to deter the criminal element. Protect your personal belongin's."

"Can't do it?"

"Shoot! I used to let my daughter play with these when she little. Undo 'em in nothin' flat."

Jordan shook his head. "Glad she's gettin' a good education."

"You got that right. She'd run you boys ragged. She learned young though. A man with a briefcase steals a lot more than a man with a gun. Plus, the law looks the other way. Might even be a ticket to the White House."

The lock popped open. The man handed it to Jordan. "If you don't mind. I'll wait here outside. Don't want to be breakin' no laws you understand? Just doin' my best for the boys in blue. Might leave me the Mace, though, case that dog get loose."

Jordan unclipped the canister from his belt and handed it to the man. "Be sure to aim it the right way, if you have to use it."

After pulling the crossbar from the door, he hung the open padlock in the hasp. Jordan stepped to the side as he reached for the door knob. "Luther, step away from the door. No tellin' what might be just inside."

The older man's eyes opened wide. He moved to Jordan's side, as the door swung open.

Jordan drew his gun, turned on the flashlight. "Police!" No sound came from the darkened house. "I'm coming in!" He stepped through the door.

*****

A voice upstairs, but Bonnie could not make out the words. He had never come back twice in one night. *Had she pushed him over the edge? Had he finally had enough? If so, what would she do?* She asked herself. Her mother and father had taught her to pray, but God never listened. *First, he took her mom then her dad. Sent her to that awful house where the man hurt her. Prayer did not work. God did not care. She had to do it herself.* Stifling a sob, Bonnie trembled as she heard the footsteps overhead. If he came down looking for her, she must get away. She could not continue waiting for someone else to save her. She looked around. *Find a weapon then attack. Hit him. Get the edge she needed to bolt up the stairs. She'd slam the door shut behind him. Trap him down in this dungeon. Then find Lester. Lester would fix this asshole's wagon.* The pencil on the desk. *Attack in the dark, stab him. Go for his throat. Maybe in the face. Drive it through his eye. A warrior like her Mom.*

*****

Meanwhile, upstairs, through the flashlight's beam, Jordan studied the furnishings. He clicked on one wall switch to test for power. After killing the light, he resumed his search. Recently remodeled, the smell of fresh paint mingled with the faint aroma of food. Furniture in good condition and set in expected places. The only exceptions were in what appeared to be the home's kitchen and dining room. The dining room looked more like a gym. It contained a weight bench and treadmill. The kitchen looked like it also served as an office and a table more appropriate in a medical setting.

A laptop rested on the desk. He didn't turn it on, wanted no trace of his visit.

He checked a trash container near the wall in the kitchen. Empty, but a fresh trash bag. Inside a cupboard, he found an opened sack filled with plastic cups and paper plates. Inside the refrigerator, a bottle of Peach Schnapps and a pitcher of what looked to be ice tea. As he closed a cupboard, a sound came out of the darkness. He trained his light around the room. Nothing. All houses made noises.

Returning to what looked like a living room, he shined the light on the bare walls—the carpet beneath the sofa, the only decoration. Not unusual for a place not in use, but still someone had been inside recently and eaten a meal.

"You 'bout done in there, Jordan?"

Jordan returned to the back door. "Guess so. Hey Luther, what about the garage? You open that?"

Jordan shined his light on the garage's lock. Luther nodded.

After replacing the crossbar in the door and re-locking it, Jordan moved to Luther's side.

"Did this one in the dark," Luther grinned as he helped Jordan raise the garage door. Inside sat the red pickup from Shining Light. The rest of the garage seemed normal.

Jordan felt the hood. "It's been driven recently. Whoever drove it must have had another ride."

Luther said nothing, just shrugged. Together they lowered the door, locked up, then strode back up the street.

Luther glanced at Jordan. "See anythin' inside?"

"Not much. Just an ordinary house. Maybe they're fixin' it up to be some kinda clinic. Anyway, thanks for indulgin' me. If you need a kind word to your parole officer, give me a holler."

After returning to Jordan's SUV, they drove away.

*****

The footsteps above stopped then the door closed upstairs. Maybe the asshole had just forgotten something. Would leave her alone? Clutching the pencil, Bonnie crouched in the corner. She waited. No more sounds. She shuffled to the light switch. Her toe smarted from where she toppled the desk chair in her dash in the dark. The sound it made as it crashed onto the floor had brought her heart to her mouth. Still, she found the pencil in the dark on the desk, but he had not come down the stairs. She set the pencil aside. Now she studied the room. Decided to plan what to do if she got the chance again.

Not just here. Maybe at the kitchen table. Stab him with a fork. Run out the door. Possibly during a workout. She might have to be very cagey to get him into that. But maybe she could. Promise to behave then clobber him with a weight or drop that bar on him.

She had no idea about the neighborhood. *Was it in the town or in the country? Either way she could avoid him. Become the warrior woman her mother had been. He looked strong and powerful, but he viewed her as helpless. This would be her edge. She would show him. Enough of being the victim, he would be her prey.*

*****

He loved the way the car leaped when he pressed the gas. The engine's hum becoming a scream as the tires broke loose from the pavement. He lifted his foot from the accelerator, watching the speedometer dip from one hundred fifty to the legal sixty-five. These brief bursts satisfying, for now, his lust for the beast's power. He could not afford to draw attention to himself by getting a ticket. Maybe he would take a week off this summer. Head out west, no speed limits there. Even if they tried to stop him, this car could outrun anything a cop might have. Except maybe an airplane. But they had more important matters to do out West than chase speeders. Yes, that's what he'd do. Might take the girl with him.

Right now she drove him nuts. He laughed to himself. She grew on you. Not like the others, but he still had the lust that could only the kill quenched. But what the hell, he loved living on the edge.

The car purred as it coasted down the exit ramp. Turning left he entered the neighborhood. No cars on the street he let the car idle in the driveway while he pulled the truck from the garage. Taking his toy for a ride might take the edge off for a while. He had much to do tomorrow.

CHAPTER TWENTY-THREE

Charmain, Archer, Collins, and Dr. Maynard gathered for their usual post-press conference meeting. Charmain turned to Dr. Maynard seated at her side. "I kinda feel sorry for Reverend Belkey. He'd really like to be more involved. He said he's sorry about not coming to us right away about the contest with the girl. He seems real tore up about it."

Collins slapped the table. "Well, I don't care how much he pushes. Except for you, I want no one but police here attached to the case. I don't see him able to offer much at this point besides prayer. Plus, we got some new information. We need to get back to his little operation."

Charmain turned to him. Her eyes opened wide. "I thought we'd ruled out Belkey, and you got the word to avoid that guy working for him."

Collins scoffed. "The one wrongly convicted for kiddy porn? The guy we so wrongly detained for questioning? Threatened us with a lawsuit for harassment if we bothered him again? You mean that upright citizen?"

Archer shook his head and snorted. "Yeah. Remember, I said you put a beard and mustache on him; he could fit the images we got from the video and the composites."

"Also, don't forget he could have spotted Belkey's infatuation with Charmain," Dr. Maynard added. "It's a stretch from kiddy porn to murder, but the guy creeped me out. So, what's this new information?"

Archer told them about the tapes from the sporting goods store. "Plus, a witness at the scene of the last murder mentioned a red pickup in the area that night."

Collins handed a printout to Dr. Maynard. She glanced at the sheet as he pointed to the highlighted area. "And this red truck with the close plate match belongs to Shining Light?"

Collins nodded.

Dr. Maynard passed the sheet back. "I agree. Looks like a good reason to go back there. Find out more about this truck and who uses it."

Collins looked over at Charmain. "So, even if Belkey's not our guy, havin' him here with us would be a problem."

Dr. Maynard leaned forward, "Even if it's not the truck that belongs to Shining Light. It might be best to have uniform patrol canvass the working girls. Show them the pictures of the truck and the killer. One might have seen it, or it might jog some memories. Or at least we'll give them a warning to look out for a John who might use a truck like that. Who knows what might come from that? Might even save a life. Who knows?"

Archer nodded. "I'll pass it on to the boss with your recommendation."

Collins stood and stretched. "Come on, Archer. Let's go see the Reverend, find out more about his truck. I'm sure he would want to know if it's bein' misused."

*****

At the Shining Light offices, Jordan discovered both the red pickup and the van gone. The tracker showed the truck parked at a Mission house. The van traveled towards the office and Charmain's car set at the police station. He now wished he had put a tracker on Hector's cycle. Seeing him close to Charmain would have put his mind at ease. She told him last night about the discovery of the bag. The fact that he had tracked the pickup to the store she mentioned had made him uneasy. He wanted to corner Bert. Maybe put the heat on him, sweat him, but first, he wanted to learn about the house he broke into last night.

After turning off the tracker, he set it in the seat passenger seat. He limped across the parking lot to the entrance. Inside, Delores sorted mail at her desk. She looked up and smiled as Jordan hobbled in. "You've missed him again. Sometimes I think Bert's hidin' from you. You give him a hard time or somethin'?"

"Not really. Do you know where he went?"

"Over to the Orange Mound house. Puttin' in a new toilet, I guess. Probably could use a hand. You gonna head over there?"

"Yeah. Unless there's somethin' else."

Delores chewed her lip as she pondered the question. "Not really. The Reverend called, said he'd be here shortly. He might know. If you wanna wait."

"Why not? Beats chasin' Bert all over town. Say I got around to most of the houses yesterday. They've been fixed up real nice."

"Bert and the Reverend are handy with that. Plus, we get help from folks at the different churches."

"I'm curious. One house over in Hickory Hill. Looks too small for a shelter, but it looks like somebody did a lot of work on that."

"Oh yeah. We take any house that gets donated, but the little ones we sell off to those house flipper folks. That one the Reverend hopes to turn into a clinic and maybe an activity center for the girls. He figures he could get Doctors and Dentists to donate time. Maybe offer free services there--another way to bring the girls in."

As Belkey shuffled through the door, both turned to greet him. He managed a wan smile.

Delores stood, scowled as she peered at Belkey. "What happened to your head, Wayne?"

Belkey touched the two band-aids stuck there and shrugged. "Cut myself shaving this morning. Nothing major." He turned to Jordan. "Not using crutches?"

"Got a walking cast now. Doc says the way I travel around, the crutches would ruin my back. Said this would be better."

Belkey yawned as he nodded. As well as the band-aids, Belkey had dark circles under his eyes. His pupils looked bloodshot.

"Wayne, you're lookin' peaked," Delores fussed as she made her way around the desk to Belkey's side. "Would you like a little tea with honey? My Mama insisted that it cured everything."

Belkey smiled. "Sure, Dee. That would be fine. I'm tired, but I might be comin' down with a bug."

"I saw you on television this mornin' with that cute little reporter. Both of you looked wore out," Delores said as she made her way to the office sink. She filled a mug with water and put it in the microwave.

Belkey turned to Jordan, looked him up and down. "This killer thing has everybody wore down. I hope it all works out soon. So, Mr. Jordan, since you don't need crutches any longer, are you going back to work?"

"Not yet. I guess you're stuck with me for a while longer. This cast isn't designed for runnin' down cattle rustlers. Is there anything I can help with besides being Bert's sidekick?"

Collins and Archer's entry interrupted their conversation. Neither detective spoke. Collins scowled, and Archer stared wide-eyed at Jordan. Archer broke the silence, turning to Belkey. "I'm sorry we were delayed, Reverend. Before we talk, I would like to speak privately with Bob here."

Belkey turned to Jordan, a puzzled frown on his face. He then turned back to Archer. "I didn't know Mr. Jordan was involved."

"He's not, officially. We're just old friends. Plus, he was the first officer on the scene at the casino killing."

Belkey turned back to Jordan, his brow furrowed. "Oh, that's right. Would you like to use my office? Delores was just making me some tea. We have coffee if you like."

Archer gave a dismissive wave. "I'm good. Don't want to upset your routine. Just want to catch up here with my old partner. Maybe Collins might, though."

Archer turned to Jordan. "How 'bout we go outside. Get out of these nice people's hair."

Jordan hobbled behind Archer out the door. Outside, Archer clutched Jordan's sleeve, scowled. "What the fuck are you doin' here? Jesus, Bob. You've got no jurisdiction. You're supposed to be on disability leave. Where the fuck is your head at?"

"I don't follow, Jack. I'm here as a volunteer. That counselor I was seein', recommended it."

"Recommended it?!" Archer stepped back. His eyes opened wide.

"Yeah. Told me doin' something for the girls in this program might help me overcome my shit-relieve the guilt."

Archer shook his head. Put his hands on his hips, then kicked at the paving.

Jordan shook his head. "Do that hard enough you'll be in a cast like me. I thought you guys had cleared Belkey. Is it the other dude? Maintenance guy? Seems to be just a peeper. Maybe cops a feel now and then from some of the girls in the program. But I'm not pickin' up killer vibes from him."

Archer sighed. Turned back to Jordan. "Shit! I might as well tell you. Char will anyway. We got some leads that put a truck belongin' to the mission in our crosshairs. A person drivin' it made some purchases tied to the case. Also, a witness reported a red truck in the area the night the last one got killed."

Jordan frowned. "Purchases? Like what?"

"Sportswear, tennis shoes, some exercise equipment. Shit! Collins said he thought you drove by us at the mall. Thought you were followin' us."

"Which one?"

"The one out East that has the big box Sporting Goods store."

Jordan nodded. "You mean the mall over there on Winchester?"

"Yeah, that one."

Jordan said nothing, stared at the ground, then looked up. "Didn't see you. Yeah, I was there. Runnin' some errands and got the cravin' for a little designer Joe from Starbucks. Cute little Barista there gives me free ones. Has a thing for cops, I guess."

Archer shook his head, then grinned. "Jesus. Ain't that fine little thing you with enough? You asshole."

Jordan shrugged, grinned. "Hey, man. It's innocent. Just cause you're on a diet doesn't mean you can't check out the menu. Anyway, you say things are heatin' up here?"

"Well, despite your failure to pick up vibes from Christian, I'm beginnin' to like him more and more as our unsub."

"Unsub? Listen to you. Makin' with the Feebie talk and all. You buckin' for the big time, brother? Hell, you don't even know what that means. Do you?"

Archer shook his head. "Shit! You're still a righteous asshole. You need to know Christian, ain't Bert's real name. It's an alias."

"What's his real name?"

Archer tapped Jordan on the shoulder. "Ha! See? That girl don't tell you everything either. Ask her. Anyway, I think you might want to put a cap on your volunteerin' here for a while. Okay?"

Jordan gazed off. Said nothing for a while. "Sure, Jack. Dyin' to catch up on the Maury show, anyway."

As Jordan hobbled to his SUV, Collins joined Archer in the parking lot. "That's the car I saw him in yesterday. You mention that to him?"

"Yeah. Said he was runnin' some errands. Stopped at the coffee shop there. Claims one of the girl's workin' there gives him coffee on the arm."

Collins scoffed. "You believe him?"

Archer shrugged.

"Shit! What's he doin' here?"

"Says it's part of his therapy. Voluteerin'. Helpin' with the girls here. Shrink saw him when he broke his leg. I was there. Convinced him to see a therapist, and the guy suggested he volunteer here- work his way through some of the shit with his daughter's death."

Collins shook his head. "Lotta coincidences, Jack!"

Archer turned back to Collins. "You talk to the Reverend?"

"Not yet. He's on the phone. Figured we ought to do it together."

*****

Once Belkey sipped his tea. Just as Delores promised, he experienced the buzz from both the caffeine and the honey hit his bloodstream. He paced his office, pondering the conversation between Jordan and Archer. He met Jordan during the operation at the casino. Also, it had been the discovery of the body that had ended the busts. He tried to remember what that gorgeous blond detective had said after Jordan failed to return. Something about a family emergency. Then Jordan said the accident that broke his leg might have been related. That made no sense. Neither Collins nor Archer seemed pleased with Jordan's presence. He wondered why? He put these thoughts aside as the two detectives re-entered the office.

"Why don't we go to my office. That way we won't bother Delores."

Once inside his office with the officers seated across from him, Belkey leaned back in his chair, steepled his fingers before his face, and leaned back. "What can I do for you?"

"We wanted to tap your brain a bit. Learn how the program runs. Understand what you do," Collins began.

A puzzled frown appeared on Belkey's face. "I'm not sure why that might be of interest."

Archer leaned forward. "We realize you want to help all you can. I'm sorry we've kinda kept you on the fringe, but that's the way the

FBI wants it. They're the tall hogs at the trough right now, and us peasants have to go along."

Belkey nodded. "So, you think I might help?"

"Yeah, we told the Feds that we wanted to find out more about your program and the girls," Archer continued. "Might give us a feel for how this guy operates. Figure out why he picks the ones he does. I mean, you know these girls well. You're the only expert I can tap without going to the brass."

Belkey smiled, leaned forward. "As I said all along, be happy to help. What can I tell you?"

"Well, you've talked in the news conferences about what the program does and how it does it. It's all been a general description. But I'd like to learn more."

Belkey described the program's history, home donations, volunteer usage, general operations, and organization.

Archer interrupted, changing tacks. "What makes the teenage girls unique from the others? Do you have any idea why he might target them instead of the more mature ones?"

Belkey paused, stared off, chewed his lip. "Of course, I would not understand why he might kill these girls. One thing the girls that age have in common is their aura of innocence. While they might enjoy the sex act, they seem to approach it with a sense of wonder, like a child standing beside a swimming pool on a hot day. The water seems inviting but appears daunting. They might observe other children playing nearby and enjoying themselves. This might give them the courage to plunge in. This might heighten the enjoyment."

"Humph! But then he kills them. He doesn't have sex with them. He's a real a sick fuck!" Collins snarled. Belkey sat back as if slapped, squirmed.

Archer, wide-eyed, snapped his head around to Collins. "Easy, man! I understand, it seems like we're spinnin' our wheels right now. The Reverend here is just tryin' to help, man." Archer turned back to Belkey. "This is how our sessions usually go. Cops like us are used to the rest of the team blowin' off steam. That's another reason we're reluctant to let outsiders sit in. Gets real emotional and feelings get hurt."

Collins winced. "Yeah. I'm sorry, Rev. This case is gettin' to me. Listen, let me go tap my kidney. Coffee runs right through me, plus walkin' around helps me cut the stress."

Collins stood and left the room, closing the door behind him. Alone, Archer resumed his questioning. "Anything else about these girls that might be unique?"

"Not that I can think of. I'm no Psychologist. Have you considered what the girls might represent to him? Could a girl that age have hurt him? Abused or humiliated him?"

"Make the killing an act of symbolic revenge?"

Belkey nodded. "I guess so. Like I said, I'm no expert, but from things I've read, that might be a possibility."

"Has any of the girls mentioned knowing any of the victims?"

"No. I've never asked them. Do you think they might tell you something more?"

Archer nodded. "It can't hurt. Who knows? If we find any that did, it might help our profiler out. We got little information right now. The more, the better. Would that be possible?"

As if pondering the request, Belkey said nothing before leaning forward, energized. "How about if we have a group meeting at each house? I can announce it, and we'll see if any of them can help. It's the least I can do, and it would help me feel like I'm doing all I can to help."

At that moment, Collins returned. "Listen, man. I know you're just tryin' to help. I wasn't barkin' at you-more the situation. We good?"

Belkey gave him a slight smile and nodded.

Archer turned to Collins. "Reverend here is gonna help us talk to the girls. Find out if they knew the victims and if so, maybe find more about each one. Might help us see the commonalities. Anything else you wanna ask about?"

Collins smiled, shook his head. After shaking hands with Belkey, they strode to the door. Archer turned back before leaving. "When can we start?"

Belkey nodded. "How about we start first thing tomorrow? I'll ask the managers to hold the first ones home from school. Girls enjoy a little hooky. We can probably do all the houses in two, maybe three days."

"Sounds like a plan. Where do we start?" After Archer had written the address on his legal pad, they left the office. As he watched the two detectives exit, Delores came to his side. "Tea help?"

He nodded.

"Let me make you some more. My, those two seemed like nice men. Especially that one from Mississippi. Seemed real impressed with what we do here. But he seemed most interested in the pickup."

Belkey's brow furrowed. "Humph."

CHAPTER TWENTY-FOUR

"God Damn It!"

Hearing the shout, Jordan hobbled as fast as he could down the hall. The home manager, Doris, at his side jogged ahead. The sound of gushing water came from the room down the corridor.

"Shit!"

When the water noise stopped, Bert appeared in the hallway, his dripping clothes left a trail on the hardwood floor. Doris shoved past Bert. Her hand clutched to her chest as she gazed into the room.

"You okay?" Jordan asked as he arrived at Bert's side.

"Yeah. Just fucking soaked." Bert turned to Doris. "Need to mop this up quick, for it soaks into the floor. If not, the ceiling downstairs might collapse."

Doris ran from the scene.

Jordan shook his head. "What happened?"

"Ballcock was no good. I turned on the water supply, and it blew all over the place."

Bert looked Jordan up and down. "Where're the crutches, stick-man?"

"Don't need 'em. Got a new cast."

"They send you over?"

"Yeah, Delores said you were puttin' in a new toilet here. Thought you might need a hand."

"Would have been nice. Reverend usually helps with these kinda chores. But he's been busy with them fuckin' news conferences." He shook his head before continuing. "Think he just wants to hang around that little black hottie they got leadin' the parade. Don't blame him, though. I'd slam the ham to her myself if I got the chance. You know what I mean?"

Bert leered and winked at Jordan. Jordan's face felt warm.

Bert shook his head. "What the hell's with you? You one a them sensitive pricks? Probably wouldn't know what to do if they handed it to you."

Jordan's legs trembled, his arms jerked as he fought the desire to reach out and choke Bert right here. Thoughts raced through his head. Before him stood the man, Archer claimed might have murdered his daughter. Now he had the nerve to make comments about Charmain. At this moment, he wanted to send Bert straight to Hell.

Doris's return with a wheeled bucket and mop, broke up the looming confrontation. "Comin' through with the mop guys! Also, Bert, the Reverend called. Wants you back at the office right away. Seems the toilet there is backin' up."

*****

As Archer and Collins strode to their vehicle, Archer tossed his notepad on the back seat. As he slipped behind the wheel, he struck the dash with his fist. "Shit! I couldn't find a way to talk about the truck without making him suspicious. At least we got an excuse to hang around the program. Interview the girls maybe we can find out somethin' that way."

"Well, I'm sorry about losin' my cool in there. I wished we'd talked a little beforehand. Mapped out a strategy, but as he was dishin' out his bullshit a plan came to me, and I just went with it."

Archer turned to Collins. A frown creased his forehead. "Whadd'ya mean?"

"Well, that old gal in the office is chatty as hell. I took the chance to talk to her. She told me about the truck. That handyman drives it mostly. Secretary said he takes it home too. The pay here ain't the greatest, and he does pretty good work. So, they figure havin' use of the truck off duty might be considered a nice perk."

Archer grinned. "They keep records on it?"

"Nah. Just receipts for fuel, repairs, and maintenance."

"How about the night of the killing. Was it here?"

"No. Secretary said our boy Bert was off sick. Thought he had it at home."

*****

The next morning Archer, Collins, and Belkey sat at the dining room table with the five girls living in the home. Estelle, the manager, scurried around the kitchen finishing the after breakfast clean up. Three girls clustered together-whispering and giggling between themselves like teammates planning a play. They stole glances at the two Detectives, and one winked at Archer. Archer shifted, uncomfortable he looked away, while Collins chuckled. He leaned close to Archer.

"You gotta fan," he whispered. Archer sneered, unamused.

The other two girls sat on opposite sides of the three. Not part of the threesome, but unfriendly to each other. The one on the left snapped her chewing gum. She seemed bored, gazing at the wall behind the officers. Her counterpart twirled her dark shoulder-length hair with her fingers. She followed Estelle with her eyes.

"Girls, this is Lieutenant Archer from the Memphis Police and Detective Collins from the Tunica County Sheriff," Belkey announced.

The three plotters stopped giggling. The two on either side stared wide-eyed at the Detectives—all silent. The detectives had their total attention.

"We're here to see if y'all can help us on a case," Archer began. The two Detectives described the case and the victims. The request for help by the officers relaxed the girls-drew them together as a group.

"I knew Bonnie. You mean that asshole has her somewhere?" The gum chewer asked. Her face flushed, almost matching her red hair.

Archer nodded. "That's right. Shows us a videotape of her every day. We're skipping the viewing this morning, so we could get with you guys. Anything you can tell us about her? Also, the other victims. Or what you might have heard about this while you were out on the streets. Anything might help us."

The girls murmured among themselves. An occasional swear word emerged. The blond in the group's center raised her hand as if in school. The other four stopped talking and looked to her. "Do you guys have any idea what he looks like?"

Collin's passed the composite sketch, then the photo across to them. All leaned close to examine the picture. The girl on the blond's right pointed at it. "It looks like Ole Horndog."

The one on the outside left stood, stepped behind the group, then peered over their shoulders. She turned to the others, "Could there be two creeps like him around?"

Estelle rushed to the table. She too peered at the image. She looked up. "The girls say he looks a lot like Bert."

The three men exchanged glances.

"Anything else?" Archer asked. Two girls shook their heads.

"Bonnie's real nice man. Real brainiac. I thought she didn't work the streets no more. Just kept Lester's books," The gum chewer added.

"That's right. We believe the guy snatched her from school after stealing Lester's car," Archer replied.

"Was he more upset about the car than Bonnie?" the gum chewer asked, then snapped her gum defiantly. The one next to her hit her on the shoulder.

"I'm just sayin'. The guys like a total asshole. At least my pimp cared about me when I got boxed around." Gum chewer protested, then shoved the other girl off her chair.

"You guys got anything to say to these gentlemen that might help? If not, keep your hands and your mouths quiet," Estelle snarled as she moved between the two scuffling girls. The girls again became quiet.

"Listen, if you can't think of anything right now, that's okay. If you remember somethin' later. Let Estelle know. She'll contact me. Right?" Archer said as Estelle nodded her head. "Believe me. If you recall anything, anything at all. Even if you feel it might not be important, let us know. We'll fit it alongside what we already know. You might be bringin' the missin' puzzle piece that gets us to this guy and brings Bonnie back safe and sound. Okay?"

In unison, the girls all nodded.

The meeting ended, the detectives and Belkey walked down the home's driveway. Halfway to the street, Bert arrived with the truck. As he emerged from the vehicle, Collins called out to him. "Nice truck!"

Bert sneered at them as they approached. "You need to talk to my lawyer again?"

"No, man, we're cool. Nice set a wheels," Collins replied, an apparent attempt at amiability. "Been thinkin' about gettin' one myself. Is that the V-8?"

Bert nodded as he retrieved a toolbox from the back of the truck.

"Stump puller, I'll bet." Collins turned to Belkey and Archer. A broad grin on his face. Puzzled, Belkey frowned. Archer winked gestured to the police car, "Let's go to the car while the good old boys discuss their Cowboy Cadillacs."

As Archer and Belkey strode away, Collins continued his discussion with Bert. As he did this, he pulled out his phone. "I'd like to take a quick video of this to show to my wife later. Is that okay?"

"What the hell. Whatever gets your rocks off? If the Rev don't mind me standin' around, I don't care. Paid by the hour, so it's all the same to me."

Collins walked around the truck holding his phone out. After he finished a complete circle of the pickup, he glanced into the cab. "Humph! Doubt that would impress her much," He returned the phone to his belt holder. "Even though it's kinda messy in there. Would it be okay if I looked around in the cab?"

"Whatever," Bert called over his shoulder as he walked away. He then punched the remote. The truck's lights flashed once, and locks popped up. "Lock it up when you're done.

In the Police Car, Archer handed a form to Belkey. "By signing this, you are givin' us permission to search the truck. Do you have questions?"

Belkey squirmed in his seat. Shot a glance out to the truck. Wide-eyed, he turned back to Archer. "Well, yes! I do! What's going on?"

"We have good reason to believe the killer has been usin' your truck. We would like to search it for evidence. Is that a problem?"

Belkey shook his head.

Archer held up his phone. "For the record, please, Reverend."

"No. Uh...no. It's not a problem. And yes, I know you are recording this conversation."

Belkey scribbled on the form, then passed it back to Archer. "You think it's him? Bert? And I let that man in our houses around these girls?" His jaw dropped. "This can't be happening. As I said, I apologize for not doing the background check...."

"In your defense, if the registry had been doin' its job, you wouldn't have spotted him, anyway. If it is him, it'll draw you a lot of negative attention, but it'll blow over. 'Specially, if you get out in front of this now. I'll make sure your cooperation is well known."

Finished with his search, Collins slid into the passenger's seat. Wearing latex gloves, he held up the bags so Belkey and Archer could view the contents. "We got the son of a bitch. This should be all we need to get a warrant for his house."

"By the book all the way," Archer picked up the car's radio microphone. "I'll get us covered for the search and the arrest." Before making the call, Archer turned to Belkey. "After we hook him up, we have to impound the truck. Uniform will come by to take him downtown for booking. We'll drop you back to the office. Like I said, when we go public with this, I'll make sure it's obvious how much you helped."

*****

Jordan used his key to let himself into Charmain's apartment. The fragrant aroma of meat roasting greeted him as he stepped inside. At the kitchen table Charmain, Tony, and Glenn, Tony's partner, shared a bottle of wine. The two men greeted him with smiles. Charmain rushed to his side, threw her arms around him, and kissed him. Taking his hand, she led him to the table. Glenn held up a bottle of sparkling grape juice. "Join us we're toasting your little woman's success."

Jordan snapped a glance at Charmain.

She beamed a big smile. "We caught him. He's under arrest."

Jordan's jaw dropped. "Who?"

Charmain tipped her head back peered down her nose at Jordan. "That creepy maintenance man at Shining Light."

Jordan smiled. "The girl's safe?"

Charmain shook her head. "Not yet. She was alive yesterday according to the video. Bert Christain or Bell or whatever his name is playin' dumb. Called his lawyer and he's refusin' to talk."

A puzzled frown crept across Jordan's face as he settled into an empty chair. "What led them to him?"

"Well, remember I told you about how he had that prior conviction. It got reversed and all, but still it looked bad. Then there's the truck. It or one like it was spotted near the last murder.

Then all those purchases at that store. Once again the truck showed up in a surveillance video at the store. It hauled one of the big items purchased. The plate was a close match to Shining Light's truck so that almost made it a sure thing."

"Yeah, Archer told me about that yesterday. Warned me off volunteerin' there anymore. I figured at worst the guy was a peeper. The managers thought he might be propositionin' some of the girls and I guess he'd cop a feel now and then. But a killer?" Jordan shrugged as Glenn filled a glass for him.

Charmain cocked her head. "Well, get this. They searched his truck. All legal. Collins found a false mustache and beard along with some brown hair tint under the seat."

Jordan's eyes opened wide as Charmain continued. "Right next to one of those phony tattoos that showed up on the video."

CHAPTER TWENTY-FIVE

As Charmain waited for the group to gather before the daily press conference, she recalled last night. After Tony and Glenn left, they had gone to bed. The triumph of catching the killer fueled her lust. She demanded and gave utterly. Jordan satisfied her but seemed distant. He listened to her talk about the success, but that was it. He attended, said little. When she remained silent, he seemed preoccupied. Surprisingly, he showed no joy in his daughter's killer's arrest.

"You ready for the big announcement?" Archer said as he and Dr. Maynard entered the conference room. Archer clad in a dark suit and tie instead of his traditional polo shirt and jeans. Dr. Maynard carried her notepad and a steaming cup, a teabag string dangling over the side.

Charmain flinched. Her thoughts interrupted.

"I'm sorry," Archer said as he sat next to Charmain, "You look a little glum. Figured you'd still be ridin' high from the bust. Or did you do too much celebrating with your honey last night? I'll bet he's over the moon about it. His daughter's killer finally behind bars."

"He didn't seem happy about it. Like he didn't care. He said he was glad, but I didn't feel like he cared."

Dr. Maynard frowned, reached across the table. Placed her hand on Charmain's. "That's common for a victim's family members. I mean, there is a relief, I suppose. Joy? For what? Their loved one is dead. Gone. They know that whatever happens to the killer, it will never bring the loved one back."

Charmain managed a weak smile. "I guess that makes sense. Thanks."

Collins entered, trailed by Belkey. Maynard glanced up; her brow furrowed again in a frown. "Reverend, are you okay?"

Paler than usual, his face looked ashen. After finding a seat, he ran his fingers through the red stubble that now appeared on his scalp. "I'm afraid all this has been a bit much. I hope we can find the girl and end all this. Especially if she is safe."

"We're sweatin' him now. DA's offerin' every kinda deal imaginable to find the girl. He already fired his lawyer. I'm sure the creep told Bell to cop a plea. Guy's stubborn," Collins added.

"So, we're using his actual name, not Bert?" Charmain inquired.

"Well, the asshole's been beggin' for attention. Chief wants him to have all he can get," Archer replied, nodding as he finished as if it provided punctuation.

Dr. Maynard turned to Collins. "What did they find in the house?"

Collins glanced down at his legal pad. "They found a ton of video surveillance gear. Cameras, transmitters. Cheap, a lot of 'em. All looked used. High-end computer with the latest photo and video editors. A bunch of teenage girl's clothes, including underwear. Bell claims he was supposed to be droppin' it off at the Mission. From charities and stuff for the girls. He picks it up and then brings it to the office. He said he had to unload this bunch at home 'cause they ran out of storage at the Mission. Does that make sense, Reverend?"

Belkey staring down at the table, lurched back in his chair. His eyes blinked several times as if awakened. "Excuse me. I'm sorry. What did you say again?"

"The clothes they found at your boy's home. He stated that he stored them there. Donated. He agreed to store 'em in his basement till the Mission had room. That right?"

Belkey's jaw dropped. He struggled for words. When he finally answered, his voice quivered, sounded weak. "I, I'm not sure.... Uh, Dee handles all that. You'd have to ask her."

Collins leaned close to Archer. "What gives with him? He whispered in Archer's ear. "He crackin' up?"

Archer shrugged.

Charmain reached across the table and placed her hand on Belkey's. The color returned to his cheeks. He seemed transformed. "Reverend, we're doin' all we can to find the girl."

"What about the computer? What did he have on it?" Dr. Maynard asked, turning back to Collins.

"Can't tell yet. There a lot of stuff on it encrypted or with passwords, so we couldn't look at it. Sent it over to Agent Rogers in the FBI's Memphis office. He promised to get on it right away."

"Mmm... I know Paul. Real techie," Maynard said with a smile, "Not been with us long. Came from the Marshals. A local hero." Just then, Collins reached in his inside jacket pocket to retrieve his vibrating phone. He turned away from the table. "Excuse me. Collins here." Collins listened, then placed the phone on the table. "Agent Rogers, I put you on speakerphone. I'm meeting here with our task force right now. Dr. Maynard from your agency is here. She just asked about the computer we brought you yesterday afternoon. What have you found so far?"

"Your guy's really been naughty. There's tons of videos. The girls all look really young. I'd guess early teens. He's filmed them putting clothes on or taking them off. Girls coming out of showers. There are even some with two girls having oral sex.

"Whoever owned this computer also edited out a lot of individual pictures of the girls. Looks like they were taken candidly in a home, not a studio.

"Also, there has been regular email correspondence with someone brokering the pictures worldwide. The computer's owner sent this other person a lot of pictures and videos. The other person talks about sales and money coming in. Plus, they got a website where they post stuff for preview and sales. I've traced it to a person in Mexico City, and the locals promised an arrest today."

"This guy we're looking at has a history of kiddie porn. Can you tell how current this is?" Archer asked.

"Yeah, the oldest is two years ago, and some as recent as last week."

Maynard leaned close to the phone. "Hi, Paul. Dr. Maynard here."

"Hey, Doc. This that serial guy your workin' on?"

"Yes, it is. Is there anything there that might relate to that case? Pictures that might be our victims or correspondence related to the case? He's been using the Internet to communicate with us."

"If you have pictures of the victims, I could try running facial recognition with them. There are a lot of different girls. Might spot it that way. I can do more looking to see if there might be stuff in other files. Even without ID on the girls, the guys in legal say we have enough to indict on the porno. That's Federal."

"We'll email you the victim pictures. Can you also send us copies of the pictures you've found?"

After a brief pause, Paul came back on. "Just sent 'em to your Inbox."

Dr. Maynard checked her phone. "Got 'em, I'll circulate them here. See if any of our people can recognize them. Also, talk to legal and get the indictments rolling. Those give us more leverage here. We need to find that girl soon. She's imprisoned somewhere. God only knows how long she can survive without him bringing her food and water. Nice work. Keep digging. Like I said, anything you can find might help us find the girl in time."

"No problem. I'll keep you posted." Collins replaced the phone in his pocket. He and Archer exchanged a high five.

"Hot damn. Now we got somethin'!" Archer held up a tiny tube no bigger than a pen cap. "This is one camera he used. They mount on little suction cups."

Collins turned to Belkey. "S'pose you could check those pictures? See if the girls might be from the Mission."

Belkey tugged at his clerical collar. The color once again drained from his cheeks. "How about if the home managers viewed them instead? They would know if they're our girls. Plus, it might be more ah, ah..."

"In keeping with the proprieties of your profession?" Charmain offered.

As Belkey glanced in her direction, his eyes lit up. The color returned to his face. "Yes! Yes...exactly!"

Maynard turned to Archer. "How about the truck?"

He smiled before talking. "The techs are findin' lots of stuff to analyze, but too early to get much of anything. Lots of prints. Ran 'em and have a few hits. Archer paused at this point. Glanced around the table, then smirked. "Of course, there's our favorite handyman Bell's, but also some matching the prostitute murdered the other day. Got some others, but we gotta check further with the rule outs."

"Excellent meeting for now." As Archer, Collins, and Belkey rose to leave, Maynard called after them. "Let the Chief know about the Federal indictment too."

She turned to Charmain after the others left. "It seems like keeping the Reverend out of the group was a good idea. I know he felt bad about not coming to us right away. That bothered him a great deal, but it seems like since we had this break in the case, he is more strained than ever. I hope we don't lose him. Of course, it appears he's still carrying a torch for you. Just a little attention from you seems to bring him right back. I hope you let him down easy."

*****

As they exited the press conference, Archer took Charmain aside. "Listen. The Reverend has been a big help in this. This thing with his handyman is gonna hurt his program's image. Right now, you have a lot a people's attention."

"No kidding. I've got agents callin' me. People wantin' interviews. The original publisher's screamin' for his book. God! All I wanted to do is help Bob get some closure with the death of his daughter. I expected nothing like this."

"Yeah, I know it might not seem to have worked for him now, but it's like the Doc said. He may not have a lot of joy about catchin' this asshole, but it should help him move on. I've seen it myself with victim's families. Bringin' the killer to justice gives them peace. Not joy. Just peace."

Charmain gave a reluctant nod. "I understand that now. He'll come around. He's gettin' counseling. Plus, he can get back to volunteering, now that Christian or Bell is in custody. But you mentioned the Reverend?"

Charmain glanced over Archer's shoulder. Spotted Belkey watching them.

Archer nodded. "That's it. I thought maybe you could drum up some positive PR for him and his program. I mean the guys doin' a great job. Maybe we can get a good spin-off of this for him and the girls he works with."

"Sure! That would be great."

Archer beckoned Belkey. When the man joined them, Archer turned to Belkey. "Like I told you, she would. Charmain's gonna use her newfound fame to get some positive attention to your program."

She grinned, punched Archer's shoulder, then hugged his arm. "Jack, you're a rat!" She turned to Belkey. "Listen, I agree with Jack. This thing with the handyman might reflect on you and your program. I'll help all I can to start gettin' the word out about the good things you're doin'. How 'bout we get together. Brainstorm some ideas for gettin' the right word out about you and your program," Charmain added, still holding Archer's hand.

A dark look passed over Belkey's face. He ran his hand over the red stubble that now grew from his scalp, then smiled. "Thank you. True, this thing with Bert is going to shed a terrible light on us, but that would take a huge load off my shoulders. Shall we start tomorrow?"

"How 'bout I call you tomorrow. This whole thing has thrown everything out of whack for me. That way, I can get a little organized. Okay?"

*****

After he tried to choke her, Bonnie refused to be around her captor. Insisted he place the food at the top of the stairs. Only retrieving it after he closed the trap door. He protested at first when she insisted on doing the proof of life video herself but finally gave in.

She now prepared to once more dine with him upstairs. Maybe exercise with him while she looked for an opportunity to attack. She kept the sharpened pencil concealed in the waistband of her trousers. Covered it with her shirt.

He had not brought the evening meal last night. *Had he somehow figured out her plan?* She wondered. *Maybe starve her into submitting to whatever he had in mind next?* He had also not come for the video. That thought scared her more. *Could he not care to show them she still lived?* Bonnie's stomach growled as she checked the mini-fridge in her dungeon. She still had some milk and a little cheese to make sandwiches with.

She sighed as she turned on the television. Last night she figured out how to unblock the local stations. One news program mentioned her. She flipped to the news channel to see what they might be saying about her today. As she watched the conference and the people on the stage, her hand went to her mouth. She burst into tears. Throwing herself on the bed, she sobbed.

"Oh God! What'll I do?" Her shoulders shook. Tears streamed down her face as she wailed.

CHAPTER TWENTY-SIX

Jordan set the bag containing the mug on Urich's desk. She looked up and smiled. "You got a present for me?"

"You mentioned you got nothing on Belkey yet."

"Yeah. Besides his graduation and stuff from that preacher school, it's like the man just dropped in from nowhere. The school doesn't do background checks. Just take the application and the guy's tuition."

Urich pulled out the school's brochure. With the brochure in hand, she read aloud with sweeping gestures for emphasis. "After the student passes their rigorous curriculum, he is ordained. At this point, successful graduates may start a church, be a missionary, or just street preach under their banner."

Finished, she tossed the brochure aside before passing Jordan a copy of Belkey's school application form. "He listed some previous experience and education, but it was all bogus."

"That cup has his prints on it. Retrieved it from the Mission's office when I reported for duty this morning."

"Thought you got warned off there by that old partner of yours."

"Yeah, but since they got their guy, I figured I was clear to go back in."

"Resume your therapy?" Urich shook her head and chuckled. "I got the feeling you don't believe the handyman Bell or Christian, whatever name he travels under, is the right man."

"Well, until they're certain, I figure it can't hurt to keep lookin'. What the hell. Ain't the first time an investigation has pounced on some poor fool that ends up gettin' cleared later. Then the guy makes millions off their lawsuit and books."

Urich picked up the bag, then rose from her chair. "Let me take this over to the crime scene guys. See what they can come up with. You stayin' for coffee?"

Jordan held up a second grease-stained white paper bag. "You bet. Brought a bribe as well."

Urich chuckled. "Irene's?"

"None other."

"I swear Charmain is teachin' you the way to a woman's heart."

After returning, Urich plopped down behind her desk and dug in the bag. The aroma of bacon filled the air as Jordan, chewing on his biscuit, took a sip of coffee.

"I guess I was born to be a cop," Jordan announced, studying his half-eaten sandwich biscuit.

After pulling out a biscuit for herself, she unwrapped it. "Cause you gotta taste for greasy food and shitty coffee?"

"That's right, rookie. Pay attention to your mentor."

She held up her biscuit. "How you stay skinny eatin' like this."

"Must be my brain. They say of all your body parts it consumes the most calories."

Urich scoffed. "Musta been somethin' you read on the Internet."

Roy appeared at the desk. "You ready to get back to work?" As he said this, he dug into the white bag on the table. Discovering it empty, he scowled. "You know it wouldn't hurt for you to kiss up to the boss once in a while."

"Sorry, Roy. Thought you'd be at some important meetin'. Didn't believe you'd be hob-nobbin with the peasants."

Roy perched on Urich's desk. "Figured you'd be out partyin' with the Memphis and Tunica folks after their big bust."

"All they've got on him is circumstantial. They find the girl alive, she can ID him. Or if later he confesses. Right now, it's not a slam dunk. I'll celebrate when they find the girl."

Roy scooted off the desk as he walked away, he called over his shoulder. "Just don't be keepin' the workin' folks away from their duties too long."

Jordan grinned. "Nice to see you too, Roy."

Urich turned to Jordan. "Seriously. What are you gonna do?"

"Hang around the Mission. Do stuff with the girls I woulda done with Jennifer. Snoop around some more. Gonna take some of 'em fishin'. Load 'em up. Go down to that pond where the big ones are. Might need some help with that, though."

Urich stopped eating. Cocked her head to one side. "How so?"

"Well, me bein' a man and all, they kinda frown on males taken the girl's out without an adult female chaperon."

"Take Charmain."

"She's got other stuff she needs to do. You need a day off, anyway. Don't tell the cattle thieves, though, they might take liberties."

Urich leaned back in her chair. Chewed on her lip as if pondering the suggestion. Grinned. "What the hell. Why not? How ya gonna haul 'em?"

"Maybe load a few in my car. Plus, the missions got that nice van. Belkey could use the truck. Impound released it. Bert won't be needin' it."

*****

As Bonnie feared, no one came the night before bringing food. With her attack plan on hold, she now plotted her escape. She studied her dungeon searching for a weakness to exploit. Once up on the desk, she found she could reach the ceiling. After removing part of the suspended ceiling, she discovered the heating duct pipes. Their paths to the floor above appeared too small for her to climb through. Perhaps she could enlarge the openings. Then she could escape.

After pulling a section of duct pipe down, she tossed it to the floor. She wiggled the floor duct, found it fastened in place. Picturing the room above, she remembered it had what appeared to be a hardwood floor. She ran her fingers across the sub flooring. Between the current hole in the wall, the floor seemed loose. Removing the floor grate might free that section. This extra six inches might enable her to wiggle through to freedom. The trick would be removing the floor grate.

She hopped from the table then examined the metal ductwork pipe. One end of each section had a sharp serrated edge to fit into the next section. She climbed back on the table holding one section. Slamming the sharpened end against the wooden sub-floor shaved some splinters from the floor. The impact cut into her hand. It would take hours of pounding to cut through the wood. No way could she do this without cutting her palm.

She hopped down again. Snatched a bath towel from the shower area and climbed back on the table. Using the towel as a pad for her hand, she swung the pipe section again. A bigger splinter tore loose, and her hand did not hurt. Energized by her success, she worked away at the floor above, confident she had a workable plan.

*****

Bert sat with his lawyer in the interrogation room while FBI agent, Paul Rogers, read from the Federal indictment. Archer leaned against the wall behind the FBI man. At the same time, Collins, Charmain, and Maynard watched through the one-way mirror. Finished reading the indictment, Rogers looked up at Bert. "Bert Christian Bell. I am arresting you for interstate trafficking in child pornography. This is in addition to the charges related to the kidnap charges that are now pending."

Finished with the Miranda warning, Rogers acknowledged the attorney's presence with a nod. "Deputy Marshals will accompany you to your arraignment later this afternoon. After that, you will return to the custody of the local authorities. I understand they are also waiting for further indictments related to murder. Be advised, the Federal government will cooperate with any deal you make with these local authorities. Especially if they result in the safe return of the girl."

Bert leaned back, glanced at his attorney before turning back to the FBI man. "But I told them! Now I'm tellin' you! I don't know anything about this kidnapped girl! If they want to save her, tell 'em to hunt down the asshole that has her."

Rogers shrugged. "Tennessee is a death penalty state, sir. Even if she's found alive, you may be subject to that as it relates to other murders in the series. If you cooperate, the Federal Government will request postponing your execution until we adjudicate the Federal charges. Could add years to your life, sir. If not, we will step aside and let Tennessee run its process."

Bert opened his mouth to protest, but the attorney stopped him by placing his hand on his arm. "You're authorized to make this deal, Agent Rogers?"

"Yes, sir, I am."

"May I have a moment to talk with my client?"

Rogers glanced over his shoulder at Archer. Archer shrugged, shoved away from the wall, and Rogers trailed him out. They joined the others at the one-way mirror. Collins slipped on headphones while switching off the speaker.

Archer turned to Rogers. "It's a dirty trick, I know, but, we gotta pull out the stops to find this girl before she up and dies on us."

Rogers said nothing, merely gazed through the glass. Inside the next room, Bert buried his head in his hands as his lawyer talked.

*****

The gravel crunched under Jordan's feet as he trailed Hector into the bar.

"Man, I thought you'd be high as a kite with them catchin' your daughter's killer," the big man said as he dropped into the booth. Jordan slid into the opposite seat, then lit a cigarette.

"Like I said until they find the girl, I'm not signin' off on their case."

Their conversation ceased as the barmaid came for their order but resumed once she left.

Hector turned back to Jordan. "Well, it must satisfy the powers that be. They dropped their protection for Charmain."

"What?!"

"Yeah, pulled outta that apartment downstairs. I followed her all day and didn't see or smell 'em."

Jordan pulled out his cell phone. "I'm callin' Archer. This sucks."

As soon as he punched in the numbers, he spoke. As he talked, his face flushed. His voice raised in degrees to a shout. Patrons nearby turned in their direction. Hector scowled, and they all looked away as if slapped. The barmaid brought their milkshakes and straws.

Jordan cut off the call. "Shit! Archer says the case against Bell just became a slam dunk. This afternoon they discovered a locker he used at the Mission. Inside they found a jar with what looked to be a tongue preserved in something. They sent it off for analysis and are confident it will match with the DNA from one victim."

Hector scowled. "Yeah, but like I said, they pulled the security this morning."

"The Chief had been screamin' about the overtime, so they thought it wise to cut back a little early. They searched the houses the Mission occupies, but need to check the empty ones too."

"So, does that mean you're standin' down?"

Jordan bared his teeth. "Not till the girl's found. No!"

"So, I'm still backin' up Charmain?"

Jordan gazed into the big man's eyes. He'd asked a lot of him. At this moment, Jordan craved a drink. He wondered if this favor might also place Hector's sobriety in jeopardy. "You up to it?"

Hector shrugged. "Things are slow at the shop. Got no waitin' jobs right now. Yeah, for a while, but I want my rate doubled. Plus, you pay for the burgers tonight."

They raised their cups in a toast, then sipped from their straws as the barmaid set their burgers on the table.

*****

Bonnie's last blow with the pipe duct exposed the final screw securing the floor grate. After tossing the pipe section to the floor, she pushed up on the register. It popped loose. Once she dropped it next to the pipe, she grasped the floor section near the wall. Fastened by two nails it came out with no problem, leaving an eighteen by nine-inch hole. Remembering the Pythagorean, she turned sideways, knowing the opening would be broadest at the diagonal. Her head passed through the opening, but not her shoulders.

"For once in your life girl be happy you don't have big boobs," she chuckled to herself. "I can squeeze them and my butt through the hole, but these damn shoulder bones don't bend." She estimated that maybe two more inches at one corner might be enough.

Her stomach growled from hunger. Her arms ached from the chopping. She sighed, needed a break, and hopped down from the table. She yawned as she took a soda and a cheese packet from the fridge. Seated on the bed, she admired her work. Her arms stiff from the day's works. Her right hand which had done most of the work looked red and swollen. Also, it felt sore. The towel provided some cushion, but still, she feared a blister might form. Switching to the left might slow her down, but would allow her to continue working, giving the right a rest. From the mini-fridge, she retrieved an ice cube from its freezer. She held it now in her right hand as she elevated it in hopes to prevent swelling. Her Mom had taught her basic first aid. As she recalled her and her father, a tear formed in her eye.

"Don't worry Mom. I'll be a Warrior princess like you."

As she leaned back on the bed, exhaustion swept over her in waves. As if they weighed a ton her eyelids drooped closed. She drifted off to sleep.

CHAPTER TWENTY-SEVEN

Jordan, Urich, and Belkey stood next to the van in the Shining Light parking lot. Belkey extended his hand to Urich. "Deputy, I'm pleased to see you again. The girl's need to spend time around powerful women. Show them that a woman can do many things. Not just be objects of exploitation."

Urich smiled as she took the Reverend's hand. "Maybe I should round 'em up and give 'em some boxin' lessons. They might enjoy kickin' the crap outta some guy in the ring."

Belkey took her hand in both of his and chuckled. "That might be a bit much. But I will consider it. Perhaps discuss it with my home managers. See what they think."

"Well, let me give that some thought myself, Reverend. I might come up with other stuff and find other women who might enjoy workin' work with the girls. Kinda like a Big Sisters thing."

Belkey's eyes lit up, and he smiled. "Oh, that would be wonderful."

"So, you've got no problem with us takin' the girls out on a fishing trip?" Jordan interrupted.

Belkey turned to Jordan. "No! Dee told me last night after I got back from the press conference. I called the homes, and here's a list of the girls who want to go and where they live." He passed the sheet to Jordan. Jordan studied the list as Urich loaded fishing gear from Jordan's car into the Mission Van.

A horn honked, announcing Charmain's arrival. She emerged from her car with a smile and a wave. As Jordan approached her, she rushed to embrace him.

Hand in hand, they joined Belkey and Urich. "Remember, I promised to help get you some positive publicity goin' for you and the Mission?" Charmain squeezed Jordan's arm. "Well, Bob told me what you all had planned today, so I thought I'd start right now."

Belkey stepped back. His jaw dropped. The color drained from his face as he glanced from Jordan to Charmain and back again. "Uh, Uh," he ran his hands across the red fuzz that now covered his skull, "What? Uh.... how?"

Charmain squeezed Jordan's hand while gazing up into his eyes. "Well, I called Catchem Lake over by Shelby Farms. They agreed to let the girls in. No charge. Supply them all with bait and tackle, like poles and lines and stuff. Coupla the local TV stations will film there. Plus, the Commercial Appeal is sending a reporter and photographer."

Belkey frowned, glanced back at Jordan. "Does that work for you and Miss Urich?"

Jordan snorted with a half-laugh. "If it doesn't, I'll catch hell later."

Urich scowled as she placed her hands on her hips. She spun around to Charmain as she spoke, she shook her finger beneath Charmain's nose as if scolding her. "My God! How could you? All these cameras and me lookin' like this?" She tossed her hands in the air.

Charmain's laughter pealed as she placed her hand on Urich's shoulder. "Relax, girlfriend. I called Paulo. He and Maureen packed up some makeup and clothes for you. And as we speak, he and Steven are rushing down here to join you. Give 'em about a half-hour. They should be here!"

Urich clapped before hugging Charmain. "Like I said, this girl is way too good for you!"

*****

Not a cloud appeared in the sky above. The sky's blue reflected on the water. A breeze whispering across the pond made ripples while keeping the heat at bay. Surrounded by cameramen, Jordan, Urich, and the three girls fished. Nearby, a reporter interviewed Charmain and Belkey. A TV camera stood by while Urich helped a blond girl bait her hook. The girl pulled a wiggling nightcrawler from the bait container. While holding it up, her lip curled. "Ew! They look so slimy, but they feel weird."

Urich chuckled as she showed with her hook how to attach it. The girl brushed the hair back from her face. Grasping the hook, she threaded the worm onto the hook while Urich instructed. "Try to get as much of it on the hook as you can. Let part of one end dangle a bit, so the fish will nibble on it like a noodle, then start gobbling it to the hook. That'll catch 'em."

Finished, the girl cast her line. Seated on the bank, she watched her bobber on the surface as she wiped her hands on her pants. Soon all three girls, Jordan, and Urich had cast their lines and seated themselves on the bank. One girl's bobber dipped below the surface.

"Pull back on your pole!" Jordan shouted as he set his down. He rushed to her side. The girl's reel squealed as the line played out. The girl tried to crank it back in.

While standing behind her, Jordan put his hands on her shoulders, "No, wait. Let him run with it a bit. When you feel him relax, reel him in. If he runs again, let him."

The line quit running out, and the girl cranked it. The water around the line boiled as a whiskered head appeared. With the hook set in his jaw, the fish shook its head from side to side before plunging below the surface. Again, the reel squealed as the fish swam away. The girl let it.

"That's right. You got him now."

The girl's tongue appeared at the corner of her mouth. She brushed the hair back from her face. A grin crept over her face as the fish now swam back towards her. The girl cranked in the line as fast as she could. As Jordan snatched up the landing net, the girl's pole bowed as the fish swam along the bank. Instead of playing out more line, the girl scampered along the bank, keeping pace with the fish. When it paused, the girl yanked on the pole, tossing the fish on the shore. Once he stepped around the girl, Jordan scooped it up with the net. After trapping the fish behind the gills, he removed it from the net, popped the hook from its mouth, and held it out to the girl. Wide-eyed, grinning, she dropped her pole and glanced from fish to Jordan, while the others cheered.

She wrinkled her nose but grinned. "Oh, my God! It's so ugly!" She squealed.

"Here, hold it like this. Careful of the head and the fins."

The girl's eyes opened wide as she slipped her fingers around the fish as instructed. As Jordan let go, the girl's arm dipped as she took the weight.

"He weighs a ton!" She giggled.

Jordan stepped back, took out his phone, and snapped a picture. He put his arm around the girl's shoulder. "Atta girl. That's the other thing to bein' a Master fisherman. Ya have to learn how to exaggerate the size and weight!"

With the TV cameras rolling, she brushed her hair back while the fish thrashed at the end of her arm.

*****

The press vanished as soon as each girl caught a fish. Jordan broke out sandwiches from a basket while Charmain passed out soda and chips. Belkey stood to the side, pacing. A bag over his shoulder, he stole glances at Charmain and Jordan. Charmain joined Urich on a bench nearby. Jordan approached Belkey, offered him a sandwich. Belkey shook his head.

Belkey gave a dismissive wave. "No thanks. My stomach's a little off right now."

"How about a pop then? Might need to re-hydrate."

Belkey sighed. "Sure, sure, okay."

Jordan strolled to the cooler and returned with a soda.

As Charmain studied the two men, Urich turned to her. "What's with the Reverend? Since the last time I saw him, he looks like he's aged about ten years."

"This whole thing put us all through the wringer. Especially him, after that taunting game, the killer did with him. Now to find out he had the man working for him?"

Urich leaned close to Charmain. "Carryin' a torch for you isn't helpin' much either."

"Is it that obvious?"

"You haven't noticed the looks he's been givin' you and Bob? 'Specially when you two are pawin' at each other."

"Tsk. We don't paw each other."

"Humph!" Urich shook her head and cackled.

Jordan checked his watch. "Okay gang. Time to wrap this up. Promised Estelle, we'd have you back by two o'clock. If we leave now, we'll make it."

One girl groaned.

"Aw, do we hafta?" another whined.

"Estelle let us play hooky from school. I'm sure she'll have makeup work waitin'," the third reminded her cohorts.

After loading up the van, Jordan pulled Charmain aside. He held her against him as his hands roamed down her back. "That was somethin' special girl. Arrangin' the press and the lake here. How about I take you to dinner tonight?"

She grinned. "I'm sure Glenn and Tony would love to see you." Rubbing herself against him, she arched her eyebrows. "My place after?"

A grin swept across Jordan's face. "I was countin' on it."

She gave him a peck on the cheek, then smiled back at him as she joined Belkey at her car.

"There's one other thing I'd like you to see," Belkey announced.

"What's that?" Charmain asked as she opened the car door.

"It's where we're gonna open a clinic. Offer medical, dental, and counseling for free to the girls from the streets-walk-in thing. I have some folks ready to volunteer there. I'd like to show it to you. Get your ideas on how to get the word out and such."

"Where is it?"

Belkey stared off as if in thought. "I'm not much good at giving directions. How about I drive? That way, if you want, we can talk, and you can take notes on the way."

She handed him the keys. As they pulled out of the parking lot heading West on Walnut Grove, neither noticed the huge man trailing them on the motorcycle.

*****

After exiting the freeway at Getwell, Belkey and Charmain headed south. As if lost in thought, Belkey said little as he drove. Only answered questions Charmain raised about the clinic. Stopped at a traffic light, he broke the silence. "I didn't realize that you had a relationship with Detective Jordan."

She chuckled. "It's more than that."

"How does that work then with Archer?"

"Archer?"

"Yes, your relationship with him. He is married."

Charmain's brow furrowed. Her head snapped around to Belkey. "Wait. What? Archer and me? Jack and I are merely friends. I met him through Bob. They were partners at Memphis. What made you think Archer and me...?"

A shiver ran up her spine. She fell silent. Remembered the taunts from the killer about her and Archer. No one knew about that outside of the team. Belkey had not been part of the group then.

Her head snapped around to him. "It was you?"

His lips drew back, baring his teeth. "You all really thought it could have been Bert?"

She reached for the door latch. Open the door, step out, escape, she chided herself. She clutched the door handle. With the car moving, it refused to budge. The image of the man in the parking lot leaped into her mind. The business card for Richard Nixon. She opened her mouth to scream. Instead, her body jolted as he hit her with the Taser, stifling sound and paralyzing in the same instant. After pulling to the roadside, he drove the syringe from his bag into her thigh, before injecting the contents.

As she drifted off, he roared. "Knew it the first time I saw you. I followed Archer to a restaurant. He met you. Saw you together. The look in your eyes. The brief peck on the cheek. Cuddling at the table. I thought you might be different. That I could persuade you to get out of that sinful relationship. Restore your virtue, Black Beauty. But no! You're a whore, like the rest!"

*****

Close behind Charmain's car, Hector peered through his goggles at the vehicle ahead. The man drove while Charmain leaned against the passenger window, talking. As they left the freeway, traffic thinned. No longer able to keep a car between them, Hector dropped back a few yards, hoping to stay unnoticed.

Ahead, Charmain lurched back in the seat as the car slowed and pulled to the roadside. Hector did the same while monitoring the car's passengers. The man moved close to Charmain. She slumped against the passenger door. Through the car's open window, he heard the man shout. Worried, Hector killed the engine, then dropped the kickstand. As he dismounted to rush to the car, it sped away.

As the car disappeared ahead, Hector leaped on the kick starter. The engine failed to fire. "Shit, you big dumb ass!" he cursed. "It might help to keep your fuckin' thumb off the kill switch." He jumped on the kick starter again. Again, the engine refused to start.

"Fuck! It's flooded!" he roared as he twisted the throttle open before leap on the kick starter again. After sputtering, the engine roared to life. Sweeping up the kickstand with his foot, he revved the engine as he released the clutch. The bike's wide rear tire screamed and smoked as he peeled off in pursuit. As if fired from a cannon, he caught the car as it traveled at the speed limit.

He now loomed on the car's back bumper. With Charmain's head resting on his shoulder, the driver glared at him from the rearview mirror. Hector swerved, gunned the engine. Pulled up next to the open driver's window.

"What's wrong? Where you takin' her, man?" Hector shouted.

The driver said nothing, bared his teeth as if snarling.

"You goin' to the hospital or what?"

The driver swerved towards Hector. As Hector wove to avoid, he braked before slipping behind Charmain's car. Once in trail, he opened the throttle to remain behind. The vehicle ahead screeched to a halt as Belkey stood on the brakes. Hector's bike slammed into it, flipping him onto the car's trunk. As the car sped away again, Hector bounced off, landing face down on the concrete.

After rising to his hands and knees, he crawled to his bike. The front forks bent back against the frame. The front-wheel now an oval. Blood dripped in his eyes as the world spun around him. He unzipped the tank bag and grabbed his cell phone. With the phone clutched in his hand, he crawled away from the growing gasoline puddle to the curb. His hands trembled as he punched in Jordan's number.

CHAPTER TWENTY-EIGHT

Jordan and Urich transferred the fishing gear from the van into Jordan's car.

"Man, what a day. Eh?" Jordan pronounced as he closed the trunk.

Urich grinned and shook her head. "Those girls all took a shine to you. I hope you realize that."

Jordan chuckled. "Yeah. That's the best I've felt in a long time."

"Seriously, though. I'm gonna do some time with these girls myself. The Reverend was right. They need to be around powerful women."

"You know some?"

Urich flipped him the bird. When Jordan's phone chirped, he retrieved it from his jacket pocket and answered. "Hector, my man. Wassup?"

As he listened, Jordan's jaw dropped. The color drained from his face. "He did what?! Shit. Yeah, I got the tracker. Listen, call 911. Fill 'em in on what's happenin'. You got the plate number? Good, cause I sure as hell don't know it, just the make and model. I got Urich here, and we'll get on it right now."

As he ended the call, he turned to Urich. "Get in the car now! The tracker monitor is under the seat. Get it fired up."

Jordan leaped into the car, Urich followed. As he started the car, both fastened their seat belts.

"Jordan! What's goin' on?"

"Just get the tracker started. I'll explain on the way!"

Dust flew in the Mission parking lot as Jordan spun the car around to face the entrance. The tires squealed as they blasted into the street. An approaching vehicle swerved, grazed a lamp post.

"Hector thinks Belkey kidnapped Charmain. Says she's passed out. When he offered to help, Belkey rammed his bike. He told me he's somewhere in Hickory Hill. I'll head there while you find her car on the tracker."

*****

The biker unnerved him. He came out of nowhere. Shouting. Offering help. Maybe a carjacker. He had shown him. Outwitted the big scum. Taught him a lesson at the same time. He hoped he broke the man's neck. He glanced at the unconscious woman beside him. Her chest rising and falling suggested she lived. Had not overdosed on the injection. He ran his fingers over her firm thighs. He wanted to do more. Soon he would.

He pulled into the driveway, then parked behind the house. Hidden from the road, but leaving the path open for his escape.

Unsure when Police search would discover this property, he hoped they started with the abandoned ones first. Delores gave them the list of those. It did not include this one. He told her not to bother, he would check it himself right away. Convinced her, this might spare the house from the damage a search might bring. Said If he found the girl, then everything would be great. He must act now.

"Why did I keep the girl? Taunt the police. Play this game with them?" He asked himself. "Now she's like a treasure. I want to keep her." He glanced at Charmain, slumped in the passenger seat as he exited the car. "But now this one. This whore. He must get her out of his system. End the obsession. After that, he would take the girl. Go somewhere else. Start over again. Who knows? If he could persuade the girl to help, they could be real partners. Yes. That would be ideal."

While he fumbled for the keys in his pocket, a hammering sound came from inside. He undid the padlock and tossed the lock bar to the ground. As he stepped inside, the noise ceased. Turning on the lights, he ignored it. He chuckled. Figured the girl might be up to some mischief in the basement. It had been almost two days since his last visit. Thought a brief break would do them both good. Besides, she would not starve. Hunger might even improve her mood.

After returning to the car, he carried Charmain cradled in his arms. After laying her on the bed, he studied her body.

"Ooh, just like Christmas," he crooned as he tossed her shoes into a corner. She groaned as he fumbled with the blouse buttons. As he lifted her to remove the blouse, she raised a hand. Swatted at his face. "No," she protested. Her voice weak, no louder than a whisper. Once he unhooked her bra, he jerked it away, exposing her breasts.

"Stop. No. Why are you doing this?" Her eyes blinking.

As he unfastened her slacks, she kicked—no energy, like a brush against his shoulder as he pulled the pants off her legs.

"I need to hold you still till I finish the rest." He tied a restraint around each of her limbs, then rushed to secure the leather restraints to the four bedposts.

"I do so want to feel that luxurious skin, but first I have to make sure you don't run away. There now that's done, I'll lock the door, so we're not disturbed."

*****

As soon as she heard the lock, Bonnie stopped her work. Setting the duct on the floor, she flipped off the light switch and hoped no light escaped from the hole she had gouged in the floor. After hearing his voice upstairs, she slipped the pencil into the jean's waistband, climbed back on the table then poked her head through the opening. From her vantage point in the living room she could see the entire house. She watched as he carried a black woman to the bed. After he placed the woman on the bed, he turned in her direction. Bonnie ducked down out of sight.

His voice carried from above. As he talked, Bonnie felt chills race up and down her spine. *What could this sick fuck be doing now?* She wondered. *Would he be replacing her with his new captive?* Curious she peered over the edge.

Bonnie recognized the black woman who now lay spread-eagled on the bed, naked. The woman from the press conference. The one who appealed for Bonnie's safe return. Her captor loomed over her licking his lips crooning. So, soft Bonnie could not hear.

*****

Jordan ignored the speed limit as he wove through traffic. Urich studied the tracker's screen. "Did Hector honestly say Belkey kidnapped her?" She asked.

"That's what he claimed. Said she looked unconscious."

"What do you suppose is goin' on?" Urich's eye glued to the tracker's screen.

"Maybe Char got sick, and he's rushin' her to an emergency room?" Jordan replied as if reassuring himself.

Urich shrugged before replying. "But you said Hector tried to stop 'em, Belkey rammed his bike and drove off."

"Yeah! But you know Hector looks kinda scary. Belkey doesn't know him. Also, Char said Belkey's under a lot of stress. Who knows? Then confronted by Hector? Coulda spooked him. That could explain things. Whatever it is, that thing will tell us where he stops. If it is a hospital, then we don't have to worry."

As Jordan blasted through a red light, a car swerved to miss them and collided with another. Cars skidded to a halt at the intersection.

Cars ahead stopped, trapped them in the right-hand lane and ahead. Jordan flashed his badge out the driver's window and leaned on the horn. The surrounding cars shifted, clearing an opening. Jordan blasted through the intersection, narrowly missing a vehicle passing through.

Urich gasped. "He stopped. It's not a hospital."

Jordan glanced at Urich, then back at the road. "Where?"

"It's in a residential area," Urich worked the keyboard on the laptop. She read the address aloud.

"I've been there. It's a house."

Images of the building surged Jordan's mind. The strange table. The exercise equipment purchase, linked to the missing girl. He recalled the noise he heard on his last visit. Could it have been the girl? Imprisoned in that house? But why take Charmain there?

I'm gettin' a bad feeling about this. You carryin'?" Jordan asked Urich.

"On a fishing outing with a bunch of teenage girls?"

"I think we should call in back-up."

"With the way you're drivin', I'm surprised we aren't leading a convoy of patrol cars already."

"Like they say. There's never a cop when you need one."

*****

As Charmain's eyes opened, the overhead light made her blink. She groaned while trying to roll over, but she remained pinned beneath the light despite her efforts. Her body ached all over.

As she turned her head to avoid the light streaming down from above, a form emerged from the darkness. As she opened her mouth to scream, the shadow covered her mouth with tape. Her words, now muffled. Squinting as her eyes adjusted to the light, Belkey's face hovered over her.

Naked beside the bed, he rubbed his penis and grinned. "Finally awake now? Good! I've got plans for you, Black Beauty. You disappointed me. You see, I knew I could eventually get you away from Archer. Make you realize that being with him was wrong. Save your soul. Once cleansed, you would want me. But no! You're already cheating on Archer. Or are you a three-some? Is that it? Well, slut, now I'm gonna give you what you deserve."

He took out another syringe. Squirted a stream from the needle, then leered. "This is a little something to enhance the experience. They call it Special K."

After injecting her in the thigh again, he climbed on the bed. Ran his hands up between her legs, forcing them further apart. She sobbed and struggled as he drove a finger inside her. Still leering into her eyes, he licked her nipples. "See! I can tell you're enjoying it already."

She screamed against the tape, covering her mouth. Tears ran down her cheeks as she shook her head from side to side.

*****

Jordan leaped from the car as soon as it stopped forgetting about his cast. "Damn!" His knee buckled. He staggered, almost falling as pain roared up his leg. After regaining his balance, he hobbled to the door as Urich called for backup on her cell.

Finished with the call, Urich rushed to his side. "Back off. Let me lead. You've got the bum leg."

"Her car's right here by the back door, he has to have her inside." Jordan scooped up the locking bar lying on the ground as Urich turned the door handle.

"It's locked!" She yelled.

She stepped back as Jordan slammed the metal bar into the door. Like a battering ram, he struck it once, then again near the lock. The blows echoed, and the lock cracked, but the door held fast. Once more, Jordan attacked the door, throwing all his weight against it. He drove the bar against it again and again until the door frame cracked. The next blow splintered it. As the door flew open, Urich lunged through.

Poised inside, clutching the Taser, Belkey hit her with a glancing blow. Still, the jolt brought Urich to her knees. Hobbling behind her, Jordan punched Belkey full in the face. His nose cracked, then he dropped to his hands and knees. Still clutching the locking bar,

Jordan raised it high over his head like a club. He brought it down across Belkey's back, driving the man flat on his face.

Urich moaned as she raised to her knees. Upright, she staggered, clutching a counter-top for balance. Jordan hobbled to the bedroom, where Charmain remained restrained on the bed. Frantic, he ripped the tape from her mouth before working on the restraints.

Belkey slowly rose to his feet, clutching the locking bar, he entered the bedroom. He brought it to his shoulder like a batter waiting at the plate for a pitch.

"Jordan behind you," Urich warned as she let go of the counter. While staggering, she approached Belkey from behind. Belkey swung the bar, striking Jordan's cast.

As Jordan untied one arm, a blinding pain in his broken leg dropped him to the floor. Charmain screamed as Belkey raised the locking bar again over his head, preparing to split Jordan's skull. Urich drove her fist into Belkey's kidneys. He yelped and dropped the bar. Taking advantage of the stun and her momentum, Urich clamped Belkey in a chokehold. His eyes bugged out as he clutched the arm around his throat. Buckling his knees, he forced Urich to support his weight. As she stooped with the burden, he kicked with his feet driving his head into her chin. As Urich collapsed unconscious, Bonnie emerged from her hiding place in the floor. With a banshee's scream, she charged. The sharpened pencil held high over her head. Before Belkey could ward off this fresh attack, she drove the pencil into his eye. He howled as it passed through the socket and into his brain. Bonnie's howl changed to a lion's roar, as Belkey collapsed to the floor.

Bonnie rushed to Charmain. With tears streaming down her cheeks, she helped Charmain remove her restraints. "I'm sorry he did this to you. You've been working so hard to help me, and this monster did this to you." Bonnie wept and held Charmain close.

Charmain stroked the girl's head. Drew back from the embrace. "How did you know?"

"There's a TV down there. I watched it all. I couldn't believe he sat right there next to you at the press conference. Looked all so innocent. What a creep!"

"Well, you're safe now," Charmain nodded towards Urich and Jordan, "They saved us both."

Jordan crawled to the bed, clutching Charmain's clothes. After pulling himself into a sitting position, he squeezed Charmain's hand. He passed the clothes up to Charmain.

As she dressed, Jordan scanned the room. "Would you believe it? Came here one night to check the place out. I was that close."

He glanced at Urich's still body. Recalled the head injury that ended her boxing career.

"Shit, he knocked Urich cold. I hope she's okay. I can't tell if she's breathin' from here."

Bonnie rose from the bed, scurried to Urich's side, crouched to put her face close to Urich. "She's breathin'."

"Good when the paramedics get here, we'll let 'em know. They'll get on it right away."

"Paramedics?" Charmain asked.

"Yeah, Urich called for backup before we came in the door. Seems like they're a long time comin' though."

Bleary-eyed from the drugging, Charmain stared around the room. Confused, she turned to Bonnie. "Listen, Bonnie, where d'you come from?"

Bonnie pointed to the hole near the far wall. "He kept me down in the basement."

Just then, Belkey's hand clenched. His arm moved, then he groaned as he struggled to rise.

"Bob! He's still alive!" Charmain shrieked.

Jordon pulled himself up on the bed. Moved as close to Belkey's prone form as he could. "Hand me the bar!"

Bonnie rushed it to Jordan. He hefted it like a cudgel preparing to strike.

"Charmain, you and the girl get Urich out. I'll try to slow him down."

Unsteady on her feet, Charmain led Bonnie to Urich's side. After rolling her over, they grasped her under the shoulders.

As he rose to his hands and knees, Belkey looked up. The pencil protruded from his eye socket. Blood poured down his cheek. He snarled, then pounced on Jordan before he could swing the bar. The bar slipped from Jordan's hands as Belkey landed on him. Astride his chest, Belkey's hand's clamped Jordan's throat. Jordan grasped Belkey's hands. Unable to pry them loose, he slammed his palm into the pencil, driving it deeper into Belkey's skull. As Belkey drew back from the punch, Jordan grabbed the pencil. As Belkey shuddered, Jordan jerked the pencil back and forth inside the man's skull, until Belkey went limp. Jordan shoved the man off, then rolled off the bed to the floor.

"Now get her out of here. I'm right behind you," Jordon shouted as he crawled toward the door, dragging the locking bar behind him. After moving Urich outside, both rushed back to grab Jordan. Bonnie screamed as Belkey rose from the floor. Jordan glanced back, then motioned the two women away. Crawling faster, he rolled out the door. He handed the locking bar to Bonnie. "Pull the door shut and put this in the metal straps!" The women followed his instructions. As the lock bar slipped in place, a loud bang followed by a howl came from behind the door.

CHAPTER TWENTY-NINE

Five patrol cars responded to the scene of Hector's crash. After seeing his injuries, they summoned the paramedics. Now Hector sat on the ambulance's back step while three officers stood on the roadside talking. The other two officers directed traffic around the downed motorcycle.

A short black officer nodded in Hector's direction. "What you make of this dude's story, Sarge."

The tall black Sergeant, his shaved head gleaming with sweat in the sun, scoffed. "Guy's got a sheet a mile long for drugs. I'm feelin' drug rip-off gone bad."

"You ain't buyin' his story?" the third inquired.

The Sergeant glanced in Hector's direction. "You mean he was tryin' to stop some dude from abductin' a woman? Claimed it's the reporter been on TV with the missing girl thing?"

"Yeah. I mean, it's pretty left field. Why concoct some weird story like that? All he needed to say is some asshole hit his bike and ran."

"Probably figured he'd get us to chase the dude down. Then we'd sweat the shit out of him."

"God Damn it I'm fine!" Hector growled at the paramedic, cleaning the cut on his forehead. The officers formed a circle around Hector and the paramedic.

"Sir, you really should go to the ER. Have the Docs there check you out. Make sure you're okay." the paramedic pleaded as he fumbled in a bag for a bandage.

Hector turned to the nearest officer. "Are you dudes gonna follow up, or is it donut time?!"

"Sit tight, asshole," the Sergeant snarled. "We've called in the info you gave us. Any unit spots 'em, they'll stop 'em."

Hector stood. Shoved the paramedic aside then marched to the Sergeant holding out his cell phone. "Here, I called him. He's Detective Bob Jordan, Jergen County Sheriff's Department. He's already pursuin' the asshole and might need backup. Unless you're too busy."

The Sergeant sighed as he took the phone from Hector and held it to his ear. He said nothing as he listened. He scowled before tossing it to Hector. "No answer. Went straight to voice mail. Relax fellah. The wrecker'll be along any time now. Let the paramedics take you to the hospital. After they check you out, you can call your mommy to pick you up."

"Eagle 57, this is dispatch. Plates come back registered to a Charmain Crump," The Sergeants portable announced. The three policemen now exchanged wide-eyed glances. Before they could say anything, a second call came in on all the officer's radios. "Be advised. Officer in need of assistance. Possible abduction and assault. Request back up. See Detective Jordan, Jergen County Sheriff at the scene." The dispatcher called out the address.

The Sergeant grabbed the microphone on his portable. "Units 15, 18, and 21 responding."

He clipped the microphone back to his belt. He cupped his hands to his mouth and shouted to the officers directing traffic. "Forney! Carpenter! You guys keep things under control here. We're takin' this call."

One paused in directing cars around the wrecked motorcycle. Gave the Sergeant a salute, then returned to his chores. The other two officers trotted to their vehicles, with Hector limping behind. Hector opened the passenger door of one car as the officer leaped into the driver's seat. Wide-eyed, he turned to Hector, his jaw dropped. "Where're you goin'?"

"You girls might need backup," Hector growled as he jumped in next to the officer. The officer shrugged, started the siren, then pulled out into traffic.

*****

Howling with rage, he turned from the door.

"When I get out of here, I'll kill you all!" He snarled.

He searched for something to batter the door down. The only way out of his perfect prison. He built it himself but intended it for others. This should not be happening. Where had he gone wrong? He asked himself. He set it up so well. Now how to escape. The weight bar rested on the bench stand. If he removed the weights, he could use the bar as a battering ram.

He staggered to the weight bench. He felt no pain, just off-balance—his left arm, limp at his side. Must be the pencil they rammed in my eye, he said to himself. He touched the fingers of his right hand to his face, now soaked in blood from the wound. Measured the length of the pencil, still protruding from the eye socket. It must have gone into his brain.

Shit! He thought he could not break the door down with one arm. Trapped, his quest for revenge now at an end. Prison would come. Next, he would never be free. He looked down at his useless left arm, barely able to walk. If so, what then? Would the damage to his brain progress? He asked himself. Would he end up a vegetable, helpless again like he had been as a boy? He recalled his taunts to the police. The mocking cry from the story his mother read to him.

"Run, run, run, as fast as you can, but you won't catch me. I'm the Gingerbread man."

That will not happen, he said to himself.

With his right hand on the weight bar, he pushed himself upright. Like a drunk, he wobbled, then staggered to the closet. Inside, the kerosene can he used for the garage heater. He shook the handle with his right hand. The sloshing inside told him it was near full.

After unscrewing the cap, he tipped it on its side. The flammable liquid spread at his feet.

He staggered back to the kitchen counter. From a drawer, he retrieved a box of matches. After lighting one, he dropped it into the open matchbox. As the remaining flared, he tossed the box into the kerosene pool. Flames spread across the floor.

As the fire roared at his feet, every nerve in his body screamed, as he did. Through the pain, her face flashed before his eyes. Hands and feet bound, his knife at her throat. Her mouth on his penis. The laughter after he ejaculated. "Next time, I'll bite it off, little brother."

He had killed her then. Tossed the knife aside, before grabbing her throat. Watched the light leave her eyes as she fought for air. "I'm about to join you bitch!" he snarled as he inhaled the flames licking around him.

*****

Jordan leaned back against his car studying his shattered cast. Urich lay in the grass at his side still unconscious. Charmain and Bonnie held each other. All stared back at the house as Belkey screamed and roared. He pounded on the doors. Smoke seeped from under the shingles on one side of the house.

Charmain clutched Bonnie to her. "Oh My God Bob! The house is on fire!" The young girl stared back at the house. All turned their heads as the sound of sirens approached.

"Hope they're comin' here," Jordan said as he looked back at the house. A tongue of flame escaped from under an eave. It grew larger as it licked up the shingles making them sag. A piercing scream came from inside the building as the first police car screeched to a halt in the street. Followed by two more. Jordan glanced at the cars and chuckled as Hector emerged from the first. "Looks like the Cavalry's arrived."

*****

As Jordan rolled the wheelchair into the hospital room, Bonnie sat up in her bed. Both she and Charmain, sitting at her bedside, grinned. "This a private hen party, or can an old rooster join in?"

Charmain rushed to his side and hugged him. "I don't think either of us chicks mind seein' you come through the door."

Bonnie, her hair tied back in a ponytail, nodded.

Charmain stepped back. Her eyes open wide. "What's with the wheelchair?"

"Even with the new cast, they told me not to put any weight on it for a day or so. Make sure any micro-fractures and the recent break start healin'."

Charmain chuckled. "I'd be happy to push you around for a few days."

Jordan nodded at Bonnie. "What about you, youngster? You okay?"

"I guess so. They wanna keep me awhile, though, make sure I'm okay."

After Archer, Collins, and Dr. Maynard entered, Archer came to Jordan's side. He tapped Jordan's shoulder with his fist. Shook his head. "You doin' okay?"

Jordan nodded.

"How about you and I go burn one on the dock? I'll take your statement, and these guys can interview Charmain and the girl?"

Jordan glanced over at Charmain. She nodded. After exiting, they rode the elevator down to the dock. Once both lit up, Archer sighed.

Jordan shook his head. "Listen. I didn't mean to walk in on this case, it just shook out that way."

Archer scoffed. "You off your patch, cowboy. You pretendin' to be the Lone Ranger or somethin?"

"If you guys are here to start some grand inquisition, I'm not talkin' till I get my lawyer and union rep."

"Relax man. Just bustin' your chops. But you're right. The shit's startin' to hit the fan. It's great we rescued these two beauties and took a wicked fucker off the table. The press is gonna love that, but the bureaucrats are gonna be on this like flies on a turd."

Jordan's phone chirping interrupted their conversation while he answered it. "Hey, Roy. I'm not sure. I was gonna check on her when I get done givin' my statement. She was still out cold when they took her away. Yeah, I'm sorry. I'm supposed to be on light duty. Shoulda talked to you about it, but..." Jordan paused. Ran his hand through his hair. "Well, I figured that takin' those girls out on an outing would be good PR for the department. You saw the news, didn't you? Well, maybe it'll air again. The other thing got a big splash. That should look good for you too! Well, I had no idea that the outing would lead to that. Memphis already claimed they had the guy."

Jordan's jaw clenched as he listened. "The tracker? Tell George it's at my place. I'll bring it in as soon as I get back in town, okay. Yeah, I shoulda checked it out, but I just wanted to mess around with it a bit. Learn all the features. Figured I'd do an in-service on it for the rest of the folks. Yes, I shoulda told you. I forgot. Thought you'd be glad. Anything else?"

He paused as he listened. "I'll tell her. Yeah, I expected nothing on it, just thought it would be good practice. Learn how to lift a print. I know it costs money. But next time, she'll know exactly how to do it, and it might lead to a conviction. Okay. Talk to you later."

Archer chuckled as Jordan put down his phone. "Your boss sounds pissed."

Jordan shrugged. "He's a politician. Plus, he's got a lot of things to worry about besides maintainin' Law and Order in the County. He's a good head, though. He'll come around."

Archer reached in his pocket. He handed a small square object no bigger than a flash drive to Jordan. "Techs found this attached to the pickup. Said it's a sender allowing the vehicle to be tracked. Heard you mention somethin' about one to your boss. Nobody knows who it belongs to or why it was stuck to the truck. You musta been usin' this for practice, like you told your boss, right? Has nothin' to do with the investigation so you can take it." Archer winked.

Jordan took the tracker from Archer. After he placed it in his pocket, he looked at Archer. "Thanks, man."

"Don't blame you for huntin' him yourself. I loved your daughter Jennifer too. If I nabbed him, he mighta had a fatal accident or resisted arrest. Saved me the temptation. Like I said, the shit is already startin' to hit the fan. Why ruin a good bust. He's dead, you know. Torched himself and the place."

"What the hell? I didn't know. They had us outta there before they went inside. Killed himself?"

Archer shrugged. "Doc says that's common with serials. That's why they've learned so little about 'em. Sick fuck! If it's any consolation, the media will make you and Urich look like big heroes. Just remember us little people in your rise to the top. Now let's get your statement."

*****

Archer and Jordan returned to Bonnie's room. Since both still gave statements, Jordan parted with Archer. He rolled down the hall to Urich's room. Inside, she sat up in bed, awake. Paulo, Maureen, Steven, and Joshua gathered around her, gazing at the television.

Jordan leaned close to her and whispered. "What did the Docs say?"

"I was lucky. A little brain swelling, but they didn't think it did more damage. The neurologist gave me hell. Told me I should wear a helmet all the time. Just in case." She shrugged. "I should get out tomorrow, but told me to take it easy for a week."

Jordan shook his head. "You mean, wear the Kevlar?"

Urich nodded.

"How we gonna do stakeouts or work undercover with you always lookin' like you're preparin' to invade Poland?"

Urich chuckled. "I'm sure there's a happy medium somewhere. Oh, shit, there he is!" She pointed at the TV as Hector's image appeared on the screen.

With his head wrapped in bandages, the big man stooped as he spoke into the short reporter's microphone. "Yeah, I was followin' this car. Recognized that reporter who used to be on Fox News. The Dude she was ridin' with did somethin' to knock her out. Yellin' crazy (BLEEP). I tried to stop him, but he ran me off the road. Probably totaled my bike. He took off then like a bat out a (BLEEP), and I'm thinkin' like what the (BLEEP). Cops come to check me out at the accident. I tell 'em what happened, and they went after his (BLEEP).

Laughter filled the room, as the interview ended. Urich and Jordan exchanged grins. "Pure unadulterated Hector!"

The image returned to the television studio. "Memphis Police trailed the would-be abductor to this abandoned house in Hickory Hills. With the abduction foiled, the suspect barricaded himself in this house. He then set it ablaze. Sources say the man died in the fire.

In other news, Police report a positive development in the case of the girl held hostage by a serial killer. Police officials will share details at their press conference tomorrow."

As Urich turned off the set, she turned to Jordan. "Lucky you got Hector on message right away. Can you imagine if they found out about us usin' the tracker?"

Jordan held up the unit Archer gave him earlier.

Urich's eyes popped open. "Where d'you get that?"

"Archer. Just now. Guess he still has my back. Partners do that."

"But what about the main unit?"

"Yeah. Roy called me already. Gave me hell for havin' it out without his knowledge or checkin' it out."

"Shit, Jordan! I checked it out. Told Roy that George and I were startin' the tractor sting again. He seemed pleased."

"Wish we'd got our stories straight before I talked to him." Jordan sighed. "Hell! He already knows I'm a screw-up. Now he's gonna know you were in on it."

Urich grinned. Batted her eyes. "Since you're my Training Officer, I have no choice but to follow your lead."

"Thanks a lot, partner. You're supposed to have my back not toss me under the bus!"

*****

The Gingerbread man task force and the top law enforcement officials from Shelby, Tunica, and Jergen County marched onto the stage. Cameras and microphones sprouted like weeds among the reporters jockeying for position before the dais. The media chattered among themselves as they waited.

The Memphis Police Director stepped to the microphone. "For the local folks, I want to introduce Mr. Lem Atkins here on my right. Tunica County Sheriff."

Atkins, his face stern, nodded to the crowd. The Director then nodded to Roy on his left. "On my left is Sheriff Roy Speck from Jergen County." Roy glared at Jordan, still in his wheelchair, and Urich at the stage's edge. Their faces, expressionless. On Jordan's other side, Archer wore a full-dress uniform. Archer leaned down next to Jordan. "Here comes the bullshit," he whispered.

The Director continued to address the throng. "Demanding attention, a vicious serial killer held a young girl from our community hostage. To rescue the girl and apprehend this fiend, we mounted a joint operation. This involved our Department and the Sheriff's Departments of Jergen and Tunica Counties. We also relied on help from the FBI.

"As you all are aware, we held daily press briefings not only to keep you informed of our efforts but also to reach out to the killer. Make him see her as a human being. Not just a pawn in his sick play for attention. At the same time, Detectives from Memphis and Tunica searched relentlessly for the girl. The operation culminated when two Detectives from Jergen County went undercover. After infiltrating the Shining Light Mission, they flushed the killer from his lair and rescued the girl. Unfortunately, the killer took his own life rather than face the consequences of his actions.

"The girl is alive and well. Currently, she is in a comfortable and private setting. I am told she is recovering from the effects of her ordeal. The officers were also assisted in the rescue by Charmain Crump." The police nodded to Charmain, sitting on the stage's edge. "While she faced a great personal risk communicating daily with the killer, she also assisted in the girl's rescue. We commend her courage throughout this ordeal. I'll take questions at this point."

CHAPTER THIRTY

A month after Belkey died in the fire, Jordan and Archer sat on Charmain's balcony. Their feet propped on the iron rail. Two open soda cans sat on the table between them. After taking a sip from his, Archer leaned back and put his arms behind his head. "Whatever the girls are cookin' smells good."

"Yeah, Charmain won't tell me what it is. Something they taught her and Cindy at that cooking school."

"Cindy said Char was doin' real good. Told me she musta' just needed the right mentorin' to take off."

A puff of smoke coming out the door prompted Jordan to look back over his shoulder. "Don't speak too soon, Jack. No sense jinxin' the thing."

"Have faith, brotha. Have faith. So, with Shining Light foldin' you gonna keep volunteerin'?"

Jordan took a sip before answering. "It didn't fold up. A buncha local churches stepped in and re-organized it. Gonna make Estelle, that one home manager, the new director. She already told me the other girls are beggin' for a fishin' trip. Plus, Urich is talkin' with some women she knows to follow up on her idea of a big sister's bunch. She already recruited that FBI guys fiance' to help out."

"Wendy?"

Jordan stretched, nodded. "Yeah, that's her."

"She's a real badass like Urich. That oughta be somethin'. Former Army Ranger before she became a cop."

"No Shit! I guess Urich wasn't kiddin' when she said she was gonna teach the girls to kick ass."

"How's the leg?"

"X-ray showed the cast could come off in about a week."

"Then what?"

Jordan shrugged. "I guess back to fightin' crime in the Delta. Boss says the DEA has been callin' him. Got concerns with things out in the boondocks. Been doin' some flyovers lookin' for dopers. What's happenin' with the Belkey case? That's gotta be the whodunit of whodunits."

"Arrogant prick." Archer snarled, "Shit, writin' them letters to himself then goin' out on that pretend hunt. Man was a real danger freak. Lester and his boys coulda killed him."

Jordan nodded. "Yeah, but it kept him in the clear."

"Doc Maynard thinks he also did it to get close to the investigation and Charmain. But that's not all. Inside the house, they found twelve baby food jars. Each one had a tongue."

Jordan's head snapped around to Archer. "Twelve? But...?"

Archer nodded. "That's right. Musta been doin' this long before he come to Memphis."

Jordan hung his head, his brow furrowed. "Do you know where he did the others? Where he came from?"

"Got a good idea where he came from, but who the others might have been before, who knows?"

Jordan stared off. "What brought him here?"

"Doc Maynard thinks revenge."

Jordan leaned back in his chair. "Revenge?"

Archer moved his chair back upright. Glanced back at the apartment door. Leaned close to Jordan. "You ain't gonna believe this shit! We got lab work back last week, and we found a buncha papers in the back a that car in the garage."

"The Italian job?"

"Yeah, Ferrari. Anyway, DNA came back. Bert, the maintenance guy, and Belkey are brothers."

Jordan's feet dropped from the railing. His chair rocked forward. He turned to Archer. "Brothers?"

"Yeah, Bert had no idea. Said he ran away years ago and had no contact with the family. Said Wayne, whose real name is Harold by the way, still lived with the family when he left.

"Said his dad was nuts. Probably PTSD. Mom was meaner in' a snake to him, same time, she favored his brother. He wasn't sure why. They looked alike, and both had red hair."

Jordan shrugged. "Belkey shaved his head."

"Yeah, but in the end, he stopped. Guess he was so fucked up couldn't trust himself with a razor. You didn't notice the red stubble?"

Jordan made a wry face. "Didn't pay much attention to him on the outing. The house was kinda dark when we tussled."

"Dad and mom got killed in a car wreck, just like Belkey said. Anyway. Get this. You know they used to call redheads, gingers?"

Jordan's brow furrowed in a puzzled frown. "Yeah, I guess so. Wait. No... No... Are you sayin?..."

Archer nodded. "Yep! Mom called Belkey her little Gingerbread Man."

"But how'd they end up here? Together? And you say Bert had no idea Belkey was his long-lost brother?"

"Belkey knew, though. Tracked him down and hired him. Found all the details in the papers in the trunk. Maybe use him as a scapegoat if things went bad here. I mean, can you believe it? Even if he left DNA, Bell would have been in the frame. Typical forensic DNA procedures wouldn't have spotted the difference. Doc Maynard figures Belkey wanted to get even with Bert for abandonin' him with his messed-up parents."

Jordan shook his head. "What about the car? That musta cost a bundle. Where'd Belkey get that kinda money?"

Archer shook his head, rolled his eyes. "After Belkey's folks died, he got adopted by a cousin of his old lady. Currency trader, money launderer, had tons of dough. According to police reports, someone broke into their house. Murdered the mother and father and their daughter. She woulda been Belkey's stepsister. Real brutal. Sexually assaulted the girl, then mutilated her. They burned the house to the ground. Belkey survived by jumpin' out a window. Family was worth millions, and Belkey got it all when he turned eighteen."

"How d'you find this all out?"

"Used the papers from the car and good old-fashioned Detective work. Boss won't let me keep at it anymore, so I'm turnin' it all over to Char. Brass says she can copy anything she wants. That'll make her day."

"I suppose, but I wish we could put this all in the rear-view mirror. She's kinda eager to head out to Chicago soon. Check on her folks and see how they're doin' with their new ward."

"How did she convince `em to take that girl? I mean her mom's great people and all, but her dad's a curmudgeon."

Jordan chuckled. "He said he'd been bored since Charmain moved out. Plus, they did a pretty good job with Char. Thought Bonnie might turn out even better. They'd learned from their mistakes. Then he gave me that evil eye, like always."

"I wouldn't take that personal. I mean, is any man gonna be good enough for his daughter?"

As the smoke detector in Charmain's apartment blared, the two women rushed out while smoke poured from the doorway. Archer's wife fanning her face. Charmain coughing.

Charmain clutched Jordan's sleeve. "I turned off the stove, but it kept burnin'. Bob, you gotta call 911!"

*****

Charmain, Urich, and Maureen prepared the catfish fillets at the kitchen counter.

"We'll work this like an assembly line in a factory," Maureen announced. Charmain, you mix up the batter. Urich, you dip the fillet in the batter and put it in the fryer. I'll supervise the cookin' and fish 'em out as they're done."

Joshua pushed a chair next to them. After climbing up, he stood on the seat. "That one a mine, Mom?"

"Yes, big man. Most of this here batch came from the two you caught."

He turned to Charmain. "Mr. Jordan said your house burned down last night."

"Not all the way. But my apartment is pretty well ruined."

Urich turned to Charmain, a mischievous grin on her face. "Jordan told me all about it."

Charmain's eyes opened wide as she stirred the batter. "He did?"

"Said your kitchen must have some kinda spell on it. Maybe an evil spirit that only wants to ruin your cooking."

"Seems that way. I mean, I had Cindy, that's Archer's wife, right there watchin' and still, it all went up in flames."

Urich dipped a fillet in the batter. "What are you gonna do?"

"I'm stayin' with Bob for now, till they fix my place. I'm glad I had insurance. What the firefighters didn't destroy the smoke did."

"How's Bonnie gettin' on with your folks?"

"She loves 'em to death. But Mom thinks she's teachin' Dad new swear words. She's not too happy with the girl's mouth at times. They put her in a private school there, and she's gettin' counseling. Dad's also gonna sue on behalf of Bonnie and the rest of Belkey's victims. Apparently, his estate is worth millions. It'll also help us find out more about his story."

Urich took the batter bowl from Charmain. She dipped the fish in it before using tongs to place them in the fryer.

Maureen peered over her shoulder. "Don't load it up too fast. Just wait until it bubbles again before adding the next one."

Urich rolled her eyes. "Yes, Mommy!"

"You better watch what you say, Aunt Chrissie." Joshua shook his finger at Urich as he spoke. "Momma wash your mouth out with soap for that tone."

"That's right little man." Maureen nodded to Urich, a smug look on her face. "See? He knows respect."

"Momma, Aunt Chrissie used the naughty finger again."

Maureen snapped around and scowled at Urich, then turned back to the boy. "Joshua, why don't you go check on the men? They might need supervision."

"Yes, Momma!"

He hopped down from the chair. With the beads in his hair clacking, he trotted out the door. Running across the deck, he leaped onto Steven's lap. "Momma says I need to come out here to make sure you all behave."

Steven chuckled as he straightened the boy's hair. "She probably right. Better you hang out with us men, anyway."

A primer red pickup pulled up in front of the mobile home. Hector emerged from the passenger door. Mary, from AA, emerged from the driver's side. Together they climbed the stairs carrying plastic grocery sacks.

Hector held up the bags. "Mary's specialty baked beans and potato salad."

Mary clutched the big man's arm and grinned. Then took her hand to brush one side of her purple streaked black hair behind her ear. Jordan stood, hugged Mary, then took one bag from Hector. After introducing the couple to the ones outside, he led Mary and Hector into the Mobile home. As soon as Hector and Jordan returned, the big man popped the top of a soda and joined them at the table. Jordan turned to the big man. "You and Mary?"

Hector scoffed. "Well Yeah! Why?"

Jordan shrugged. "I guess I thought she had better taste. That's all."

Hector glared at Jordan, then grinned. Flipped Jordan the bird. "Nice to see you too!"

"You shouldn't do that." Joshua shook his finger in Hector's face. "Momma don't hold with bad words or naughty fingers." Hector's eyes opened wide while the others chuckled.

"So, what about your bike?" Jordan asked.

Hector eyed the group, especially Joshua. Squirmed in his chair. Uncomfortable. "Engine's fine. Frames all uh... messed up. Gonna get enough money from the settlement to get a... swell frame. All a... tricked out."

The big man's discomfort at controlling his mouth made Jordan grin. Hector said no more, appeared content to listen to the conversation. Once Jordan lit a cigarette, he turned to Paulo, who moved his chair to avoid the smoke. "So, you all set for the big fight."

"Si! Then we can start workin' up to the main event."

"Main event? I thought you might hang it up."

"I meant the wedding. That's all my mother talks about. Ayee." He rolled his eyes. "Night and day. On and on. I had to quit takin' her calls."

Steven scowled. "That why she buggin' me all the time?"

Silent, Paulo gave Steven a sideways glance.

Steven scowled. "Come on, man! When I agreed to do your security, I didn't know that included dealin' with your Mom!"

Paulo threw up his hands. "Okay. How 'bout I give you a raise. Eh? I mean, you a scary dude, man. You never have to lift a finger, just give 'em the look. You know? That's usually enough."

"That won't work with your Mom. She knows I'd never hit a woman. Sides, she probably could wop my behind, anyway."

"Fine, then do like I do. Don't take her calls." Paulo reached for his soda and raised the can to his lips.

Steven scoffed. "She said I do that, she gonna go to Christine."

Pop sprayed from Paulo's mouth. He coughed and beat on his chest, trying to catch his breath. Wide-eyed, he stared at Steven.

Jordan laughed, leaned close to Paulo. "Listen, Paulo, you're just gonna have to face it. Like most men, you're in a no-win situation. There's only one way to survive."

Turning to Jordan, Paulo cocked an eyebrow. "Oh yeah? What is that?"

"It's your answer to everything. The true key to man's marital success."

He grasped Jordan's arm. "Okay! Tell me."

"Learn how to say this. Repeat after me. Okay?"

After leaning close to Jordan, he raised both eyebrows. "Yeah. Yeah! I'm ready. Go on!"

"Yes, Dear."

FROM THE AUTHOR

I hope you enjoyed this story as much as I did bringing it to you. If you liked it please leave a review on line. It might guide others to the experience you had here. To see what other works of mine you may enjoy go to my website at:

https://richardpowellauthor.com/home/

Browse through the site and if something appeals take it home and enjoy. Also you can email me at: richp470@gmail.com. I love to hear from readers and answer all emails myself. As an added bonus I am including here the opening chapters of the next book in the series. Just turn the page and enjoy. Take care and hope to hear from you soon.

JERGEN COUNTY WAR

Richard Powell

CHAPTER ONE

The sound of a shell being jacked into the shotgun's chamber and the press of the barrel into his back prompted Detective Bob Jordan to turn. "Goddamnit Mike, watch where you point that thing."

The young deputy behind him in full battle dress raised the barrel and mumbled into his respirator mask. Jordan reached out and pulled it down from the man's face. "I told you to leave that off till we're ready. You wear that too long in this heat, and we'll have to call in the paramedics for ya."

He glanced past the young man. Sheriff Roy Speck looked back at him wide-eyed. Sweat poured down the tall man's forehead. He leaned close to Mike's ear. "Stay here while I talk to the boss."

After crawling around Mike, he checked Roy's body armor. "I know you say leaders lead from the front, but this time stay to the back. The rest have done this before, so you can see how it's done. Goin' through the door on a bust is a risk, but these Meth labs usually go down quietly. We bang on the door, and the folks inside either let you in or come out. They don't want any gunplay inside cause of the volatile fumes. It's valuable stuff, but it ain't worth dyin' for."

Roy nodded. His hand trembled as he popped a stick of chewing gum in his mouth. "How's Mike doin'?"

Jordan gripped an errant strap. Threaded it through the correct buckle then pulled it tight. "Well, he's eager I give him that."

"Yeah, reminds me of a pup I'm trainin' right now. Eager as hell for the hunt. Howls when I don't take him with the older dogs, but he can't hold a point. Wants to flush the birds right away."

Jordan shrugged. "I'll give him the word. Make sure he follows me and the DEA boys. He'll be all right. This is just his first bust workin' with me. Wants to put on a show for the boss."

After turning Roy around, Jordan checked the straps on the other side. Finished he moved around Mike.

The young man grinned. "Let's take down these mother fuckers."

Jordan turned to him. He pulled the man close, his lips to the young man's ear. "Act like you been here before. Listen, put that on safety right now and keep your finger outside the trigger guard. I don't wanna be pickin' buckshot outta my ass. You're behind me. So cool it. Okay?"

"Just sayin' man! I'm ready to Rock-and-roll."

Jordan sighed then crept up beside the DEA man scanning the scene with binoculars. Jordan took a deep breath and wiped the sweat from his eyes. He glanced up. The morning sky hazy, the grass still damp with dew-soaked his clothes. Ahead a mobile home sat with a pickup parked beside it. "Got anything?"

The DEA man turned to him. "Nobody on guard outside. Pass the word. Watch for trip lines. They might have booby traps. Try to follow in my footsteps."

Jordan returned to Mike and Roy. "Mike, you follow me. Roy, you follow him. The DEA boys are leadin' the way. Try to follow in my footsteps. Watch for wires or fishin' line strung across the trail in front of you. Might have booby traps. Some might be deadly. We back up the DEA. If there's a fight, let them start it. Don't you guys do anything till I tell you? Got it?"

Roy grinned. "Ten-four, Bob."

Mike said nothing stared ahead. Jordan elbowed him in the ribs.

"Ow! Dammit. I got it," Mike whined.

All slipped on their respirators before donning their helmets. The group slipped up to the trailer. The DEA men stopped outside the door. The others fanned out behind, weapons trained on the door. Assault rifle in hand, the agent banged on the door. He pulled the respirator away from his face. "DEA, come out with your hands up!" He turned to his colleague at his side. "Door opens out. Rams no good we need the crowbar."

As the man replaced the respirator, no response came from inside. The other DEA man tossed the battering ram aside. As he pulled the crowbar from his tool belt, the battering ram landed, and a string snapped. Hissing flame as it rose, a rocket launched behind them and burst with a loud bang. The two DEA agents dropped to the ground. Mike leaped around Jordan. At the base of the steps leading to the door, he yanked it open. An explosion roared. Mike's helmet with his pulped head inside flew backward. His headless body toppled back off the steps. Buckshot from the trap gun snapped branches in the surrounding trees as the blast echoed. Before the smoke cleared the upper part of another man's body tumbled down the stairs. Clad in heavy boots, his legs stood in the doorway.

****

Daren slammed on the brakes as the rocket soared overhead. As he peered ahead, an explosion roared.

"Shit!" After slamming the gearshift into reverse, he backed up to the highway. His foot stomped on the accelerator, and he raced down the road to a driveway of an abandoned house. Stopped behind the house, he clutched his assault rifle as he leaped from the vehicle then sprinted back down the road.

What had gone wrong? He asked himself as he moved to the site. He placed the rocket outside to give them a warning in case somebody snuck up on the property. Harvey said other gangs might hear about their operation. Might move in. Take their product. At first, the cook, Beau, laughed when he rigged up the trap gun. Said if he wanted to catch some 'z's while Daren ran to town to fetch their lunch he would just use the lawn chair outside. Beau had never experienced the gnats and skeeters in these parts before. He soon realized sleeping in the out of doors would not be an option unless he wanted the bugs to carry him away. Today he had not laughed as Daren rigged the booby-trap.

Daren chuckled. Now maybe he would see I was right. Give any other gang invadin' our turf a real nasty surprise. If that didn't send 'em home lickin' their wounds it also gave Beau a warnin'. Wake him up from his nap, grab his gun, and stand his ground. Give me a chance to move in from behind. Teach these encroachers a lesson.

At the gravel road, he hopped the fence and dashed through the corn. As he neared the trailer, he slowed. Controlling his breathing, he listened. A moaning came from ahead. On his belly, he crept to clearing's edge and peered through the grass. DEA and Sheriff's men stood outside the trailer. One agent sat on the steps moaning and rocking while staring straight ahead. The trailer door stood open, but he could not see inside. The Sheriff wretched behind the trailer. Another Sheriff's man scanned the perimeter as he talked on a phone. Beau, the cook from Biloxi, was not in sight. As Daren backed away from the scene, sirens wailed in the distance. After creeping away, he rose to his feet and sprinted to the gravel road then jogged back to his truck. An ambulance and a Sheriff's car roared by the abandoned farm their sirens wailing. Daren's truck roared out of the farmstead in the opposite direction almost colliding with a speeding car with a flashing blue light on its dash. After swerving to avoid it, Daren flipped the other vehicle the bird in his rearview mirror. As he drove down the highway, he kept below the speed limit. He pulled out his cell phone hit one on the speed dial, the other end answered at once. "Daren, you better be callin' me to arrange a delivery."

"We gotta problem."

"Problem?"

"DEA and the locals just busted the lab."

"No pig fucker. You gotta problem. I loaned you my best chef and all the finest ingredients. You promised me a shipment tonight."

"But everything was at the lab. I'm sure they've got it."

"Hey man. You wanted to be the big guy. Enforcer for Jergen's County. You supposed to bring me solutions, not problems."

"Man they got the cook. I gotta get him out before we can make a batch. That's gonna take time. What I was gonna bring tonight would have been about two grand worth. How 'bout I bring you the money. Then you can make up for the shortfall from your other suppliers."

"That two grand is wholesale. Now you're sayin' I gotta go out on the retail end to make up for it?"

"Okay. How about three?"

"I want ten."

Daren gasped. "Ten? I can't pay more'n five."

"Like I said you gotta problem. I'll take five now as a down payment. The rest next month. If we have a problem, then I'll send Frankie up. He'll straighten it out in person."

"Listen what about the ingredients? I'm gonna need more. I'll need equipment too. The law's got all of mine."

"Your problems are givin' me a headache. Next, you wanna take out a thirty-year loan?"

Daren sighed. "No, I'll talk to the old man. Maybe he needs work done. Just let me know how much I'll owe, and I'll have it for you."

"You gonna cross your heart and hope to die? Or give me the Boy Scout promise?"

"Whatever."

"Let's say If we're not square at the end of the month Frankie will come up and charge you a finger. Your run out of fingers? Well, you got toes. Now get lost before I lose my temper." The other end cut off the call.

****

Ah yes, here it is, Parker said to himself as he pulled back the sheet covering the model of his latest property development. Jason Estates, named in honor of his late partner. The homes on the estate sized lots and with their accompanying attractions would sell like funnel cakes or deep fried Oreos at the Mid-South Fair. They had been partners in other projects. Gotten rich together since their early twenties. He had even been best man at Jason's wedding. Once over a single malt, Jason said they were like brothers. Parker clapped him on the back and laughed, "Like Frank and Jesse James? They only stole from the rich. Some say we steal from everybody."

Like Northfield, Minnesota had been, for the James's Gang, the Tunica casino had been a ride too far for the duo. Problems with the site caused compromises in the construction. The downsizing forced by the construction changes prompted their investors to bail. Jason's disappearance on a Gulf fishing trip kicked in their Partner Life Insurance enabling him to escape bankruptcy and save their assets. Jason's unfortunate accident left him free and clear of the Casino's problems, but now he owed a debt. Free now to make the deals he loved, he wondered how he would repay his new benefactor. The intercom's buzz interrupted his thoughts.

"Mr. Parker, the fire chief called. There's a serious incident on the Clovis property and thought you needed to go there."

"Did he say what was goin' on, Marie?"

"No, Sir. Just that some people got hurt out there real bad. Might have been Sheriff's people."

"Shit! That's all I need" he thought to himself as he strode to his car. A linchpin for his new development, it had taken him months to secure the property from the Clovis estate. With the deal closed, he thought his problems would be over. With luck the incident might have occurred on the farmstead, it's abandoned buildings a problem. He advised the probate attorney to let that part go back to the county for back taxes. Let the citizens of Jergen County cover the cost of cleaning up that mess. After all his planned development would bring employment and income to the folks of the county. So while making him and his investors wealthier they would reap a windfall from it as well.

As he roared out of the parking lot, he tossed the blue flashing light on his dash. One perk of being Chairman of the Board of Supervisors. On emergency county business, the light ensured he could travel well above the posted speed limit. After all, swift executive action saved the county money and lives.

As he came to the gravel road leading to the property Parker swerved when a pickup emerged from an abandoned farm on the paved road. Intent on his turn ahead he failed to notice the driver just flipped him the bird in his rearview mirror.

After turning on the gravel road he slowed, his vision obscured by dust hanging in the air kicked up by the emergency vehicles. He passed the parked DEA, and Sheriff's vehicles then turned into the farmstead. Two ambulances and a sheriff's patrol car sat in the yard their light bars flashing.

Paramedics attended to the Sheriff and one DEA man. Jordan talked to a paramedic with a black body bag at his feet. The coppery odor of blood, feces, and vomit filled the air. A severed torso lay on the trailer's wooden stairs. The sight of two bloodied legs encased in work boots standing in the open doorway made his stomach churn as he approached. He focused on the Sheriff, pushing the sight of the body parts from his mind. As he joined them, Roy rose to his feet. He stumbled as he made his way to Parker's side.

Parker scowled. "What happened, Roy?"

The tall Sheriff ran his fingers through his hair and surveyed the scene. "I'm sorry, Larry. It's been a shock. DEA found a Meth Lab here. We backed 'em up on the bust." He nodded to the body bag. "We lost Mike. Trap gun inside the trailer. Killed a guy inside as well."

"Meth lab! Shit! I told Bill to get on this tax forfeiture down here six months ago. Knew shit like this would happen if we didn't tear stuff like this down. I'm sorry about your man. Anybody else hurt?"

"DEA man kinda shook up. Blast almost took him out. I got sick, but the guys here gave me a shot. I'll be okay."

"Well call me if you think the Supervisors need to get you anything. Okay?"

"Thanks, Larry. Will do."

As Parker made his way back to his car, he felt a bounce in his step. This incident might be just what he needed to get the change they wanted in the Sheriff's Department. "Yep," he said to himself, "Roy Speck's days might be numbered."

****

The tall man behind the counter peered into the box before him. The obese man on the other side wore a cap turned backward. As he removed it the man sighed, ran his fingers through his hair then pointed at the box. "Mr. LaPlage those dishes been in our family for generations. They's antiques."

LaPlage snorted. As he looked up, he fingered the shoulder straps on his bib overalls and studied the man before him. "Lester, I can buy ones just like 'em at Walmart for no more than ten bucks for the box."

The man reached into the box. Pulled out a plate. After turning it over, he pointed at the bottom. "See that? Made right there in England. Real China. There's the date. See?"

"If they're worth so much, maybe you oughta sell 'em on eBay or one a them other places. Hell, next week the auction house is havin' a sale. That might get you more."

"But I need the money now for my kid's school lunches."

"Lester, if that's the deal, school'll give the kids lunch for free. You just gotta talk to 'em."

"My people don't take charity, rather have 'em go without."

LaPlage shrugged. "Tell you what. How 'bout I lend you the money. You leave this here for security then you pay me back in a month. Course there'd be interest."

"How much?"

LaPlage ran his fingers through his snow white pompadour. Fifty bucks at ten percent a week compounded."

Lester thrust out his hand. "It's a deal."

LaPlage stared at the man's hand yet made no move to shake it. "Course we gotta fill out the paperwork." LaPlage set a form on the counter. As he filled in the blanks, he talked aloud. "This says I agree to loan you fifty dollars for thirty days at ten percent interest. Your offerin' up this box of dishes as security for the loan. Should you default, that's fail to pay back the money. I get to keep the dishes and dispose of them as I see fit. Also, I can have these here things insured in case somethin' happens. Like my place catches fire or someone breaks in and steals 'em. If that happens, you don't owe me a cent. It's five dollars for the coverage. I deduct it from what I give you today. Course it's not required, but if this stuff is as valuable as you say it would be worth it."

"That sounds steep. Let's gamble on it."

LaPlage pointed to the form. "Just check off here then initial it that I offered, and you declined then sign it."

As the man signed the paper, LaPlage counted out the money on the counter. After the man left, LaPlage carried the box to the back room. He seated himself before a laptop. While his fingers raced across the keyboard, images of china dishes appeared on the screen. As he clicked the mouse, he held a different piece up to the screen.

"Bless your heart, Lester. You were right. Got twenty-five pieces here. Ten plates at two hundred a piece. Soup tureen. Whoo-wee! Five hundred. Gravy bowl 'nother five hundred. Covered butter dish, three hundred. Salt and pepper shakers, a grand. Ten napkin rings at twenty-five a piece. Four thousand three hundred. The entire ten piece matched set worth twice that. But at auction, the price may be higher."

He carried the box to a section by the loading dock. As he turned around Daren strode through the door. LaPlage shook his head. "Heard on the scanner 'bout the mess out at the Clovis place. They're sayin' got two dead. Didn't say who, but I think one's a cop. What the hell happened?"

"Beau'd been up all night cookin' so while he took a nap, I ran into town to pick up food. Cops showed up before I got back."

"Now what?"

"The folks in Biloxi are blamin' it on me. Told me I gotta cover the cost of the loss. Ain't built up enough cash flow yet to cover it."

"How much we talkin'?"

"Ten total, but they agreed to five right now, and the rest paid as we get back in production."

LaPlage made a wry face. "These the folk's in Biloxi? Those Crown fellahs?"

Daren nodded. "Yes, Sir."

"When they need their five grand?"

"Tonight."

LaPlage shook his head. "You sure you ain't gettin' in over your head?"

"No Pa. Honest, it seems like a great chance for me to make it big."

"Even though you're only my stepson, I feel an obligation to help you along. If nothin' else to please your Ma. But there ain't no handouts. Man's gotta work for what he gets."

LaPlage pointed to the stack where he had placed the dishes. "You take that stack down to our warehouse in Biloxi. That job oughta be worth five grand easy."

"Is this a burglary?"

LaPlage scoffed. "Less you know the better. Just load it up right after dark. Should be able to make Biloxi in good time."

TO CONTINUE THE TALE, FOLLOW THE LINK BELOW:

https://www.amazon.com/gp/product/B07GM19RF1/ref=dbs_a_def_rwt_hsch_v_api_tkin_p2_i2

Made in the USA
Monee, IL
11 April 2021